the »»» DIE ««is CAST

by Frank Lyons

Copyright © 2012 by Frank Lyons.

All rights reserved.

The Die Is Cast is a work of fiction.
All of the characters and events portrayed
are fictitious and any resemblance
to real people or events is coincidental.

Book cover design by Timothy Van Hyfte.

The Die Is Cast is available for purchase on Amazon.

The author may be contacted at fwlyons4@mchsi.com

ISBN-13: 978-1481226431

ISBN-10: 1481226436

For Jean M. Lyons

Without her technical advice and assistance,
The Die Is Cast would have been scrawled
on a writing pad with a quill pen.

CHAPTER ONE

The black, armored town car nosed into the basement of the imposing Manhattan headquarters of Titan Motors Corporation. Justin Cairncross closed his laptop computer, stepped from the back seat, walked several feet to the elevator, and sped in whispery solitude to his suite on the fiftieth floor. Although the affairs of Titan Motors, where Cairncross was the chairman of the board of directors, awaited his attention, his first priority was to attend to an imperative matter for American Semiconductor Corporation, known around the world as AMSCO. Cairncross was a member of the AMSCO Board of Directors.

As he passed his assistant's office, he said, "Good morning. Call Robert Drood at AMSCO in San Francisco and tell him to meet me here in my office right away." Drood was the CEO of AMSCO. "Have our chief legal counsel here to witness the meeting, and tell a security officer to stand by. Let me know as soon as you've set up the meeting."

In a short time his assistant confirmed the arrangements. Cairncross said, "Good. Now call Ken Yee at AMSCO, and tell him to be here an hour before my meeting with Drood." Yee was the second-highest-ranking officer of AMSCO. "And set up a teleconference for late in the day with the executives who report to the AMSCO CEO. Tell them all to talk to absolutely no one—especially Robert Drood—about the teleconference. Note that my office is calling the meeting. Yee and I will participate. Interrupt whatever I'm doing today if any difficulties arise."

Dennis Curran, a mid-level AMSCO employee, observed the flurry of actions precipitated by the bombshell information he had presented to Cairncross during the last several days. Cairncross stuck his head into Curran's temporary office and said, "Dennis, can you stick around for a while? I may need you." He did not wait for an answer. This was Curran's first visit to the Titan Motors headquarters offices and the first time he ever met Cairncross.

He now understood what it was like to be the CEO of the largest corporation in the world and a board member of AMSCO, the pre-eminent Silicon Valley company. When Drood and Yee received calls from Cairncross's office, they rearranged their schedules and agreed to scurry to New York as if they were prefects summoned to Rome by Caesar.

Drood and Yee reacted differently to their unusual calls from Cairncross's office. Drood speculated on the reason for his call: Could it be that Cairncross is going to ask me to be the CEO of Titan Motors? His retirement at the end of the year is public knowledge. I thought a few years ago when I was elected CEO of AMSCO, I had reached the peak of my business career, but this would be a far grander position. What a wonderful way it would be to celebrate my forty-first birthday!

He ate lunch and had a company driver take him to the AMSCO hangar to board the Boeing Business Jet waiting to fly him to New York. The aviation dispatcher had cancelled the plane's previously scheduled evening flight to Rome when Drood requested the plane.

Yee could not guess why Cairncross called him to New York. He thought: I'll just have to wait until tomorrow to learn his purpose. But it is strange for me to receive a call from the most influential member of the AMSCO Board of Directors. Although I'm a top AMSCO officer, my position seldom warrants meetings with Mr. Cairncross.

He walked at a measured pace from the AMSCO high-rise office building in San Francisco's financial district to his modest flat in a building he owned in Chinatown, ate lunch with his wife, and inspected his garden and birds. The garden, with birds chirping in their cages, was his place for tranquility and contemplation. He called a cab to take him to the waiting Learjet he had leased for his flight to New York. He did not order an AMSCO plane because of Cairncross's instructions on strict confidentiality.

When the plane reached flying altitude, Yee stretched back in his seat and relaxed. He regretted he wouldn't be able to walk downstairs to the back room of the ground floor restaurant of his building after supper for a cup of tea and a few games of Zheng Fen or Luk Fu with his Cantonese-speaking buddies. It was the year of the rooster on Chinese calendars—2005 on western calendars. One of the characteristics of the rooster is its devotion to friends. Although Yee was close to his friends, he let them believe he worked at AMSCO as a China/U.S. liaison engineer.

He knew a man in Manhattan from his home village in Guangdong Province of China. Maybe when he was in New York he could meet him and chat about the explosive transformation unfolding in China since their boyhood.

Curran called his boss, Carly Jackson, at the sprawling new AMSCO computer chip manufacturing factory outside Dublin, Ireland. He said,

"Carly, you better take this call on your secure phone line." She transferred the call and they continued, "All hell is going to break loose here tomorrow. Mr. Cairncross is going to drop a blockbuster bomb based on the information I presented to him."

"What's he going to do?"

"I'm sorry, but I can't give you any details now. He told me not to talk to anyone and to be sure there are no leaks. I'm disregarding his direction by calling you; I just wanted to warn you to be on standby tomorrow for the news."

"Okay, Dennis, but let me know what's happening when you can."

"I'll call you as soon as the news goes public, Carly. Please call my home and let Mary Catherine know I plan to take an evening flight home to Dublin in a couple of days. I'll send her flight details when I receive a confirmation."

CHAPTER TWO

Forty-one years earlier in Cork, Ireland, on November 15, 1963—one week after John F. Kennedy's assassination—it all began. Mary Drood, with the assistance of the community midwife, gave birth to her first child, a son she named Robert Garrity Drood.

The midwife was accompanied by her cousin, a sprawling frog of a woman with saddlebag cheeks, gray hair hanging down her back like a curried horsetail, and a head crammed with thousands of years of Celtic lore on foretelling the future. The cousin was proud of her time-honored profession as a soothsayer. During the birthing, she sat at a table in the tiny kitchen studying her cards and paraphernalia and sucking her lips over toothless gums while she contemplated the destiny of the newborn baby.

Mary's life-weary mother had been summoned. She sat unsteadily and morosely by, sipping from her glass of gin.

When the midwife finished her work, she nodded permission for the soothsayer to see the baby and Mary. She stood, assumed the bearing of a bishop, and entered the bedroom.

She examined the baby and intoned, "Robert Garrity Drood will acquire wisdom from the 'Salmon of Knowledge' like the legendary boy Fionn millennia ago when he tasted fish from the River Boyne. As with Fionn, the magical salmon will bestow onto this child knowledge of all things and the judgment of Solomon; and he will travel from Ireland to a distant place where he will become the chosen ruler of many people in many lands; and according to the custom of the salmon, he is destined to eventually return to Ireland, the land of his birth."

Mary shuddered and demanded, "How do you know these things?"

The soothsayer answered, "The Lord gave me the gift to foretell. It has never failed me. The foreordained destiny of Robert Garrity Drood is as inevitable as the tides of the restless seas and orderly movements of the heavenly bodies."

Mary sighed and turned her head on her pillow as she relaxed her aching body and cuddled her beautiful son. Although she was of the modern generation that doubted the prophecies of soothsayers, she had an uneasy feeling this weird witch may have indeed predicted her son's destiny.

As the midwife and the soothsayer departed, the midwife whispered, "I hope Mary's mother is up to caring for the baby for the next few days and she lightens up on the drink. I watered down her jar of gin."

"God knows George Drood—the most worthless husband I ever laid eyes on—will be of little help if he even bothers to come home," the soothsayer responded. "When St. Patrick drove the snakes from Ireland, he overlooked the likes of him."

Mary thought about her husband not being with her to share the birth of their son. When she told him she was pregnant and they would have to marry, he urged her to go to England where abortions were legal. Her strong Catholic faith did not accept abortions; she declined.

She wished their relationship could have remained as it was when they met in the country dancehall near Ballincollig. They were together every weekend when he came home to Cork from his travelling job and she was free from her domestic work in the McClellan household. It all seemed so grand. But their relationship started to unravel when she foolishly believed his promises of love and marriage and went with him to his hotel room after a wedding dance. They gave no heed to the caution of the bishop: "During the interval between the dance and the dawn, the devil is busy."

Mary finally dozed while her mind thrummed with a verse taught to her by her Irish-speaking grandmother: *"In minic a chealg brithra mine cailin crionna"* (Many a girl lost what can't be bought with money. And all because of words, sprinkled with honey.)

A year after Robert was born, Mary gave birth to a girl named Bridget. She was colicky—a heavy burden day and night. Robert added to the domestic turmoil with his limited need for sleep, his high energy level, and his extraordinary alertness.

George dreaded coming home on weekends to their steamy little flat. Mary was run-down with the "twenty-four-hourness" of caring for their children. George was happy to return to his job away from home on Monday mornings.

After a weekend of Mary's despondency, Bridget's crying, and Robert's demand for attention, George reached the end of his tether. Mary's visiting brothers added to the household turbulence with their beery needling about his shortcomings. George had never forgiven them for the beating they gave him until he agreed to marry their pregnant sister.

George stopped coming home. To protect himself from further verbal abuse and harm by Mary's brothers, he sent home weekly remittances in envelopes without a return address. In his final letter to Mary, he wrote:

> Mary,
>
> I lost my job and can't send money any more.
> Tell Robert and Bridget I love them and think of them every day.
> I'm sorry for the way things are turning out.
>
> George

CHAPTER THREE

After George Drood's last letter arrived with his final remittance, Mary could scarcely care for her two children. She worked to scratch out a living but could not earn enough to pay the rent. After months of delinquency, the landlord sent her an eviction notice.

In desperation, Mary tried to think of another place to live. Returning to her childhood home in Farrenree was a possibility although a poor one. Her parents slept in a tiny space partitioned off from the parlor with a blanket and her brothers on cots in the loft over the kitchen. The only place for her and her children would be the small parlor, watched over by a gloomy, candle-illuminated statue of the Blessed Virgin Mary. Returning to her family and enduring the sullen atmosphere of hopelessness in their cramped home would be a nonstop nightmare. There had to be a better place for her to live.

In the middle of the night, she thought of an answer. Her former employer's wealthy landlord husband, Brian McClellan, owned a stud farm with an abandoned barn in a secluded area near the Cork city limits. McClellan seldom visited the farm. It was unlikely he would know if Mary moved into his old barn.

Mary and her children sneaked into McClellan's barn where she hoped to live until she could find better accommodations. When the derelict barn was built, it was finer than many houses. Now, rank grass and tall weeds surrounded and partially hid it. Curling paint fell off to the touch, loose windowpanes rattled in the wind, and the neglected roof leaked. Rafters and sills were daubed with detritus from insects, birds, and rodents. Mary and the children swept it out and occupied one horse stall and the tack room with the smell of previous occupants still permeating the air. The loft contained musty hay; Mary heaped it around their living space to insulate against the cold. A two-lid cast iron stove and broken cots and chairs, previously used by the horse grooms, remained. Mary brought with her a kerosene lamp, rudimentary cooking utensils, and frayed blankets.

She obtained firewood from dead tree branches around the barn and water of doubtful purity from a nearby livestock well. She became adept at devising traps for catching careless rabbits and curious pigeons. The St. Vincent de Paul Society was her source for used clothing.

When Mary cooed to the cows in the adjacent field, they became docile. "Nice old girl. Let me rub you and take a little milk in my pail. It'll relieve the pressure and make you feel better. There, there—the dairyman won't notice. Now, that feels better doesn't it?"

Robert, who was now five years old, puzzled Mary. He asked questions beyond her ability to answer, spoke with the vocabulary of a gifted teenager, read with ease, and effortlessly learned the Irish language any time he could coax her to speak it. When Mary left for a St. Vincent de Paul store visit, he said, "Mother, will you bring me more books? I've read the ones you brought on your last visit. I don't care what they are about; I like to read them all. And bring Bridget a doll if you can find one. You know how she loves them."

Mary took in mending and needlework to earn money for basic necessities, but it was difficult to sew in the uncertain light of the kerosene lamp. The quality of her work suffered, and orders dried to a trickle.

Robert and Bridget were closer to each other than puppies in a litter. They shared all of their secrets. Robert explained to Bridget, "When I grow up, I'll be famous like the people in my books."

"And when I grow up, I'll marry a man with a nice house and have lots of children," said Bridget. "I know this is true because my dolls told me so."

When Mary became depressed coping with her poverty, Robert and Bridget combined their efforts to perform the household duties they were capable of doing. Robert comforted his mother by making up imaginative and complex stories that went on until she grew weary of hearing them.

CHAPTER FOUR

While touring his farm on horseback, McClellan noticed a smoke plume coming from his barn. When he investigated, he discovered Mary and her children living there. "Who are you?" he bawled. "You have no authorization to be here. Get off my property within the hour, or I'll call the garda (police)."

"Don't you remember me, Mr. McClellan? I was Mary Garrity when I used to work in your household for Mrs. McClellan. Please let us stay. We'll not damage your barn. We've no other place to turn."

"That's not my concern. My barn isn't the rescue mission. Get out—now!"

When Mary saw McClellan swaying in his saddle, she knew further appeal would be useless. Mrs. McClellan had always failed to influence him when he drank.

Mary moved her family out of the barn to an abandoned van in a secluded copse of trees. Sleeping in the cold, damp van was impossible. She was desperate and could not think clearly. In the hope that McClellan would not find them again if she concealed the smoke by using the stove only at night, Mary and the children sneaked back to reestablish residency in the barn.

A few weeks later, McClellan found Mary and her children had returned to his property. He came into the barn and slowly sized Mary up from head to toe with lecherous, reptilian eyes. He said, "How badly do you want to continue living here?"

"Oh, Mr. McClellan, I'll do anything you ask if you don't force us to leave."

He said in a thick voice, "I'll let you stay if you make yourself available to me any time I come for a visit."

Mary was horrified at McClellan's humiliating proposition but could not think of an alternative. Finally, she shamefully nodded her consent to his detestable offer. He said, "I'll return late tomorrow night—be ready for me."

As McClellan buttoned his riding jacket and pulled on his gloves, he noticed Bridget. He tousled her light, curly hair and said, "Now, aren't you the pretty little lass. Come over here and turn to the light so I can see you better."

Mary was appalled she had agreed to become McClellan's mistress, but what other choice did she have? Going to the authorities risked losing her children to a foster home; the thought horrified her. How could the merciful Lord in heaven let this happen? How could a person's life be so miserable?

McClellan came on his dreaded visits several times a week. He showed up one night drunker than usual with his expectations revved up to full throttle. Mary pleaded, "Oh, please don't be rough with me tonight."

McClellan mocked her. "A little pain adds to the pleasure. I'll treat you like I do any other filly I own. The deal we made was for you to use my barn and for me to use you. You have no other place to turn for help. You are soiled goods for anyone else after what you do here with me. Besides, I know you really like it. Now, if you give me a wild enough ride around the stable tonight, I'll bring you a basket of provisions on my next visit."

After he left, Mary stumbled outside and retched. For days she remained in a state of despondency and could barely care for herself and the children.

Robert confided to Bridget, "I wish Mr. McClellan didn't come to visit Mother. When he took her to the cubbyhole over the tack room last night, I heard him hurting her. I know he wants us to call him Uncle Brian, but I don't want to; I know he isn't our real uncle. I don't like him. And I don't like to see him always touching and rubbing you."

When Robert started attending school, he was transformed. Absorbing his lessons was as effortless for him as blinking. He remembered everything he heard or read and solved mathematical problems before the schoolmaster finished posing them.

After Robert's first day of school, he exclaimed to his mother and Bridget, "My schoolmaster knows everything. I think teaching is the grandest thing a person can do. When I grow up I'm going to be a schoolmaster too."

In November, after a night of shivering in his cold bed, Robert developed a respiratory infection that kept him home for several days.

When he returned to school, he asked his schoolmaster, "Mr. Tweedy, can you give me the lessons I missed when I was sick?"

"Why should I bother?" he snarled. "You miss school without permission; you disrespect me and your classmates by coming to school looking like your clothes came from a dustbin; you have no home address—God knows how you must live; and you come to class without paper and pen. I prefer to spend my time with the scholars who are not going to squander their lives living on the dole and spending every quid they earn drinking themselves to kingdom come."

"Sir, that won't happen to me; someday I'll be as famous as a king; you just wait and see."

When Robert went home he said, "Bridget, my schoolmaster is the worst man in the world. He smells like a bag of dirty laundry. I know he doesn't like me because he always gives me a dirty look when I answer his questions faster than the lads who are his favorites. I thought he was going to hit me yesterday when I showed him a mistake on his answer to a mathematics problem. And today he wouldn't give me the lessons I missed when I was sick. When I grow up and become famous, I'll come back and show him how wrong he was about me."

In mid-December Robert raced home from school to tell Bridget, "The schoolmaster said there will be a Christmas party at school. The lads who were there last year said it'll be a grand affair with fine decorations and exciting games. I wish Mother wasn't feeling so bad since Mr. McClellan's last visit so she could tell me what they do at parties. I can hardly wait. When it's over, I'll tell you all about it."

On the day of the party, Robert's classmates came to school in their Sunday clothes with little presents for the schoolmaster and favors for each other. The schoolmaster treated the class to crackers that they pulled apart causing a popping sound and revealing tissue paper hats, face decals, or festive geegaws.

Robert arrived empty handed wearing his usual hand-me-down clothes. As the children romped around the decorated classroom, Rinty Donlan, one of Robert's older classmates, noticed him wearing the castoff shirt his mother had donated to the St. Vincent de Paul Society when he outgrew it. "Hey lads, look at Robert," he screeched. "He's wearing my old, hand-me-down shirt from last year. Now isn't that a great joke?" The classmates laughed and howled in derision. The schoolmaster ignored their merciless mockery.

Robert ran from the school seething with shame and resentment. When he stumbled on the stone threshold and scraped the skin from his shins, he could not hold back the tears.

When he returned home, Bridget asked, "How was the party, Robert? Tell me all about it."

"It was nothing. I don't know why everyone gets so excited about parties. I hate them. If there's ever another one, I won't be going to it."

CHAPTER FIVE

McClellan came to his barn for a daytime visit. He hid behind the bushes and watched until he saw Robert leave for school and Mary go out on an errand. He had spied on the barn for several weeks until he learned Mary and Robert's normal schedules. Mary locked the barn door and told Bridget not to let anyone in unless she knew them.

McClellan tied his horse to the gate post, patted its neck, and knocked on the barn door. Bridget unlocked the door when she saw who it was. "My mum is not home now, Uncle Brian," Bridget chirped.

"That's all right, Bridget. Uncle Brian is here to see you this time. Come over here and sit on my lap. It's nice and warm in front of the stove." He stroked her hair and rubbed his cheek on hers. It was the first time she ever smelled a man's cologne.

"I brought you some presents because I love you so much. And I want you to always remember how much I really like you. Now, you must come upstairs to the cubbyhole with me to open your presents. We'll be cozier up there alone."

Bridget and McClellan climbed up the rickety ship's ladder to the cubbyhole. He sat beside her on the cot while she opened her presents. She squealed when she saw the doll and sack of sweets, "Oh, Uncle Brian, these are the finest presents I ever got."

"I'm happy you like them, Bridget. Now Uncle Brian wants you to do something very special for him. It probably will seem new and strange to you, but it's the way big people show their love for each other."

Returning unexpectedly early from school, Robert heard Bridget's unearthly screams. He grabbed a rusty-tined pitchfork and scrambled up the ladder to protect her from her peril. He smelled the rank mixture of sweat and cologne when he entered the cubbyhole. McClellan reared and lunged and grunted like a rooting hog as he defiled Bridget. Robert was horrified. He did not understand what was happening, but he could see it was loathsome and disgusting. "You stop hurting Bridget!" he screamed.

Robert's adrenaline surged as he attacked McClellan with the pitchfork. He gashed his shin from knee to ankle with a slashing swipe and with a hard thrust, poked the fork tines deep into his white bare rump and the back of his hairy upper thighs. McClellan rolled off onto the floor and roared in pain. While he was tangled up in his trousers, Robert beat him on his back. When McClellan was able to stand and hoist his trousers, he grabbed a brass-knobbed horse harness hame from a wall nail and beat off Robert with vicious blows to his arms and head. He stopped swinging at Robert because he knew he must immediately visit his doctor. "If you ever do that again, you little sod, I'll poke a fork tine up your little arse."

McClellan was terrified he might have contracted lockjaw from the dirty pitchfork tines. He knew farmers in the community who died of the disease after minor barnyard accidents. He would tell his doctor his horse threw him, and he landed on a pitchfork.

In spite of his haste to seek a doctor, McClellan waited long enough to say, "If either of you tell your mother or anyone else about this, I'll come back and slice off your mother's ears and nose."

In his pain and anxiety, he did not think about how the children could avoid explaining their appalling condition to their mother. He felt no remorse or concern for his heinous crime. He looked at his rape of Bridget the same as his abuse of Mary; he had merely collected payment in kind in lieu of barn rent. He was a throwback to the old days when landlords claimed the "Right of the First Night" with brides, servants, and girls.

McClellan left Bridget rolled up in a ball sobbing and Robert sitting against the wall massaging his goose egg-sized bumps. He scraped his knees while he slid down the ladder, limped to the gate post, and clawed his way up onto his horse. He rode away carrying his weight on one stirrup and his rump skewed to one side of his saddle to ease the pain. The blood flowing from his wounds drained into his boot and made his foot feel sodden and warm. Mary was delayed in returning home. When she looked at Robert and Bridget's faces, she could immediately see something terrible had happened.

Bridget was traumatized. When Mary talked to her, she could only stare back. Mary surmised what had happened and confirmed her suspicion when she examined Bridget and the gore on the cubbyhole cot. Robert was frightened and uncommunicative.

Neither Robert nor Bridget could comprehend McClellan's revolting atrocity, and they wouldn't talk to Mary about it because of his promised reprisals.

Mary stayed awake all night with her mind in turmoil: How can a man think of such obscenities—but he's not a man, he's a reptile. He's too rich for the garda to take action against him, and where would the money come from for me to hire a solicitor. And who'd believe the witness of children? If only my brothers had not emigrated, they could pulverize McClellan or fix him so he'd not be capable of doing such a filthy thing again. Sooner or later, the pervert will be back for more. Sweet Jesus in heaven, is there not some way to end this nightmare?

Bridget and Robert arose the next day with a permanent marker indelibly branded into their minds of the horrible day of McClellan's beastly visit.

When Bridget could function again, she burned McClellan's presents in the stove and spent hours scrubbing and bathing trying to expunge the stain of his defilement.

Robert fanned out the cubbyhole to rid it of the smell of McClellan's sweat and cologne. He wondered if McClellan could have bled to death from his pitchfork wounds; if he did, he deserved it.

Robert's mind flooded with self-recriminations: Why did I loiter on the way home from school and fail to protect Bridget? Why did God allow a wicked snake like McClellan to crawl into our family? And why wasn't my father here to take care of us?

Robert was consumed with guilt, frustration, and rage. He couldn't understand why there was such injustice and evil in the world.

He reasoned that if he didn't love Bridget and his mother so much, he would not feel so unbearably bad when terrible things happened to them. In the future he would stop loving them; he would build a wall around himself impenetrable to feelings and emotions. But it made him feel hollow to think of living without his sister and mother's sustaining love. He felt like he was in a room where all of the familiar furnishings were removed leaving him with emptiness.

A grim specter now perched on Robert's shoulder always ready to recall to him the horror of Bridget's assault and his mother's abuse. It took sinister control of his psyche and emotions. It had the power to override the logic of his intellect. And he was powerless to dismiss the sinister fiend.

A military combat physician would have noted Bridget had most of the characteristics of shell-shocked soldiers: fatigue, listlessness, apathy, masklike face, slow speech, headaches, poor memory, no sense of responsibility, and hopelessness about the future. As long as she lived, the trauma from her rape would control her life. She would loathe her hideous assailant and an uncaring God—and at times even herself.

McClellan did not come back for the next several weeks, but Mary knew he would return when he healed from his pitchfork wounds. She thought of how she had prepared for his next visit: Of course, I will never leave Bridget home alone again. And I bought a guinea cock to give a raucous day or night warning at the first sign of the arrival of a stranger. And I placed a honed butcher knife under my pillow. If McClellan touches me again or tries to harm my children, I will cut him to shreds even though I know the consequences can be dire. Somehow I must soon find a way to vacate the barn and go elsewhere to live—but how?

CHAPTER SIX

Mary stopped receiving the sacraments of the church because of her feeling of guilt for the sins she thought she was committing and her doubts about a God who would allow her family to live in such misery. She despaired at the loss of her sustaining faith in her church and in God. The ossified parish priest who harped on the wickedness of sex intensified her despair and guilt.

Mary's brother, Liam, periodically wrote to her after he went to Chicago. He was the only other person in the Garrity family who shared Mary's good nature. He sent his pencil-scrawled letters to her at the parish rectory because she had no other postal address. When she sporadically attended mass, she stopped at the rectory to check the mail spread out on the long hall table. It was a tradition for Irish emigrants to communicate through the parish priests stemming from the times when literacy, except for the clergy, was rare.

Boom economic conditions prevailed in Chicago after Liam arrived from Ireland; his factory employer offered him long working hours and paid him good wages. He had little desire for material possessions; he saved a large portion of his earnings. Part of his savings made the down payment on his modest three-bedroom house. He could not believe his good fortune at being blessed with such a fine property.

Liam dated Debbie, the barmaid from his neighborhood tavern. Debbie displayed her delusions of social grandeur and tacky taste by wearing flashy clothes and gaudy makeup when they attended romance movies and ate at the neighborhood eateries.

When Liam attended a three-day course at a trade school to learn how to read technical drawings, Debbie told her friends, "Liam's company done sent him to an important school where they learned him a lot of technical stuff. I think they're getting him ready for a big 'permotion.'" Her IQ was on par with the temperature on a cool day. Behind Debbie's back, her friends mocked her affectations.

Liam could have done better at finding a girlfriend, but the search would have taken more effort than he was willing to exert. Debbie could see a marriage proposal from Liam was not forthcoming, so she told him, "Something's wrong with them there pills I been takin'. I think I got a bun in the oven."

The deception worked. Liam and Debbie married in St. Patrick's Church followed by a raucous reception in the beery back room of the saloon where Debbie was employed. She wore a garish, overpriced wedding dress she had ordered from an ad on the back page of an *Exotic Romance* magazine. She fibbed to her friends, "Me and Liam's goin' to take one of them there Caribbean Island cruises for our honeymoon; you know, the kind where they give you all the free food and booze you want." Her friends winked at each other.

After the wedding, they drove a few miles to Gary, Indiana and checked into the honeymoon room of a fleabag motel. The mirrored ceiling and candle on the edge of the bathtub differentiated it from the normal rooms. The regular motel clients were truckers who used the rooms while they waited, with their diesel engines idling, for their turn to load steel on their rigs at the Gary and East Chicago mills. On weekends the mills curtailed shipping operations, so the room rates were reduced. The bedding reeked of cigarette smoke and blast furnace effluent.

After Liam read one of Mary's despairing letters, he wrote to her, "Come to Chicago, Mary; you can live with me and Debbie. I'll send you the passage money from my savings account. You and your weeuns will be safe here. And it will be grand to see you and hear your voice again."

Mary hesitated because of fear of the bustle of life in America, but she was even more fearful about McClellan returning. After she reflected on her children's peril and her revulsion for her relationship with McClellan, she wrote, "Dearest Liam, We'll come over as soon as we make the arrangements."

Mary called on Mrs. McClellan to ask her to drive her and her children to the Shannon airport, a three-hour drive from Cork. She hoped Mrs. McClellan would recall the favor she once promised for helping straighten out her daughter Kathleen during her rebellious teenage phase. Mrs. McClellan was unaware of Mary's tawdry liaisons with her husband. "Of course I'll drive you, Mary dear," said Mrs. McClellan. "I've owed you a favor for a long time. Thanks to your influence when you worked here, our Kathleen redirected her life. She's now married and raising a lovely little girl." As Mary left the house, she paused and gazed at the sunny vegetable garden where she had worked for so many happy hours.

Mary found a pair of battered, but serviceable, suitcases at the St. Vincent de Paul Society and packed them with her family's scant clothes.

She made a final visit to her childhood home in Farranree where she filled an empty medicine vial with a pinch of soil and picked a bluebell to press between the pages of her prayer book.

Mary recalled the Sunday afternoon walks with Liam on her days off from work. He made her split with laughter when he told her his earthy stories in Irish. Liam was a good man and Mary loved him dearly. As Mary departed from her ramshackle home in the barn, she tacked a note on the door for McClellan to read:

> *Your repulsive behavior would turn the stomach of the devil. May the Lord in heaven have mercy on your filth-stained soul when you must give him an accounting for your disgusting life.*

A surge of relief swept over Mary when she realized she would never again need to succumb to McClellan's slimy touch and fear what he might do to her children. She hoped their new home in America would allow Bridget and Robert to forget the horrors of his assaults.

Mary and her children met Mrs. McClellan at the crossroads close to the barn for the drive to Shannon. During the ride, they sat in silence. Mary's only movement was a nervous tapping of the sign of the cross with her fingertips on the middle of her chest at each church they passed. Mrs. McClellan stayed with Mary at the airport until she completed the check-in procedures.

As a final gesture of good will, she went to a money exchange kiosk and converted Irish notes netting one hundred U.S. dollars. She slipped the unfamiliar money into Mary's damp, shaking hand. Mary was so overcome with gratitude and excitement she could only stare at Mrs. McClellan and, with trembling lips, whispered her thanks.

The meadow green Aer Lingus plane descended through the clouds, swooped down the runway, and edged to the terminal gate like a majestic Argonaut from another universe. Mary's knees felt so weak she had to sit. She could not believe a thing so fine could be Irish, and she would soon be boarding it. The perky flight attendant directed Mary and the wide-eyed children to their seats.

As the plane sped down the runway and rapidly gained altitude, Mary clutched her rosary and murmured, "Jesus, Mary, and Joseph, protect us during our trip." The sleek Boeing 707, with its gracefully flexing wings, climbed over the Aran Islands off the west coast of Ireland and nosed out over the Atlantic heading for far-off America. Mary dared to look out the window at what she guessed would be her last view of Ireland.

The children sat clutching their armrests in anxious silence until the whine of the engines subsided to a soothing white noise; then they slept. Mary sat rigid with worry about her decision to join the never-ending Irish diaspora and the new life she would be starting in America at the age of 26 in the year 1970—the beginning of Richard Nixon's presidency.

CHAPTER SEVEN

Debbie jerked the back screen door open and waved a bank statement in front of Liam when she saw him coming home from work. She demanded, "What the hell is this here big check to your sister for? It damn near wiped out our bank account."

"It's for air tickets for Mary and her children to come to Chicago. They're being molested by the skunk who owns the barn where they live. They need to get out of there right away."

"Who the hell do you think you are spendin' our money without my okay?"

"Calm down—it's my money; I saved most of it before I ever met you. I don't pee my money down a rat hole like you do when you buy all of that tacky junk you keep hauling home."

"Well, the money became half mine when we got married. You just wait until they try to come into this house; I won't let them set foot in the door."

"The hell you won't. The house is mine, and I say who comes and goes. In fact, I told them they could live upstairs until they get settled."

"You rotten Irish bastard, I can't believe you did this without talkin' to me first. Don't expect no meals on the table or any more humpin' until they've cleared out of here."

"If you think that's a threat, you fat cow, it isn't. The swill you've been dumping on the table lately isn't fit for the dogs, and a sneeze is more exciting than what I've been getting from you in bed."

A few days after Mary arrived in Chicago, Liam took her for a walk through his neighborhood and a talk as they sat on a park bench. Liam remembered Mary's mirth when he used to take her for Sunday afternoon walks in Farranree while giving her the stories from his pub. He now told her the gossip from the factory where he worked, but this time in the South Chicago accent he had acquired. When they spoke of past times in Ireland, they switched to the Irish language.

When Mary stopped laughing she said, "That was my first all-out laugh in a year."

As they arrived back at Liam's house, she squeezed his arm and said, "Liam, I love you so much. I can't imagine why you're so kind to me. And may God and the Holy Saints in heaven always bless you."

Robert, who was now seven, saw the move to America as an opportunity to distance himself from his miserable past life in Ireland. He hoped he could also separate himself from the ever-present specter perched on his shoulder ready to remind him of McClellan's lechery.

Mary landed a room maid job in a nearby Howard Johnson motel. She and her children seldom saw Debbie except on the weekends when she was not working at her evening bartending job.

When Mary arrived in Chicago, she investigated St. Patrick's parochial school for her children, but she found it was inferior to the public schools because of limited budgets and crowded classrooms. She learned the priests in America did not have an autocratic hold over their parishioners like they did in Ireland. They could not demand that parish children attend parochial schools. Mary enrolled Robert and Bridget in the public elementary school.

The children soon shed their Cork brogues, but Mary never changed hers. The children were relieved they were no different than their classmates. Within weeks, Robert academically eclipsed every student in his grade. Bridget was an average student, and her teachers needed to coax her to perform in class.

"I just can't stand it no more with that lot in our house," Debbie whined to Liam after a quarrelsome weekend. "I never have a minute to myself, and you always defend them crummy kids. You did it yesterday when I caught them pokin' fun at me about my weight and clothes. And you think it's amusin' when your sister looks down her nose at me like I was a disease you get from a toilet seat."

"I'm getting near the end of my tether with your bitchiness," Liam fired back. "If you ever have an outburst like this again, I'll throw your big butt and your cruddy junk out onto the street." Debbie seethed with resentment but backed off because she knew she could never find another man as good as Liam.

When Mary saw Debbie working herself up, she would say, "I think we'll go to our rooms. The children have homework."

Mary's income from her job, supplemented by her tips, and the ever generous hand of Liam, allowed her to provide a better life for herself and her children. For the first time in their lives, they were well-fed, properly clothed, and medically treated.

No children with new bicycles were ever more joyful than Robert and Bridget when, on a Saturday afternoon, Mary took them to a Sears and Roebuck store and bought them complete new school outfits.

Robert was so overwhelmed at his good fortune, he stayed in his room all evening staring in disbelief at his crisp new clothes spread out on his bed. He wished Rinty Donlan and his Cork classmates could see him in his new jacket with the Chicago Cubs team logo emblazoned on it.

Liam chuckled and said to Mary, "Robert and Bridget are prouder than freshly white-washed pigs with their new clothes. You sure are lucky to have such nice-looking kids."

Debbie's hostility intensified as she became surlier and heavier while Mary's pleasantness continued and her trim figure remained unchanged. The unfavorable contrast was a threat Debbie could not bear. Mary sensed that for Liam to maintain his marriage, she and the children would have to move out soon.

Mary attended Sunday mass at St. Patrick's Church in the hope that she could recapture the simple comforting faith of her youth and for a little social life in a safe environment.

Matt Dolan was one of the St. Patrick's regulars and a lifelong parishioner. He was an attractive, agreeable man, a little older than Mary, with simple tastes and a cheerful personality. When he talked, he had a peculiar way of turning his head to overcome his developing deafness from the crashing hammers at the forge shop where he worked. He regularly drank coffee and ate doughnuts while he sat with Mary and her children in the church hall after mass.

Matt screwed up his courage to ask, "Mary, we're having a Christmas supper and dance next Saturday night at my union hall. I'd be proud if you'd go with me."

"I'd be happy to go with you, Matt; I've seldom ever eaten a meal outside of home."

When Matt introduced her to his workmates, he couldn't have been more pleased if he had a date with Cinderella.

After several dates, Mary could see Matt's growing interest in a closer relationship. Mary's affection for Matt grew slowly. It was her first experience with a man, other than Liam, who was not wretched.

Matt and Mary wed with Father Hannigan officiating. After the church ceremony, they held a subdued reception in the church hall and departed for a four-day honeymoon trip to Milwaukee, the farthest Matt had ever traveled from home. They drove in Matt's four-year-old Plymouth sedan; Mary thought it was a grand car.

Liam had a heavy heart when Mary moved out of his house. He would now have only Debbie's dim-witted, crabby companionship. Debbie did not find the relief she expected. The main target for her nastiness was gone, and all of the food cooking and house cleaning was now up to her.

Mary and her children moved into Matt's modest, story-and-a-half, 1920s bungalow he inherited when his mother died a few years earlier. Behind the house were a spacious yard and a single-stall garage with access from the alley via two narrow paved strips.

Matt was content with drinking a couple of beers at the neighborhood tavern on Saturday nights, bowling on Wednesdays with his pals from the forge shop, and following local sports on TV. His demands on Mary were minimal. He adored her and could not believe his good luck that she had married him. She was grateful for the stability he brought to her and his kindness to her children.

Mary asked Matt to build a picket fence around an unused area in his back yard so she could grow a garden as she once did when she worked for Mrs. McClellan in Ireland. Before she planted vegetable seeds, she sprinkled her vial of Farranree soil over the surface and raked it into the rich Illinois earth. She removed the pressed Irish bluebell plant from her prayer book and buried it in a shady spot in hope the clinging seeds would germinate.

While she gardened, Mary could escape into her private world. Matt enjoyed teasing her by asking, "Are Mrs. McGregor and Peter Rabbit going to spend the afternoon in the garden again today?"

Whatever Mary wanted for her children was okay with Matt. Several months after their marriage, Bridget said, "Mother, I am so happy that Matt doesn't hurt us like Uncle Brian used to."

One of Robert's few precocious classmates with a literary flair had read most of Charles Dickens's books and remembered the title of his unfinished novel, *The Mystery of Edward Drood*. He said to his pals, "Hey, listen to this you guys, I read this here book about a weirdo named Edward Drood. I think Robert must be one of his relatives. Anybody who can brown nose the teachers like he does and get all of them compliments for good grades looks pretty weird to me."

Robert said, "Think about how this stick feels across your choppers the next time you tell anyone a lie like that again you stupid sod." The Dickens reader left the schoolyard by ambulance. The attending physician at the hospital emergency room removed two dangling teeth and sewed up his lip with six stitches.

At her lunch table in the faculty room, Robert's teacher said to her colleagues, "Robert Drood is my new student from Ireland. He has the most enormous learning capacity I've ever known. I accused him of inattention after reading a poem to the class yesterday. He recited it back verbatim. And yesterday he came into my room while I was entering a list of numbers on an adding machine tape. He scanned the tape and told me the correct sum faster than I could punch the total key."

While Robert's classmates read comic books, he read electronic magazines containing information on rapidly evolving computer designs and software development. He bought electronic components and constructed his own rudimentary computer in his room.

The school principal called Robert to his office and said, "I hear you're good with computers, Robert. I'm studying small computers for possible use for school record keeping. An electronic company wants our school to be a beta site for testing its new line of computers and software. Will you help us learn how to use the computer and evaluate it?"

"Sure, I'll help you, sir," Robert replied. "May I start now?"

Robert's school principal asked Mary to come to his office for a conference. He said, "Mrs. Dolan, Robert is a problem student. He disrupts his classes with sarcastic remarks and pranks. His teachers can't control him. We think he's bored because his school assignments are too easy for him. I believe we should move him ahead to a higher grade."

Mary said, "Sir, Robert has always read and talked like an adult. He reads all the time and remembers everything. His bedroom is always piled full of books. Moving him forward a grade is okay with me."

Robert graduated soon after his twelfth birthday.

Father Hannigan visited Mary at her home. While he drank his tea, he said, "Mary, I have heard reports that Robert is a stellar student. I think we should find a way for him to attend a high school that can advance his remarkable learning talent. An old friend is a Jesuit priest and teacher at the St. Ignatius Preparatory School for gifted children on the north side of Chicago. He claims its graduates can pass the entrance examinations to any American college or university. The school attracts students who have both academic and athletic talent. Robert is blessed on both counts."

"Oh Father, that isn't possible. Matt and I can't afford to pay the tuition for a private school."

"But I think it is possible, Mary. St. Ignatius reserves a few scholarships for gifted students whose families can't afford its hefty tuition. If it's alright with you, I'll talk to my friend about Robert's remarkable talent."

When the St. Ignatius admission officer visited Robert to confirm Father Hannigan's claims about his academic superiority, he interviewed several of his teachers. "How would you sum up Robert's academic talents?" he asked his eighth grade English literature teacher.

"I can best answer your question by quoting Oliver Goldsmith: 'And still they gazed, and still the wonder grew, that one small head could hold all he knew.' Robert is the most intelligent student I've known in my twenty-five years of teaching."

The admission officer then interviewed Robert. "I hear you're a well-informed boy, Robert. I'm going to ask you several questions. Take whatever time you need, and feel free to use paper and pencil to work out the answers. I'll start with several mathematics and science questions. What is the square root of 337,561?"

Robert promptly answered, "581."

"Correct. Now, what is the full name and atomic number of the element 'Rh' as shown on the Periodic Table of Elements? If you can answer part of the question, it's enough."

"Rhodium. Forty-five," Robert replied without hesitation.

"Now, I want you to tell me the author of several quotations: 'Tho' I've belted you and flayed you, By the livin' Gawd that made you, You're a better man . . .'"

"That would be Rudyard Kipling, sir," Robert interrupted.

"And now this one: 'Beware when the great God lets loose a thinker on the planet.'"

This obscure quotation took Robert several moments of thinking before he answered, "I think it was Ralph Waldo Emerson."

"That is also correct."

Before the admissions officer left, he hinted, "There should be no problem for you to enroll in St. Ignatius."

During one of Mary and Father Hannigan's periodic visits, Mary said, "I've never forgotten the soothsayer foretelling Robert's destiny at the time of his birth. The first part of her prophecy is now proven. He indeed has the wisdom of the 'Salmon of Knowledge.' She also foretold that he will be the leader of many people in many lands and will return like the spawning salmon to his birthplace in Ireland. Father, do you think the rest of her prophecy will also come to pass?"

"We must wait and see, Mary. I'm a strong believer that our lives are more complete when we listen to all of the voices that speak to us. Everything can't be explained by scholars and scientists."

CHAPTER EIGHT

When Robert enrolled at St Ignatius, he found most of his classmates—whose parents could easily pay hefty tuitions—were from posh northern Chicago suburbs: Evanston, Wilmette, Winnetka, and Lake Forest.

An upper-class student mentored Robert on St. Ignatius traditions. He said, "Robert, here at St. Ignatius we all must wear gray blazers, black shoes and trousers, white shirts, and red ties. And we get along a lot better if we show an attitude of respect to our teachers. Actually, most of them are quite good."

Robert said, "That all sounds pretty dumb to me, but I suppose I can do it if I have to."

The apparent wealth and power of the families of Robert's classmates amazed him. Detractors called St. Ignatius students "The Roman Legion" because of the Roman numerals after many of their names.

When classes commenced, Robert was momentarily challenged. He now had to concentrate rather than brush by information and have it automatically implant itself in his mind. When he gave a small amount of time to proper study, he again excelled even in the competitive environment at St. Ignatius. A teacher observed, "Robert Drood accumulates knowledge like a puddle collects rain in a cloudburst."

He was disdainful of his teachers. On the surface he treated them respectfully, but inside he smugly thought none held a candle to him for intelligence.

He reached his six feet three inches mature height and maximum athletic agility early. His sports skills rivaled those of older classmates. Football gave him a visceral thrill because of the mauling he could give his opponents. His coaches had limited success in tuning down his unnecessary aggressiveness and tendency to be a loner on the football field.

Matt Dolan could see little reason for education beyond that required to operate the machines at the forge shop where he worked. Nevertheless, to please Mary, he set up a small upstairs study cubicle for Robert who breezed through his homework and read voraciously on his favorite subjects: mathematics, science, history, and philosophy.

While at a St. Patrick's Church basement rummage sale with his mother, Robert noticed four volumes of boxed books entitled *The World of Mathematics* by James R. Newman. He bought the volumes for a dollar and read and reread them with the enthusiasm of a child hearing favorite nursery stories. With this small library of books, Robert thought he had found the mother lode of mathematical and scientific knowledge. The books clinched his decision to pursue mathematics and science for his profession.

Robert's physics teacher spent a class period explaining the complexities of light in terms of wave mechanics and photons while writing mathematical formulas and drawing sketches on the blackboard. Robert read an electronics magazine throughout the lecture and occasionally glanced at the blackboard.

His apparent inattention and disrespect irked his teacher. Near the end of the class he asked, "Mr. Drood, can you be so kind as to tell me anything at all about today's lecture?"

Robert flipped his magazine aside, strode to a side blackboard, and rewrote the mathematical formulas and redrew the sketches. "Now, do you want me to summarize your lecture or repeat it verbatim?" he asked. His admirers envied his panache; however, his more perceptive classmates recognized he was showing off his parrot-like memory and not necessarily demonstrating a talent for creative thinking.

Robert's good looks, athletic capability, and academic talent made him the alpha person of his class. But the closeness of friendships with his classmates was proportional to the degree to which he could exploit them. He manipulated friendships with classmates who had rich, indulgent parents to ensure access to weekend cottages and boats and invitations to posh birthday parties and social events. Exposure to wealth and affluence, a new experience for Robert, became increasingly appealing to him. He never revealed his humble origin to his classmates. None ever met his family or visited his home.

The specter perched on Robert's shoulder always stood ready to recall the horrors of his past, and no amount of intellectualizing could dismiss it. When he received kudos for outstanding schoolwork or sports achievements, terrifying recollections of his miserable childhood in Ireland intruded and dampened the glow of success. He was cheated out of the euphoria he deserved for his achievements. He had an irrational fear his good fortune was a mirage that would fade away, and he would return to the deplorable conditions of his youth.

Robert imagined his mind consisted of two chambers. One contained concrete elements controlled by reason and logic. This chamber was as easy for him to understand as mathematics and science. The second chamber contained his mysterious psyche controlled by dark, unbridled forces. He was denied access to it, and yet it could control and dominate him. Even though he had abandoned belief in the Catholic faith, he beseeched God and the Holy Saints in heaven to intercede for him in dispelling the grim specter that controlled the dark chamber of his mind. He sustained himself with the hope that his crushing burden would lift when he grew older, and the dream that the people who abused his family in Ireland would be brought to justice.

While scanning a book of poetry one evening in his study cubicle, Robert read a verse by Sylvia Plath that he thought she could have written for him:

> *I am terrified by this dark thing*
> *That sleeps in me*
> *All day I feel its soft, feathery turnings, its malignity.*

For the next several weeks, when Plath's verse again turned over in his mind, he felt faint and shuddered.

In Robert's junior year, he was short of money for a school dance. He hid in a closet until the administrative staff went home for the night, and with the light from his flashlight entered the school offices. He jimmied the lock on the office petty cash box and pocketed two hundred dollars. His school identification card fell from his pocket marking him as the thief.

The school authorities handled the theft without police intervention. Robert was apologetic and contrite to the school discipline officer. The officer, who had been around a long time, wanted to take harsh action, but the school authorities decided to excuse Robert based on his apparent contriteness and in light of it being his first identifiable criminal offense. His star athletic capability also influenced their decision. The discipline officer muttered, "I'll bet my reputation young Drood will steal again but on a far grander scale."

In his last year at St. Ignatius, Robert was invited to a rich classmate's town club for dinner and dancing. After an evening of drinking, he turned nasty and taunted and mocked his debutante date. "How does it feel to wear clothes that cost a working man's annual wages and travel the world like a member of a pasha's harem—all on your daddy's credit card? Does it make you feel like a parasite or a princess?"

She tried to brush him off by changing the subject assuming his remarks were due to drinking too much. Robert persisted with his needling, "If you run out of things to do with your old man's money, you could invest in a boob enhancement and a nose job. It would do wonders for your appearance."

"You lift bad manners to new heights," she snapped. "You should take a good look in the mirror when you strut around looking like a peacock with your 'attitude' pasted across your face. You think you deserve credit for your intelligence and appearance, but you don't any more than I deserve credit for my father's wealth and affluence. I've had enough of your boorish behavior; I'm taking a cab home."

When Robert sobered up the next morning, he called his date to apologize. She would not accept his phone call. He was appalled he had done something to himself that caused him to lose control of his most-cherished possession: his mental capability. He made a resolution to never again drink immoderately.

Robert took enormous pride in his appearance. When he studied his well-proportioned profile in a mirror, he imagined his nose should be less aquiline and his chin slightly more prominent. He listened to his voice on a recorder and thought he detected a slight stammer. He would have these defects corrected when he earned enough money to hire a plastic surgeon and a speech therapist. Every time he looked in a mirror he posed like he imagined he would look when he became famous.

One of the few girls who was not gaga over him said, "Robert, you always look like you're sizing others up and proclaiming your superiority over them. Your mouth's becoming twisted into a permanent sneer." Uncharacteristically Robert heeded her criticism. He spent hours practicing in front of a mirror and was successful in softening his scornful and cynical expression.

Robert gave meticulous attention to his clothes. His daily brushing, pressing, and shoe shining of his school clothes made him look like he was perpetually prepared for inspection by his drill sergeant. His one set of non-school dress clothes made him look like a store window display. He stood while riding to school on the bus to prevent wrinkles in his trousers and to avoid the possibility of sitting on a dirty seat. Some of his classmates called him "The Mannequin."

When he walked, he leaned forward several degrees as if he were on the verge of breaking into a trot. He did everything at flank speed; he was obsessed with speed, orderliness, and efficiency.

The school counselor met with Robert to discuss his schoolwork and deportment. "Mr. Drood, you're gifted with a superior intellect and excellent athletic abilities, both of which you use effectively. But I hear frequent criticism of your arrogance and disrespect for your classmates and teachers." Robert bridled at the counselor's criticism, but held his tongue. The counselor knew Robert admired Benjamin Franklin so he suggested, "You should reread the part of Franklin's autobiography where he speaks of 'dropping the habit of abrupt contradiction and positive arguments in favor of a more diffident demeanor in putting forward opinions.'"

Robert returned to his counselor the next week and said, "Sir, after rethinking the passages you mentioned in *The Autobiography of Benjamin Franklin*, I've tried to follow Franklin's example of being more understanding of the views of others. Thank you for your advice; it's been valuable to me." Robert's contriteness was feigned; he only said he agreed with his counselor because he did not want any black marks on his record.

Shortly after his sixteenth birthday, he graduated with some of the highest grades ever recorded at St. Ignatius Preparatory School. The administrator mailed a graduation ceremony invitation to Mary and Matt. Robert did not want to introduce his "plain Jane" mother to his classmates' "fancy shmancy" parents, and he dreaded the possibility she would bring Matt along in his cheap blue suit, out-of-style necktie, and scuffed brown shoes. Even worse, he feared he would speak with his shop floor grammar and express his viewpoint in labor union rhetoric. He intercepted and destroyed the graduation invitation.

CHAPTER NINE

With Robert's perfect SAT scores and outstanding athletic ability, every college and university where he applied for admission courted him. When he explained his meager financial circumstances, all offered him scholarships or grants.

Robert accepted the engineering scholarship offered by MIT. He soon found, for the first time in his life, his academic capabilities were not superior to all of his classmates; some of them also had perfect SAT scores.

The MIT competition stimulated Robert. He tracked the grades of his ablest classmates and was not satisfied until he could top them.

However, he soon realized that many of his nerdy classmates would not be a socially competitive challenge for attracting girls when he heard one of them use the dopey pickup line, "What are your SAT scores?"

Bridget's academic performance was less exemplary. She had the intellect to perform well, but the trauma from her childhood rape lowered her self-esteem and her ability to concentrate. Her wrong kind of friends led her to drink, drugs, and flings with boys she met in unseemly hangouts.

During her last year of high school, Mary received a call from the school nurse, "Your daughter's on her way to the hospital. She slit her wrists in a toilet stall; a classmate found her before it was too late. We think she'll recover. The ambulance is taking her to Trinity Hospital. It should be there in fifteen minutes." After Bridget healed and was counseled by a psychologist, she dropped out of school. Matt found a job for her in his factory shipping department.

The human resources department of Union Electric Corporation, the largest electrical and electronic equipment manufacturer in the world, maintained a close relationship with MIT faculty. The professors helped Union Electric identify stellar students for part-time employment during school breaks with the hope that they would be hired permanently upon graduation. The company courted and hired Robert as an intern while he was still in college.

During a school break, he helped write a creative report defining a business opportunity for a complex new product. He wrote the algorithms upon which the business model for the product was based and described it in easily understandable terms.

His manager said, "Robert, I want you to present your report to some of our executives."

After the presentation, his manager said, "Your presentation went over so well it's creating 'buzz' all over the place. We're going to move you around to different departments to broaden your work experience."

Chicago became a closed chapter of Robert's life. Because his family could no longer be beneficial to him, he seldom visited them.

During a rare holiday visit, Mary told Robert the story of his birth: "When the midwife finished her duties at the time of your birth, she sent her cousin, a soothsayer, to my bedside to foretell your destiny. She said you would have great wisdom, rule many people, and return to Ireland. From your grades, I can see the first part of her prophesy has come true. Father Hannigan and I think the rest will follow."

"Mother, you've told me this story before. Only the Irish can come up with that kind of claptrap. Next, you'll tell me about the pot of gold at the end of the rainbow and banshees that howl in the night to announce death."

"We'll wait and see, Robert. I'm betting on the predictions of the soothsayer."

The job at Union Electric provided money for Robert's personal needs, but he was always short of money for luxurious splurges. He added to his income by gambling where he won much of the time by memorizing cards and calculating statistical odds. Some of his game partners were convinced he cheated and quit playing with him.

Robert also earned money by tutoring undergraduates in mathematics. For some inexplicable reason, teaching touched a primordial need within him and gave him a surge of fulfillment. His normal impatience and arrogance subsided while he taught.

The universities and colleges near MIT in the Cambridge and Boston area abounded with affluent female students. Robert dated one of them long enough for her father to assess his career potential. He said, while lubricated with a drink too many, "Robert, I may be jumping the gun, but from what my daughter tells me, it won't be long until you're engaged. We have an opening in management and on the board of my company. It's a growing company; we are up to fifty million dollars of annual sales. We almost control the highway road sign market. I think you're the man for the job. How about me setting it up for you?"

"That's a generous offer, sir, but let's hold off until I'm further along with my studies." Robert did not mention that his career goals were far more ambitious than running a small corporation that manufactured a dull, low-tech product. He had no interest in an engagement, and he imagined employment in a family firm would be a caged existence that would prevent him from being the sole decision maker for his professional life. He soon ended his relationship with the daughter.

Robert always dumped women soon after they slept with him, and he had his fill of luxurious weekends at their parents' Cape Cod or Hampton estates. His conquests of women only gave him momentary gratification followed by a feeling of emotional hollowness. Because he did not have the capacity to bond with anyone, he ended his affairs with no more remorse or emotion than a bird swallowing an insect.

A classmate observed, "Robert Drood will not give the time of day to people who were not up to his intellectual standards, but he will abandon all restraint to chase anybody with wealth, fame, or influence."

Robert graduated summa cum laude from MIT, Class of 1985, with a degree in physics; it was during the presidency of Ronald Regan. He went on to earn a master's degree in mathematics at Stanford in California and returned to MIT for a Ph.D. in physics. He supplemented his technical education by simultaneously sprinting through Harvard's MBA program.

After a round of graduation partying, Robert thought about his career and the next phase of his life. He was now twenty-four years old, superbly educated, and ready for full-time employment.

He had no doubt it was his destiny to become supremely successful. He wrote a step by step career plan for becoming the chief executive officer of a major corporation before he was forty, wealthy before fifty, and then on to a second career—possibly in the federal government at the cabinet level. He also devised a matrix showing the requisite factors required for success and his self-evaluation for each factor.

One of Robert's classmates saw his career plan on his desk and read it. He said to a friend, "I read Drood's career plan that he left out in the open. I wouldn't be surprised if he left it there to be read as a kind of bragging document. He rates himself high on all factors required to quickly rise to the top of a major corporation. I agree with the high ratings he gave himself for intelligence and communication skills. But he didn't have an item for 'capability to relate with others'; if he did, I'd have given him a big fat 'F'."

His friend replied, "Drood will likely follow his plan and become a big success, but I don't want to ever work within a country mile of the bastard and his bloated ego. I never trusted the guy. When you first meet him, he appears to have everything going for him, but you soon discover he's only a well-programmed robot. A conversation with him is more like an adversarial confrontation between opposing lawyers in a court room. Some awful thing must have happened in his earlier life that made him lock up all of his emotions in a safe."

CHAPTER TEN

▶ ▶ ▶

Drood received generous job offers from dozens of firms following his interviews with them. After evaluating the offers, he accepted the one from Union Electric. He already knew the company from school break work assignments and liked its emphasis on management development. In June of 1988, he began working in its advanced research division in Albany, New York.

Union Electric expected its scientists and engineers in this division to perform significant original work with minimal direction. Robert soon discovered, in spite of his high intelligence, he did not have the singular spark required for basic, original technical thinking. However, he did excel in communicating complex ideas among the sometimes myopic worlds of engineering, manufacturing, and marketing. He facilitated bringing several profitable new products—invented by others—from concept to market in record time.

Union Electric executives were accustomed to hearing technical presentations as lugubrious as funeral orations. Robert's presentations contained a livelier theme. He introduced a new type of light bulb with the opening line, "The Lord said, 'Let there be light.' With our new illumination system, we can boast we have exceeded his promise." He brashly killed an unfavorable joint venture proposal by saying, "Union Electric needs this venture like a deer hunting party needs a bugler."

Executives looked forward to hearing Robert's refreshing style and technical clarity. After his presentations, it was not unusual to hear them whisper, "Who is this young guy? I'm going to transfer him to my division." His nickname became "The Speaker."

After six months in the advanced research department, Robert transferred to the strategic business planning department at the posh company headquarters in Manhattan. He soon exhibited a rifle-shot sense for identifying businesses with strong, profitable market potential and developed comprehensive plans for rapidly developing them.

Robert worked intensely while in his office, but seldom took a briefcase home. He used nonworking hours for exercising in his gym, reading, and dining in topnotch restaurants—usually with a stunning woman.

Wealthy, sophisticated women with entrées to concerts, plays, and art shows dominated Robert's Rolodex file. He was attracted to any woman who spoke of high society, fame, or wealth.

He occasionally met men after working hours for sporting events or dinners. After he dined with several work colleagues, one said, "Spending an evening with Drood makes me feel like I'm having a poor work performance review. I think I'll be occupied the next time he calls."

With Robert's considerable paychecks from Union Electric, he engaged a plastic surgeon to correct minor—almost imaginary—defects in his nose and chin. The surgery marginally improved his appearance. He also hired a speech therapist to help him eliminate a scarcely noticeable stammer. The small improvements further inflated his already enormous self-image.

Robert knew it was risky to work too long at corporate staff jobs where he would become an overpaid "suit" wearing five thousand dollars' worth of tailor made clothes and shoes. He maneuvered his way to an assistant manager position for a specialty silicon chip factory—commonly called a fab—near Poughkeepsie. Along with the appointment came the promise that when he learned the ropes, he would likely become the fab manager with full profit and loss responsibility—a prerequisite for significant career advancement.

For the first few days on the new job, Robert memorized fab reports on manufacturing, quality, and product development. And he reviewed the personnel records of all of the managers and a cross-section of the eight hundred wage employees. A long-time employee said to Robert's secretary, "Young Drood can recite more employee names and fab operation facts than I can after working here for years. When he reads or hears something, I think he presses his personal save button to store it away in his mental server for future retrieval."

After a session with Robert, an older manager grumbled, "With young 'Hot Shot' Drood's trick memory, he can spew out facts as if he were reading from a report. He thinks we're supposed to be impressed, but I'm waiting to see how he performs when we have the next manufacturing crisis in the fab."

Robert's boss and the fab human resources manager met to discuss the best way to counsel him in the face of mounting employee disrespect. The human resources manager was a congenial woman with no further career aspirations. They decided she would talk to Robert.

"Robert, the culture here in the fab is laying speed bumps in front of you. Most of the employees are not from the competitive halls of academia you're used to. They want to do a good job, but they want to do it in a nonconfrontational environment. They are put off by your cerebral style and lightning speed. They think you're trying to 'hot dog' them."

"Well, if they can't keep up, isn't that their problem?" Robert snorted.

"One of the jobs of the human resource manager is to facilitate harmony among the employees. I can't change all of them, so I thought if I appealed to you, you might agree to trim your sails. You don't need to impress the employees. They will follow your leadership if you just show some understanding and consideration for them. Will you please think about what I'm telling you? I suggest we meet each week for further feedback."

During the next several days Robert thought about his meeting with the human resources manager: What does that aging broad know about executive behavior? And who does she think she is to act like a school counselor? What a sow. But on the other hand, she's probably the spokesperson for the fab manager. Offending them is a good way to be scrubbed from the high potential promotion list. Kissing butts and slowing down to accommodate this bunch of rustic slope heads is apparently the price I must pay to keep on the fast track.

In less than a year, the Poughkeepsie fab manager was promoted to a new job. By this time Robert had improved his image among the employees. At twenty-seven, he was promoted to fab manager—the youngest in the company.

Social life in Poughkeepsie was a letdown for Robert after New York City, but he would endure his sentence and do his time because he did not expect to be there long. Being single and attractive with a high-level job gave him universal entrée to society in Poughkeepsie, but few of the opportunities interested him. A dinner party that included discussions of the high school athletic teams and the host's children bored Robert. He frequently spent his weekends in Manhattan in the company of women with invitations to velvet-rope events.

George Winthrop, the CEO of Union Electric, was renowned for monitoring and challenging exceptional employees. He believed in giving jobs to high-potential people before they had adequate experience and testing them to see how fast they could master the new jobs. When they demonstrated success, he moved them on to even more challenging jobs—often in entirely different fields.

After a year in Poughkeepsie, Robert's boss wrote his work performance review. He was dissatisfied with Robert's frequent absences on Monday mornings and Friday afternoons. The fact that he returned after a weekend brimming with ideas did not mollify him. He also did not like the stories he heard about Robert's bloated expense accounts and high living. On the other hand, he could not overlook his success in improving the profitability and quality at the Poughkeepsie fab.

Although Robert's boss wanted to note his personal deficiencies in his performance review, he did not. Robert was on the fast track promotion list, and a negative review could slow down or halt his rapid career growth. It could also be detrimental to his own ambitions. Recently a manager wrote a negative performance review on an elite employee. When it passed over George Winthrop's desk, he noted the review writer showed poor judgment for evaluating exceptional employees. Robert's boss concluded his review with a note: "Robert Drood is a superior employee who is ready for promotion to a position of expanded responsibility."

The performance reviews of high-potential employees were routed to George Winthrop. When he read Robert's review, he said, "Let's move Drood to an overseas position. Find a spot for him in Asia. That's where our fastest business growth is."

Robert, who was now twenty-nine years old, received an offer to become assistant managing director of the Asia-Pacific Office in Tokyo. The mission of the office was to assist all divisions of the company with their Asian investigations and ventures. Although its mission was vaguely defined, the office was widely recognized as a valuable and effective force.

Robert analyzed his new job offer. It was a good fit with his career plan even though some traditional executives thought employees were odd who accepted overseas assignments where they must work with strange people who jabber instead of speaking English; eat with their left hand or with chopsticks; and measure things with the metric system. Robert had a broader viewpoint: he accepted the offer.

CHAPTER ELEVEN

Thomas Scott, the AMSCO Asia-Pacific Managing Director, was a veteran from the earliest Union Electric overseas ventures. His English still retained the flat accent of the prairies of eastern Colorado where he was raised on a ranch; he still "warshed" his hands; and flew to "Warshington" to testify before international trade commissions. He still called creeks "cricks." He knew enough of a dozen languages to move around the world with confidence and ease.

Scott liked to have smart, high-energy people work for him. He could stand warts on employees if they could effectively work with limited direction while under pressure. He tethered them with a long rope and watched to ensure they stayed within his loosely defined bounds. If they strayed too far, he gave their rope a jerk to pull them back into an acceptable orbit. If they went beyond prudent limits again, he sent them home with a letter for their performance file that would cause time-out for maturing before further career advancement.

Scott's advice to new employees who showed a tendency for elevated egos consisted of telling them an often repeated ranch aphorism his father told him at thirteen when he sent him into the corral to break riding horses, "There ain't a horse that can't be rode or a cowboy that can't be throwed." An employee kept a list of Scott's rustic aphorisms and an explanation of their meanings; the list helped non-American employees understand him.

For his first several months in Tokyo, Robert spent his spare time studying the cultures and histories of Japan, Korea, China, and other Asian countries. He expanded his rudimentary knowledge of Japanese and within a year could speak with functional fluency. He set a goal to expand his vocabulary by one hundred words each day. Okiko Ogata, an employee of the Tokyo office, taught him Asian social customs and business protocols.

Robert quickly adjusted to the culture of Japan and the other Asian countries where Union Electric conducted business. After a short break-in period, Scott gave him negotiating assignments. He learned to negotiate with a balance of toughness and respect for tedious Asian business customs. His instincts were good for deciding when it was time to reach agreements or to abandon business propositions.

After Scott saw several of Robert's business presentations, he called him to his office and said, "Robert, I'm going to cut you loose and have you make more presentations to our company executives. You can convince a shooting gallery duck it's going to die of old age. You better memorize the air schedules to New York, London, and Sao Paulo. From now on, you're going to do a lot of your sleeping in airplane seats. Fly Singapore Airlines when you can; they fold their seats into sleeping berths."

Many of the officials of the Asian companies who dealt with Union Electric belonged to prestigious social and sporting clubs in their respective countries. They used the clubs primarily to entertain business clients. A call from Robert announcing he would be in town precipitated weekend agendas of lavish entertainment. He could always devise a business reason to travel to an Asian country when special events were scheduled. Scott drove his employees hard for work results, but he never interfered with their travel plans. Because he disliked traveling, he could not imagine anyone ever taking a nonessential trip.

Hong Kong became one of Robert's favorite cities and a frequent destination for his business travels. Hong Kong business associates provided boundless entertainment and pleasures for their visitors. Although Robert understood the stringent Union Electric policy forbidding favors or gifts, he interpreted it to suit his inclination for self-indulgences.

Many Chinese men are dedicated, high-stakes gamblers who bet on anything imaginable; even which raindrop will roll down a windowpane fastest or which sugar cube will attract the first fly. Horse-race gambling is a favorite. Selecting winning horses is not based on bloodlines as is normal for westerners. The Chinese determine winners based on a combination of luck, incense smoke, calendar dates, and ancestral names. Several of the Union Electric suppliers belonged to the Happy Valley Race Club on Hong Kong Island and the newer hundred million dollar Shatin Club in the New Territories. They were always happy to provide Robert and his guest with premium racetrack seats.

While at a race, a Chinese business associate said, "Robert, I take your money to betting window for you and pick winning horse with my proven methods. You wait in seat until I come back."

The associate added his money to Robert's, bet on every horse in the race, and assigned the winning ticket to Robert. When he returned after the race he said, "Robert, I delayed by a jam-up in aisles. You lucky man. You win big time."

Robert guessed how his host had manipulated the tickets in his favor, but he let it stand because his weekend expenses were so enormous even his padded expense account could not absorb them.

One of Robert's regular Hong Kong companions was Chen Li Maranhes, an exquisitely beautiful employee of Cathay International Airlines. Her mother was Chinese and her father Portuguese. She dealt with her clients every day in Portuguese, English, Mandarin, Cantonese, and Japanese. Robert squired her to the racetracks and other destinations in a chauffeured Rolls Royce limousine from the Peninsula Hotel garage. He always stayed at the majestic Peninsula in suites with nightly rates equal to a month's wages for a U.S. factory worker.

At the end of their weekends together Robert usually said, "Chen Li, I want you to select a gift to remember this weekend. Have you a favorite shop?"

She always replied, "Oh, no, Robert, I don't want a gift. My weekend with you was enough." But she then signaled the chauffeur, whom she had pre-instructed, to drive to a classy boutique on Nathan Road or Mody Road where she had already earmarked an expensive designer outfit or jewelry and negotiated a slice of the purchase price for her purse as a payoff for bringing in a live customer.

After the first several weekends with Chen Li, Robert called her and asked her to arrange his future visits to Hong Kong. By then she knew his taste for lavishness and his capability to pay the price. And she also knew where to find the best—and often obscure—places for exotic entertainment and pleasures.

During a weekend date, Chen Li said, "Robert, I heard a man speak of the great companies in Silicon Valley in California and how he made big money on their stock. Can you please explain this to me?"

The next day Chen Li bought a few shares of stock based on the information she had solicited from Robert. She also gathered financial advice from her other VIP visitors to help her select stock for her growing and profitable investment portfolio.

A visiting Union Electric executive said to Robert after a series of mind-numbing Asian negotiations, "I don't know how you do it, Robert. You sit through all of that time-consuming, dull nonsense day after day as if you have nothing better to do with your time. You keep a dozen negotiating tracks in your mind at the same time. Then at just the right minute you bundle a bunch of them together in a way that is advantageous to Union Electric, and they agree to a deal."

Union Electric was accustomed to sending teams of people to Asia to participate in prolonged contract negotiations. Risk aversion was so paramount in the Union Electric culture that many good business propositions were delayed until they became stale. The company was tagged with the slogan: "Union Electric analyzes until the opportunity dies of boredom or old age."

Robert found a way to speed up Asian negotiations by allowing only a few well-informed Union Electric people to participate in meetings. He usually insisted on leading the negotiations himself. He had seen too many people wander offtrack and become tied in knots by clever negotiating adversaries.

When a team of Union Electric people arrived in Asia without adequate preparatory work, Robert canceled their planned meetings and sent them home. A few days later, their senior vice president called him and fumed, "Who do you think you are, the emperor of Japan? Well, your empire doesn't extend to my division. You had no authority to cancel meetings and send my people home."

"Then don't send people here who are ill-prepared," Robert snapped. "I'm not their nanny. I won't allow our company to be embarrassed and ridiculed because your people come here unprepared to face a group of superbly informed negotiators who know everything about our business and about us down to our collar sizes and zip codes. I did you a favor by canceling the meeting. Your people would have been as defenseless as trout in a net. Send them back here after they properly prepare for the trip. I will then help them in any way I can."

Robert continued to be called The Speaker because of his skill for presenting Asian business opportunities to Union Electric executives. To goad cautious executives to make prompt decisions, Robert sometimes opened meetings with a Shakespeare quotation:

> *There is a tide in the affairs of men,*
> *Which taken at the flood, leads on to fortune;*
> *Omitted, all the voyage of their life*
> *Is bound in shallows and in miseries.*

Staid executives bridled at being told by a brash, young man when they should make decisions, but they usually refrained from comment because they did not want to confirm the implication they were either incapable of making timely decisions or too dense to understand the meaning of a lofty quotation.

Robert's peers resented him seeking the limelight, but they knew the wisdom of never running counter to fair-haired boys on the rise who might soon be their bosses. Privately, Robert's peers admitted he was unequaled at digesting and articulating complex information. One of them, who remembered a line by Homer from a college Greek classics course, recited: "His speech flows from him sweeter than honey."

When Robert moved to Japan, Okiko Ogata impressed him with her intelligence, aggressiveness, and business acumen. She was from an ancient, prominent Japanese family that realized, after the chaos of World War II, the old ways of Japan were doomed and the ideas of the West would dominate the world. The family educated its children and grandchildren in America. Okiko attended high school and college in the U.S.

When Okiko returned to Japan after college graduation, Scott hired her based on her knowledge of Japanese culture, intelligence, education, and supreme self-confidence. She immediately showed promise as a savvy business person. It was not evident to most people that Okiko's well-manicured fingernails were razor-sharp talons she could use with speedy, and sometimes deadly, effectiveness in business negotiations.

Robert took Okiko with him on a trip to visit Lodestar Limited in Korea. Lodestar, an enormous international industrial firm, was a high-volume supplier of small transmissions to several divisions of Union Electric. A contract for them to design and manufacture a complex new transmission was under way. Union Electric engineers were uneasy about Lodestar's lagging schedule and difficulty in meeting the demanding new transmission performance and quality specifications.

During the visit, the Lodestar executives gave an upbeat presentation to Robert, Okiko, and the accompanying engineers demonstrating that their work was progressing satisfactorily; they said technical requirements and delivery schedules would be met.

Okiko slipped out during a lull in the meetings to visit the transmission engineering department and test shops. She found, contrary to the assurances given in the conference room, there were still formidable difficulties to overcome. When she shared her observations with Robert, he became uneasy. "Okiko, what do you suggest we do to bring Lodestar back on track?"

"Let me loose with those Korean blockheads for several more visits and I'll either have them back on schedule or recommend cancellation of their contract."

"Okay, Okiko, go for it. Incidentally, the Koreans and the Japanese don't seem to be too fond of each other."

"The Japanese consider Koreans a low social caste fit only for menial work. And the Koreans still remember Japan's unspeakable brutality during World War II. However, the Japanese have learned to tolerate the boisterous aggressiveness of the Koreans, and the Koreans accept the stoical calmness of the Japanese. But it is a mystery to the macho men of Lodestar why a Japanese woman like me is allowed to represent Union Electric. They can't stand it."

The Lodestar officials were in for a shock when Okiko returned for her next visit. She met with the project executive and bluntly stated her demands. "I want you to schedule overtime until the project is on schedule and I want you to put in a new project manager—one who doesn't lie in the conference room about work status." The executive was nonplussed and refused Okiko's demands. The project executive seethed to a colleague, "I won't take orders from that Nipponese bitch whose highest responsibility, if she worked for Lodestar, would be to fetch us our tea. If she didn't represent Union Electric and such an important contract, I'd dump her out into a compost pit on her skinny Armani-clad butt."

Okiko called the Lodestar division vice president, Lee Yoon Woo, to press her demands to a higher level. She restated her position and bluffed him into believing she had the authority to cancel the Union Electric contract if he didn't agree to her demands. "I'll be in your office tomorrow at 7:30 a.m. to hear your response to my requests," she said.

The next morning, to Okiko's surprise, Lee Yoon said, "Miss Ogata, we have evaluated and considered your constructive suggestions since yesterday. We have decided to accept and execute them. Please assure Dr. Drood and the Union Electric engineers we'll deliver on time and according to the contract specifications. We invite you to return at any time to monitor our progress."

Okiko refrained from giving her well-deliberated outburst of invective and threats. She surmised Lee Yoon and his staff had worked much of the night in a flurry of nasty accusations before deciding on the response he had just given. "I think you have made a wise decision, Mr. Lee Yoon," Okiko said. "I'm hopeful we'll never again witness your project manager giving a report in the conference room that varies from the actual work status. I'll be back again in two weeks to monitor your progress."

When Okiko returned to Tokyo, she said to her brother, "Those Kimchi-eating (spiced vegetables) bastards at Lodestar are not fit for tilling a Japanese rice paddy. I sure enjoyed seeing them gag when I kicked their fat Korean asses."

Okiko wrote lucid reports on each of her Lodestar visits and how she forced an underperforming supplier to fulfill its contract. When Lodestar delivered the promised transmissions on schedule, Okiko received favorable comments in the Tokyo office and from the Union

Electric transmission users around the world. Scott wrote a note on the margin of one of her reports: "Looks like Okiko can put lipstick on a goat."

Because of Okiko's decisive performance on her work assignments, Drood and Scott set up a two-month schedule of working visits for her to Union Electric factories in the U.S., Europe, and South America to advance her career development.

When Okiko completed each segment of her trip, she invited the visited executives to a dinner organized according to her knowledge of international and Japanese business etiquette and hospitality. She presented to each guest a small, exquisite gift in a silken bag. After dinner she gave a well-reasoned speech on how Union Electric could further capitalize on alliances with Asian firms. Okiko made it clear she could capably represent their interests in the Asia-Pacific office.

When she returned to Tokyo after her round of visits, Drood received a number of positive feedback messages. Robert shared some of them with Okiko, declared her fully fledged, and ratcheted up the scope of her work responsibilities. He also shared another of Scott's comment written on the border of one of the laudatory letters: "Okiko got more notice on her visits than Lady Godiva when she took her celebrated horseback ride while clad only in her flowing blond hair."

Robert let the proper Union Electric people know identifying Okiko for her stellar performance and the plan for her career development was done on his initiative. He wrote a positive work performance review that led to her promotion.

Since Robert came to Tokyo, he developed a near obsession for buying antique Japanese art, but he was often delinquent with the payments. He was so long overdue in paying a large invoice to an art store that the owner came to Scott to seek his help in forcing payment.

Scott responded by talking to Robert and making his point with a homey story about a Texas rancher who got into financial trouble. The rancher's banker said, "Charley, it looks like you're going to go broke if you don't stop trying to buy up all of the land in Texas."

The rancher replied, "Oh, that's not my plan; I'm only trying to buy all the land that's adjacent to mine." Robert understood the point of the story, paid his bill, and temporarily curbed his runaway acquisition of Japanese art.

For years Scott invested in Union Electric and other successful companies. Because of the steady increase in stock prices, he was a wealthy man. At fifty-eight, he announced his retirement.

Scott had a high regard for Robert's capabilities. His aggressive performance reminded him of his own rambunctious behavior when he was a young man. He recommended Robert as his successor, and the officers of Union Electric concurred even though he was only thirty-one years old.

During the year after Robert became director of the Asia-Pacific office, he reported business handled by his office had increased forty percent. There were those who said he was a master at amplifying the facts, but if they challenged his claims, he smothered them with supporting evidence and data. He was gaining a reputation for obtaining exceptional results in a complex business environment.

Robert spent an evening in his flat thinking about his career status. His work opportunities and experience were in line with his career plan so far. He was still on the management fast track list, but it was time for the next step. If he was not offered a promotion to vice president soon, he'd look outside the company for a better job. The grapevine had it that he was being considered for promotion to a higher level. A little patience was in order—but not for very long.

Robert was startled late on a Friday evening when he received a call from George Winthrop's administrative assistant. "Dr. Drood, Mr. Winthrop wants to see you in his office in New York as soon as possible."

Robert replied, "I'll be there Monday if I can cancel some meetings and book a short-notice weekend flight. Can you tell me why Mr. Winthrop wants to see me?"

"He'll tell you when you arrive," the assistant replied. Robert knew the culture of executive assistants; they wouldn't reveal unauthorized information even if encouraged by fingernail removal.

CHAPTER TWELVE

In New York on Monday morning, an assistant escorted Robert across the acreage of George Winthrop's exotic-wood floor and Persian carpets to his pool table-size desk. The desk was clear except for a thin folder. Winthrop said, "Good morning, Robert. Thanks for coming here on short notice. I've been hearing lots of positive 'buzz' about the work you've been doing in Asia and the benefits to the company." He extracted a green bulletin, the standard document for high-level executive appointments, and said, "I want you to read this before we post it."

When Robert saw the green bulletin, the only color used for top level appointments, he took it with a firm hand, but a rising pulse, and read it:

Bulletin No. 67-8916

UNION ELECTRIC COMPANY
Electric Plaza
321 Broad Avenue
New York, NY 87932 U.S.A.

February 12, 1996

Appointment: Dr. Robert G. Drood
Vice President, Supply Management

Effective immediately, Robert Drood is appointed to the new position of Vice President, Supply Management.

A high percentage of the materials and components used in Union Electric products are purchased from outside sources. The board of directors has decided this portion of our cost should be consolidated and overseen by a corporate executive. By consolidating the purchasing functions, substantial savings and quality improvements are anticipated.

In the eight years since Robert joined Union Electric, he has held a variety of positions in the company. Most recently he was the Director of the Asia-Pacific Office. Previously he served in other company capacities including manager of the Poughkeepsie silicon chip fab.

Robert's education, experience, and successful performance of his various assignments well qualify him for this challenging new assignment.

He will report to the Office of the Chairman.

George Winthrop
Chief Executive Officer

Although company green bulletins are written like obituaries, they are the ultimate scorecard for career success.

With his usual self-confidence, Robert said, "Mr. Winthrop, I appreciate your confidence in me, and I'm grateful for the appointment."

Winthrop responded, "I trust you'll bring our supply management processes up to the standards of other world-class manufacturers in short order. We've all read about the concepts of just-in-time delivery and six-sigma quality levels, but we've been too slow in introducing them throughout Union Electric and with our suppliers."

Robert said, "I have some rather aggressive ideas on how to do it after seeing what is happening in the best Asian companies. How long a rope do I have for making changes?"

"Take all the rope you need. The board and I understand there'll be 'wigs on the green' when you start making drastic changes. Get started as soon as you wrap up your affairs in Tokyo. Good luck to you Robert. I know you'll be as successful as you've been with all of your past assignments."

Along with the promotion to vice president, Robert received a hefty salary increase. He needed it to support his lavish lifestyle.

Company executives believed Okiko Ogata had the knowledge and vigor to direct the rapidly expanding Asian business. They appointed her to succeed Robert in the Union Electric Tokyo office.

Several procurement managers met with Robert soon after he took over his new job to object to his aggressive new directives. Robert cut them off. "When George Winthrop told me to improve procurement, he didn't mean you had a vote on it. You roosted on your perches for the last five-to-ten years like hunting falcons with blinders while you allowed our suppliers to loaf. I've pulled the blinders off and started the hunt for improvements. Let me know tomorrow morning if you want to unreservedly participate in the hunt or not. If not, I have no place for you in my group."

One manager resigned. When he handed his resignation letter to Robert, he said, "I prefer not to have to come to work each morning holding the neck of a broken bottle in each hand."

Union Electric was an old company with many supplier relationships in place for decades. In the past, if a procurement officer pushed too hard on an established supplier, a discrete call to his boss was enough to diminish the pressure and ensure the traditional relationship remained undisturbed. The relationships resembled *keiretsu,* the comfortable interlocking arrangements that exist in Japan among large companies, suppliers, and banks.

According to a Union Electric policy, business relationships should be good for all parties. Robert interpreted the policy to mean they should be ninety-five percent good for Union Electric and five percent good for suppliers. Established agreements were canceled if suppliers did not submit to Robert's drastic new criteria. He applied his new procurement polices with the gracefulness of a chain saw.

If suppliers did not understand the new criteria, Robert sent in a training team to educate and assist them. But the training teams often acted as intimidators. They were usually as welcome as an anxious father when he shines a flashlight into the window of a parked car of teenagers in lover's lane.

Some suppliers resisted the nullification of their contracts with lawsuits, but they found they couldn't afford to hire squads of lawyers to counter the enormous legal resources of Union Electric. After several rounds in courts and the prospects of an uncertain future, most gave up and succumbed to Drood's new rules.

Some Union Electric executives and almost all of the suppliers objected to Drood's aggressive initiatives. George Winthrop, who was under intense pressure from his board to reduce costs, ignored the calls from his executives and suppliers requesting that he rein in Drood. Some of his critics called Drood "The Impaler."

He set up an analytical system for evaluating each supplier. If anyone used judgmental criteria not on the decision-making spreadsheets, he said, "Show me the item on the spreadsheet for 'Supplier is a Nice Guy' or 'We Owe Him a Favor.'" The engineers with MBAs who reviewed supplier selection decisions were called "The Enforcers."

Sam Tucker, Senior Vice President of the power generation division, received an invitation for a round of golf from his old friend, Bernie Goldman, the CEO of a major supplier to his division. Goldman complained about the undue pressure by Drood's procurement group. Tucker replied, "I'll look into it."

Tucker met with Robert and said, "Bernie Goldman has been a long-term supplier to my division during good and bad times. The pressure your group is placing on his company is too severe; let up."

Robert said, "Sam, we've examined the contracts with Goldman's company. They aren't cutting it. We intend to terminate Union Electric's business with them."

Sam shot back, "Damn it, I run the power generation division, and I'm directing you to work out the problems with him."

"Sam Goldman's company has failed to perform. In a few days a contract will be signed with an alternative supplier. Your personal relationship with Goldman is not a factor in our evaluation."

Sam raged, "George Winthrop will be advised of your high-handed refusal to execute my decision."

Robert cut him off. "I'm confident he'll agree our stockholders shouldn't have to accept a disadvantageous business decision based on an old-boy relationship."

Several days later Tucker barged into Winthrop's office and gave him an impassioned explanation of his encounter with Robert. He hinted of resigning if Drood was allowed to dismiss Goldman's company. "Sam," Winthrop said, "I support Robert's decision to discontinue doing business with Bernie Goldman based on the benefits to our company from a new supplier and our urgent need to reduce costs."

Even though Winthrop was displeased at Tucker's attempt to override Drood, he let it ride in consideration of his achievements and tenure with the company.

Tucker was surprised Winthrop already knew about the switch of suppliers. It then dawned on him Robert had trumped him by going to Winthrop first. He now realized he had jumped into a high stakes political cockfight and been out-spurred by a superior adversary.

A few weeks later George Winthrop heard of Tucker's continued resistance to Drood. He reached under his desk and jerked up his socks, his ultimate gesture of annoyance. He could not tolerate Tucker's challenge to his authority or allow Drood's cost-cutting initiatives to be blunted.

Winthrop called Tucker to his office. He said, "Sam, when you came to me to protest the termination of the contracts with Bernie Goldman's company, I decided to support Drood's decision. You have flouted my decision ever since. Your obvious insubordination and conflict of interests are unacceptable. We like constructive dissent in an open forum but not when handled in the manner of a resentful school boy. We are at an impasse; it is time for us to part ways."

Tucker had not been so severely talked to since his first days with the company when he worked for a bull-of-the-woods factory superintendent. He was furious, but before he could voice his protest, Winthrop pulled a green bulletin from his desk drawer and handed it to Tucker. He frowned when he read the first line of the bulletin and then gasped and paled.

Bulletin No. 67-9012

UNION ELECTRIC COMPANY
Electric Plaza
321 Broad Avenue
New York, N.Y. 87932 USA

January 10, 1997

Retirement: Samuel Tucker
Senior Vice President, Power Generation

Sam Tucker has elected to retire after 28 years of service with Union Electric.

Sam started his career in manufacturing. He then transferred to our Corporate Planning Department followed by a series of manufacturing management positions before returning to corporate headquarters to be Vice President, Manufacturing. He was later promoted to his current position.

He led the Power Generation Division during a period of major domestic and international growth.

Sam and his wife Betsy plan to enjoy their hobbies and pursue private interests.

George Winthrop
Chief Executive Officer

Tucker regained his composure and sputtered, "But George . . ."

Winthrop cut him off. "Sam, this decision is irrevocable. You know the culture and the rules here and you violated them—badly. I had no other choice. Now, go to the human relations department. The director will go over a fine retirement package and some related legal matters with you. I wish you all of the best and a long retirement." Tucker's career was over at Union Electric. He had no further recourse.

Executives throughout Union Electric who read Tucker's terse retirement announcement understood he was fired. The informal, but accurate, gossip network would soon spread the information all over the company and supplier chain that resisting Drood's purchasing initiatives was to risk career setbacks and contract terminations.

The wiser senior officers understood Robert's violent tree-shaking activities were necessary. They knew they could tune him down later if he created too much havoc.

Robert lost no sleep over the actions he was taking to fulfill his objectives. He could ruin careers and bankrupt suppliers with no more emotion than a predator stalking and catching its prey. He reasoned his actions were a zero sum proposition. For every failed career or dismissed supplier, there were equal offset benefits to others who were more worthy. He thought he was doing what other lax executives should have done long ago.

When Robert moved back to New York from Tokyo, he reviewed his old Rolodex file of women friends. Almost all of them had moved or were no longer in play. He developed a new computer list of eligible women.

Robert started thinking about his dating relationships in a different light. Although he had little interest in marriage and its restrictions, he knew most executives his age were married; marriage to a trophy wife with good looks and a high-visibility profession would serve him well at business functions.

CHAPTER THIRTEEN

Robert spotted Sarah Silverton while he sat alone eating an after-work steak dinner at Gallagher's Restaurant. Since she returned to New York from Tokyo, Sarah was the international marketing director for her bank. They warmly recalled their brief dating time when they both lived in Tokyo.

Robert called her the next day, "Sarah, it was good to see you again last night and relive our good times together in Tokyo. I'd like to see you again. How about going to the theater with me Friday night?"

"I'd love to, Robert."

They started to date regularly. Sarah had entrée to posh social affairs in Manhattan and weekend invitations to country estates, partly due to her job but also because of her parents' wealth and social position. Robert loved exposure to her world of sophistication, money, and good living. He was fascinated with rich art collectors and high rollers who lived on family trusts. As Sarah and Robert continued to date, their photographs frequently appeared in newspapers and on magazine society pages.

They fell into a comfortable relationship. During a weekend ski trip in Colorado, Robert said, "Sarah, I'm getting lots of good vibes about the benefits from us being together and because we seem to be a good fit. During the Union Electric executive dinner we attended at the Plaza last week, even our CEO, George Winthrop, gave me an 'atta boy' for my good taste in selecting you as a my companion. And more important than that, I'm getting very warm vibes myself every time I'm with you. Sarah, will you marry me?"

"Oh yes, Robert, even though that is probably the most left-handed marriage proposal any man ever made. What took you so long to ask? I've loved you since our first date in Tokyo. I'm sick and tired of the singles life. It will be so nice to settle into a homey lifestyle. Let's call my parents to tell them now."

When Robert read the wedding invitation list prepared by Sarah and her mother, he crossed off his own mother and his sister. Sarah said, "Robert, you can't do that; they're your only family!"

"They'd be like fish out of water; I'll tell them when we return from our honeymoon."

Robert and Sarah had long ago abandoned their family religious traditions. Their wedding was a secular ceremony performed under tents on the rolling lawn of the Silvertons' sprawling East Hampton estate. Sarah's parents pulled out the stops for the wedding and reception; Sarah was their only child.

After a two-week honeymoon in a friend's mansion in Cannes, Robert and Sarah returned to New York to live temporarily in Sarah's rented apartment. They soon bought a spacious condominium on the twentieth floor of a building overlooking Central Park and hired an interior decorator to furnish and decorate it. With their heavy travel schedules and evening business commitments, they used the condominium mostly for sleeping and reading the Sunday edition of *The New York Times*.

Robert gauged success by the size of his paycheck, the number of times his picture appeared in *Fortune* and *Forbes,* and the lines written about him in the *Wall Street Journal*. Robert and Sarah remained childless; they were unwilling to accept the necessary compromises to their work and lifestyle if children came into their lives.

Robert soon tired of marriage. He traveled continually and took diversions with other women along the way. Sarah found their marriage did not provide the tranquility she had hoped for. She discovered she had judged Robert mostly as a corporate executive, not as a husband.

As they stood waiting for their limo after a Metropolitan Museum of Art fund-raising ball, Sarah and Robert had a ferocious dust-up. Robert snarled, "You spent the entire evening being a bitch. When our vice chairman and his wife asked us to have a drink with them, you acted like a Yiddish sow with your overly endowed snout stuck up in the air. You didn't utter five civil words."

Sarah retorted, "And when your supercilious Grand Pooh-Bah and his pinch-nosed wife condescended to have a drink with us, you acted like a peasant bowing and tugging his forelock in the presence of the high and mighty seigneur. Well, I won't kiss anybody's tushy."

Their verbal donnybrook continued after they returned to their condominium. Sarah unloaded pent-up observations and emotions she had been accumulating for a long time. "The great Dr. Robert Garrity Drood looks into the mirror each morning and sees a man who is movie star handsome and intellectually superior to most people, a boy-wonder executive, and a magnet for attracting women. The mirror betrays you, *Herr Doktor*. When I look at you, I see an emotionally underdeveloped boy still trapped in the miseries of his Irish childhood; a boy too psychologically stunted to build human relationships; a boy who prides himself on his great mind but in reality only has a superior memory; and a boy who wags his tail and salivates like a dog in the company of any bigwig—or even a nobody—if he or she happens to have money or fame."

To Sarah's amazement Robert did not interrupt her tirade. She continued, "I thought I married a man, but I married a boy consumed by his inflated ego and constricted by emotional scars from the past. I know you're tormented by terrible demons from listening to you talk in your sleep. I once suggested you seek help from an experienced psychologist to free you from your torturing demons. That started a weeklong domestic battle. I thought our marriage would lead to a tranquil life, but instead it could be the basis for a soap opera script. We can't go on this way."

Sarah's voice softened. "Why do you always lock me out, Robert? It isn't natural to never speak of your past and to always keep your emotions bottled up. I'm your wife; if you'd share whatever is eating at you, maybe I could help you."

Sarah braced herself for Robert's counterattack, but he half closed his eyes, shook his head, and left the room.

Robert sat in his study staring out the window into the darkness as he thought: Until now, I believed my emotions were safely stored in my impenetrable inner mental fortress; I felt violated when Sarah clearly and accurately pointed out my problems. I can't bear it, and I can't explain why I feel this way. Her offer to listen to my problems is not unreasonable; why can't I let her do it? Why can't I turn the clock back to my childhood and the security I felt when I shared my aspirations and inner thoughts with Bridget? And why can't I be like other Union Electric executives with trusted colleagues who they can unload on for relief when the going gets tough? And why is the emotional side of my mind always strewn with uncontrollable psycho-forces? God in heaven, why does my life always have to be such a torture chamber?

Sarah waited for Robert for over an hour. She peeked into his study, but did not intrude when she saw him holding his head in the semidarkness. She thought she caught a glint of reflection from a tear on his cheek. She went to bed because she needed rest for a demanding business meeting the next day.

In the morning when Sarah got up, Robert had already left for work. She found a Post-it note on the refrigerator:

Sarah,

I have caused you distress you did not deserve. I wish I could explain.

Robert

Several days later Robert and Sarah met after work at the Plaza Hotel bar. They decided the best course for them was to live apart for a while, but through the arrangements of their secretaries, they would attend business and social functions that required the appearance of a marriage. Robert moved to a residential hotel.

He continued to milk his expense account to the limit and use all of the perks of his corporate position. He reveled in company jets, hotel suites, lavish parties, glitzy women, hobnobbing with VIPS, and international travel. His division financial officer said, "Robert, your expense account claims will not stand up to an audit. I think you should control your travel costs and reduce your expense account claims."

"You have spent your life counting things and deciding if the creative work of others conforms to your bean-counter rules," Robert sneered. "You never participated in the design, manufacture, and sale of anything. You're a non-value-adding expense to the company. You have no basis for challenging me on what it takes to fulfill my responsibilities. You should stick to operating your cash register. I also suggest you read the reports on the mounting benefits to the company from my group's initiatives."

Robert continued to spend outrageously. He took to getting two hundred dollar hair stylings every ten days. Each of his bespoke suits from Gieves and Hawks at No. 1 Savile Row in London cost six thousand dollars. He frequented fitness clubs that employed voluptuous female trainers and masseuses who provided him unlimited attention and services in anticipation of his hundred dollar tips.

Robert's expanding scope of expensive self-indulgences had few restraints. His philosophy on personal budgeting followed that of Winston Churchill and Thomas Jefferson, also a pair of spendthrifts whose outlook was: Needs and interests—not the resources to pay for them—should determine expenditures.

Robert's job gave him the opportunity to travel the globe. He found constant travel and red-carpet receptions exhilarating. With his ability to sleep anywhere and do most of his administrative work via telecommunications, his physical location was flexible. A colleague who did not have his stamina said, "A trip with Robert Drood is a death march."

Another said, "Yeah, he's like a shark; if he stops moving, he'll die."

Robert kept tenuous contact with his mother and sister. Mary regularly wrote to him, but he seldom responded. His feelings toward his mother and sister were ambivalent. Although he disassociated himself from them, he dreamed of the love they once shared. He could not reconcile his conflicting emotions. On the rare occasions when his mother and sister occupied his mind, he dismissed them with a note and a thousand dollar guilt check.

Robert received a distressing letter from his mother:

> Dearest Robert,
>
> I have some sad news. Bridget had a nervous breakdown. She was engaged to a man who seemed to treat her well, but she found out he only wanted to marry her in the hope he could dip into your bank account. All Bridget can think of is that someone has again violated her.
>
> Since she broke up with him, she's traumatized like she was when she was assaulted in Ireland. Matt and I had to put her in a group home for women. The psychologist doesn't see hope for much improvement. Matt and I are paying her bills, but our savings are going fast.
>
> I hope you can find time to write or call. I miss you so terribly much.
>
> With all my love,
>
> Mother

A few months later a drunken motorist hurled Mary into the path of an oncoming truck when she stepped from a bus. Bridget came to the funeral, but became frightened of the crowd; her attendant took her back to the security of her home. Robert hurried into town several hours before the funeral on a company jet.

Uncle Liam Garrity came alone to Mary's funeral. He had at last thrown Debbie out of his house. He was in deplorable physical condition from heavy smoking and a life of hard labor in a poor working environment.

Robert said, "Matt, from now on send me Bridget's group home bills—and here's a check for Mother's tombstone. I want you to inscribe on it: 'The creatures in her garden weep at her passing.'" Robert talked at the top of his voice for Matt to understand him; his years working in the din of a forge shop destroyed most of his hearing.

Matt was inconsolable. He could not imagine returning to the hollow life he lived before his idyllic marriage to Mary.

Robert left for a meeting in San Francisco shortly after Father Hannigan intoned the traditional ancient burial prayer: "May Mary's soul and the souls of all the faithfully departed rest in eternal peace. Amen."

After Mary's funeral, Robert reduced his communications with Bridget to annual Christmas and birthday cards selected by his secretary. Matt neglected himself and died a year later.

Eighteen months after Robert became a Union Electric vice president he made a presentation to the corporate senior executives claiming enormous cost reductions since he took over the supply management function of the company. Even though his savings claims were somewhat "fluffy," George Winthrop accepted them and promoted him to senior vice president.

CHAPTER FOURTEEN

Winthrop summoned Robert to his office. Recently Robert had several acrimonious disagreements on supplier selections with company executives so he guessed Winthrop was going to tell him to ratchet down his aggressiveness. Instead Winthrop said, "Robert we're promoting you to executive vice president of the electrical and electronic division."

The electrical and electronic division was the largest division of Union Electric. If it were spun off into a separate company, it alone would be one of the largest industrial corporations in the world.

Winthrop, assuming Robert would accept the promotion, continued, "The electrical and electronic division hasn't been fired up to its potential for a long time. Either fix the underperforming business units or get rid of them. I'll accept a high level of turmoil while you're reinvigorating units, but the board and I will have no tolerance for a fall-off in profitability. Now go out there and rattle the cages."

"I'll be saddled up and moving on the new job in a few days," Robert said. "And thank you for your confidence in me."

"You deserve it, Robert. Your performance record made this an easy decision to make."

A fat salary increase came with the new job. It momentarily rescued his sinking personal bank account.

Sarah had only seen Robert a few times since their estrangement. She called him and said as cheerfully as if they had never had a harsh word between them in their lives, "Most of the business news services in the country have reported your promotion. This clearly puts you in line for the CEO job when it's available. May I take the newest Union Electric super-hotshot to dinner to celebrate? I promise I'll leave the hatchet buried."

"Sure, Sarah, if I get to pick the dessert."

Sarah still loved Robert. Neither had made a move to dissolve their dysfunctional marriage since he moved out.

They maintained civility during their dinner and concluded it with coffee in their condominium. Neither had serious affairs going at the moment, so Robert spent the night with Sarah. She invited him to vacate his hotel suite and move back with her. They reunited but remained silent on subjects they both knew would lead to dust-ups.

For several months, Robert had been test-driving a Bentley sport coupe. He decided to reward himself for his promotion by buying it. The window sticker showed a list price of $295,000 including perforated Connolly hide upholstery, racing style dash and instruments, twelve-cylinder turbocharged engine, and custom-made Louis Vuitton luggage for a precision fit under the trunk lid contours. He convinced Sarah to pay half the cost.

A few weeks after Robert took over the electrical and electronic division, he called a staff meeting. "We're going to redesign each business unit in our division. We'll imagine our businesses do not exist and on a clean slate we'll reinvent them like we would envision them if we started over again from scratch—especially in regard to profitability. We need to do this because most of our business units are underperforming when compared to our competitors. We're going to make plans that will give us revenues, profits, and customer satisfaction equal to or better than those of our best competitors. If we're unable to devise suitable plans for substantially improving any of our business units, we'll sell them or shut them down."

Robert showed PowerPoint slides defining the weaknesses of each business unit. He said, "The vigorous planning exercise we're going to undertake will be exciting and it'll stretch us all. But while it is going on, it is imperative that our current profitability does not fall off."

Two of Robert's senior vice presidents were pleased with his direction. They had been chafing at the bit for more aggressive planning during the recent status quo leadership of Robert's predecessor. The division controller was also on board with Robert's new direction. She had already developed data showing how much each business had fallen behind. She showed her information to Robert during their first meeting and was elated to have a boss who would listen after she had been rebuffed for so long.

James Shaw, marketing and sales director, was depressed because Robert was chosen instead of him to head his division. He stayed home and brooded for two days and returned to work belligerent and uncooperative.

The talented young consultants hired to facilitate the planning project helped define a number of new market opportunities—many of them in Asia. Shaw told his subordinates, "This is the hare-brained aberration of a pampered bunch of Ivy Leaguers with hundred dollar red silk neckties. The closest they ever came to business experience was when they wrote their copycat Harvard MBA case studies. These whiz kids think we can just wish for more market share and it will magically appear. When they come around to show you their fancy presentations and seek your support for their unsubstantiated sales and profit increases, act cooperative, but don't agree with them."

When Robert heard Shaw was dragging his feet, he called him to his office and said, "James, you're defending the status quo. It's because of the inadequate status quo that I commissioned the planning project. For you to stick to our current inadequate way of doing business is to admit our competitors are superior to us. The planning team's improved sales projections are logical and valid. I've directed them to proceed with their planning based on the improved figures."

Shaw could not believe Robert had accepted the planning team's higher sales projections without his endorsement. He gripped his chair arm with his left hand and described a circular pattern on the table with his right index finger. Robert noticed in previous meetings he did this when he was riled up. Shaw blustered, "Based on my thirty years of experience in marketing and sales, I'm convinced the planning team's sales projections are too aggressive. We have tough competitors, and they won't let us invade their markets. I can't agree with such pie-in-the-sky projections because I know they're impossible to achieve. You made a mistake to agree to those figures." His fingertip was now making circles on the table at a furious rate.

Robert had considered relieving Shaw of his position for some time. While he expanded his justification for maintaining the current sales figures, Robert cut him off. "James, your logic is flawed. You speak of your thirty years of experience; however, only a little of it was in Asia and that's where the large improvement opportunities are. You're unwilling to understand the arguments of people who know the Asian market. We're at an impasse, not only because of this issue, but because you've blocked every other initiative I suggested since I took over this division. I'm unwilling to proceed down this path any longer. You can either retire now with a generous financial package, or we can work out a special nonmanagement work assignment for you. Think about it overnight, and let me know in the morning which alternative you want to take." Robert dismissed Shaw by turning to his computer and reading his e-mail messages.

Shaw was stunned at Robert's harsh response. He knew a special nonmanagement assignment meant sitting in a small office in an obscure location with a shared low-level secretary and an inbox full of trade magazines. He'd no longer be invited to meetings and his phone would seldom ring; he'd be a pariah.

After a night of rage and finally fear, Shaw decided he would work on Robert's terms. He contritely came to Robert's office the next morning and said, "It's true I was disappointed at not getting the job to head the electrical and electronics division. I let it cloud my judgment. I thought about it all night. Robert, I apologize for my outburst yesterday. I'm now willing to put it behind me and sign on to your leadership and the sales projections of the business redesign team."

"James, you've burned your bridges. No matter how much you say you want to sign on to our new ways of doing business, you'll only be able to passively function. You're not up to the new challenges. I urge you to go to the human resources department to iron out a retirement package for you. It'll be generous, and I think you should take it."

Shaw turned white and his throat constricted. After several moments of staring at Robert, he pulled himself together enough to stand and walk to the executive men's room. He looked into the mirror until he regained his composure and headed for human resources. The human resources director showed him the retirement package Robert had worked out with him several weeks earlier. Shaw accepted the package and left the building. He raged at how unjust it was for a young hotshot to end his long career with the cavalier manner of a work-gang overseer.

After Shaw left, Robert stared into the windows of the sleek office building across the avenue from his office. He always heard firing people was the hardest thing a manager ever had to do. He wondered why they considered emotions when they made business decisions. Firing James Shaw was little different for him than handling any other routine business matter.

When the business redesign project was completed, it included a plan for improving most of the units of the electrical and electronics division. Those that could not be brought up to the company's strategic and profitability standards were spun off or shut down. Robert's subordinates, who delivered the results projected in the new plans, were praised and promoted. Those who did not were removed like weeds hoed from a garden.

Battles with competitors were fierce when the new plans called for invading their market shares. Several that Robert wanted to keep were too tough to overcome. In these cases, Robert manipulated the data. Since he learned about the flexibility of accounting practices, he could force income statements and balance sheets to dance to any tune. George Winthrop and the board applauded Robert for the way he directed the electrical and electronic division.

On a Friday evening, Robert glanced at the stack of phone messages accumulated on his desk. Normally he ignored calls from headhunters, but he recognized one in the pile from a respected executive recruiting firm. He tucked it into his shirt pocket when he left his office for the weekend. He wondered what position the recruiter needed to fill.

Over his evening drink in his condominium, Robert assessed the status of his professional life. Sarah was away on a trip to Moscow. He was now thirty-seven years old. He had the broad experience required for becoming the Union Electric chief executive officer. However, several others in the company had similar status to his, and more could catapult ahead during the remaining seven years until George Winthrop's mandatory retirement. If Robert waited for Winthrop to retire, it would be four years beyond his long-standing goal for becoming the CEO of a major firm before he was forty. He left the recruiter's note in the middle of his study desk.

At 3:00 a.m. Robert awoke from a nightmare sweating and trembling. His unwelcome demon had appeared again out of the cellar of hell to drive jagged shards into his brain. He could still see that slimy snake McClellan on top of his sister and hear the disgusting sounds of him violating his mother. He thought: Why couldn't I have found a way to protect my sister and mother when they needed help? And where was my irresponsible father? And why did my schoolmaster and classmates write me off as a nonentity? Why must I incessantly relive these miserable memories? If there was a merciful God in heaven, why didn't he intervene? And why does God not rid me of this evil demon—this hound from Hell?

Robert went to his gym for a ferocious physical workout, the only way he knew to bring his sinister demon to heel.

CHAPTER FIFTEEN

A major business magazine listed American Semiconductor Corporation as the largest silicon chip manufacturer on earth. The company's commonly-known brand name, AMSCO, was as ubiquitous as Coke, Ford, and Sony.

Thirty-two years earlier in 1967, John Stepanek and Adam Budak founded AMSCO in San Francisco. Stepanek was a humble man from the hardscrabble, coal-mining mountains of West Virginia. Budak was raised in a grubby, pollution-saturated industrial town in Poland. When he was a teenager, he stowed away on a decrepit cargo ship sailing from Gdansk on the Baltic to New Orleans on the Mississippi. After nearly freezing and losing two toes and his right index finger during the wintry crossing, he found asylum in the U.S. Stepanek and Budak became friends while earning their PhDs at Berkeley.

Stepanek was the Chief Executive Officer and Budak the Chief Operating Officer of AMSCO. They were so closely linked, they functioned as if they were co-CEOs. Rank and protocol were of little interest to them.

They regularly met early in the morning at Mother Garvey's Café for coffee and again late in the afternoon in one of their work cubicles. Conversations were usually devoted to competitive threats and the design and manufacturing of silicon chips. On Monday mornings, they prefaced their discussions by announcing how many minutes it took them to solve the crossword puzzle in the Sunday edition of *The New York Times*.

Stepanek, who was fifty-five years old, told the AMSCO board he intended to resign to pursue philanthropic interests. The board had little concern because it anticipated a seamless transition to Budak when it elected him CEO. The company was in a temporary period of tranquility with a growing share of the expanding international silicon chip market.

Budak leaned into the pilot's compartment of the AMSCO Gulfstream jet plane to speak to the pilot an hour before landing at the Pitkin/Sardy Airport near his Aspen retreat house. "I sure hope we can land at

Aspen this evening. My family's waiting dinner for me. If we have to land in Denver it'll take at least four extra hours of driving."

"Yes, Dr. Budak, I understand," the pilot replied. "We are keeping a close eye on the weather and evening landing conditions. At the moment there are snow showers and the visibility is 'iffy.' We'll be arriving a half hour after sunset, and with only a single seven thousand foot runway and precipitous terrain, we must use extra caution."

"Of course; I know the landing decision is yours alone."

The forty-five-year-old captain had accumulated nine thousand hours of total flight time including two thousand hours on a Gulfstream. The thirty-year-old first officer had half the flying experience of the captain. The captain, who was recently hired by AMSCO, was anxious to please Budak.

As the plane neared Aspen, the captain turned around and said, "Dr. Budak, I've reviewed the latest controller data; landing conditions have improved. We're going to land at Aspen."

"Wonderful. This is the best news I've heard all day."

Just before touchdown the tower controller saw the G-IV go into a steep left bank. "What's that Gulfstream doing?" he yelled.

"It's going to crash," his partner screamed and alerted the fire and rescue units.

Two thousand feet short of the runway, the plane's left wing clipped the rock-strewn terrain. Airplane and body parts were scattered from the point of impact to the vertical opposite side of a gulch. Fire from the burning fuel-drenched trees was visible for miles.

The investigation of the accident by the NTSB (National Transportation Board) declared the crash was due to pilot error.

The tragic death of Budak staggered the AMSCO Board. They revered Stepanek and Budak for their singular combination of technical knowledge and business acumen. They thought of them as the Wright brothers of the information technology industry. To lose one was an acceptable risk; to lose both could be a tragedy.

Years earlier when Stepanek and Budak were young men just out of graduate school, they developed a relationship that allowed them to seamlessly work together. In the beginning days of AMSCO, they devised a stream of breakthrough products. Although they successfully exploited each of them, they worried they might not always have new products in the pipeline to replace older ones when they became obsolete. They sensed chips could be the long-lived, fundamental core of computers, and if they focused AMSCO efforts on that one device, the company would enjoy unlimited success.

Stepanek and Budak met with their key designers and strategic thinkers to seek their ideas on what the fundamental core product would be. The group consisted of some of the most brilliant and imaginative minds in the industry. Stepanek and Budak liked working with brilliant and occasionally half-mad people. They worked in an egalitarian atmosphere where ideas were judged on their merits without regard to the rank of the team member who put forth the ideas. They listened to the group's wide-ranging outpourings but reached no consensus on the best core product to pursue.

Stepanek and Budak collected the information from their strategy meeting and went off to a secluded hotel on a remote Baja California beach. They spent the weekend reflecting on the list of ideas suggested by their staff and made their decision on the singular core product they thought would ensure the long-term prosperity of AMSCO. They came back from the weekend with a draft of a strategic document on a single sheet of paper. Stepanek typed the document, because he had all of his fingers:

John Stepanek
Adam Budak
July 18, 1985

MEMORANDUM
AMSCO STRATEGY

ASSUMPTIONS

(1) Moore's Law (transistors in computer chips will double every two years) will continue to prevail for an indefinite period of time.

(2) During the foreseeable future the silicon chip market will continue to grow at a rapid and steady rate.

AMSCO STRATEGY

(1) AMSCO will focus its resources on designing, manufacturing, and marketing silicon chips for application as microprocessors.

(2) AMSCO will maintain its competitive advantage by improving silicon chip designs and manufacturing processes at a significantly faster rate than its competitors.

(3) AMSCO will discontinue assigning resources for most non-silicon chip products.

They showed their document to the company strategic planners and senior officers. Although some had doubts, enough of them supported it that they presented it to the board for approval. It became a watershed event in the history of AMSCO as well as the chip industry. The simple document was recognized to be one of the more prophetic business strategies ever written. With the new strategy, AMSCO swamped their competitors with a tsunami of nearly flawless, low-cost silicon chips.

The AMSCO strategy heralded a long-term growth with revenues doubling every three-to-four years. AMSCO became the dominant chip supplier to the world with seventy-five percent of the market. After investors realized the brilliance of the strategic plan and saw the results in consistent revenue and earnings growth, AMSCO stock appeared in the portfolios of even the most conservative investors. The stock price rocketed and many employees and investors became millionaires; a few became billionaires. Stepanek and Budak's seminal strategic document—still showing saltwater marks from the Baja California beach hotel where it was written—hangs in the AMSCO boardroom.

After Budak's death, Stepanek told the board he would remain as CEO for a short time, but his earlier resignation announcement still stood. The board reviewed and interviewed several internal AMSCO candidates for the CEO position, but none survived the interviews.

They hired an executive recruiting company, Easter, Langely, and Jackson, to find a new CEO. Easter, Langely, and Jackson, with its headquarters in New York City, was not the largest firm in the executive recruiting business, but major firms usually selected it for recommending candidates for their senior positions. Their officers maintained close relationships with executives in high positions throughout the world and often got early wind of those who were restless and ready to move on to greener pastures.

The AMSCO Board of Directors consisted of eleven members. Stepanek, since the death of Budak, was the only member who was also an AMSCO employee. Many of the outside board members were renowned for their work in scientific and academic fields—one had been awarded a Nobel Prize—but they were limited in industrial corporation experience. Justin Cairncross, CEO of Titan Motors, was the board member with the greatest industrial management experience. He served on, and dominated, the powerful nominating and audit committees.

When Easter, Langely, and Jackson received the assignment from AMSCO for recommending a new CEO, they developed a comprehensive list of high-potential candidates. They boiled it down to a short list of fifteen. Robert Drood was on the list. Their experience indicated only three or four candidates from their short list would agree to discuss the available opening. Timing was an essential factor. If an executive was recently passed over for a promotion or was bored with his or her work, it was an opportune time to call.

Robert reread the note on his desk from Edward Easter. The note said to return his call at any time.

On a Saturday morning while unshaven and in his bathrobe, Robert went into the den of his condominium with a cup of coffee and *The New York Times*. He eased the door shut so he would not waken Sarah and called Easter. He answered the call from the breakfast room of his Greenwich, Connecticut home.

When Robert identified himself, Easter said, "Dr. Drood, we've been hired to recommend a CEO for a well-known international company. We think you're the right person for serious consideration. I'd like to send a messenger to you today with a nondisclosure letter for you to sign. When you've signed the letter, the messenger will give you a file identifying the company and providing selected information. When you've read the file, and if you wish to proceed, please call me to set up an introductory meeting." This was the kind of no-wasted-time conversation Robert liked.

"That sounds fine to me, Mr. Easter. Please send the file to my condominium."

"We have your address; our messenger will be there by noon today. Enjoy your weekend."

The messenger arrived in the marble-walled lobby of Sarah and Robert's condominium just before noon. After a call to Robert, the security officer sent his assistant and the messenger to his condominium on the twentieth floor. Robert signed the nondisclosure letter and took the information package to his study. When he read American Semiconductor Corporation was the company searching for a new CEO, he audibly inhaled. The opportunity to succeed the legendary John Stepanek and Adam Budak was only a dream for most executives.

On the following Tuesday, Robert called Easter. "It would be convenient to meet you in San Francisco where we'll have more security, on Friday afternoon in three weeks. I'll be returning from an Asian trip and stopping there for the weekend." Robert also had another motive for meeting in San Francisco. He planned to spend the weekend with Paula Jefferson, a sleek, twenty-eight-year-old account manager from the firm that was handling a Union Electric advertising campaign.

Easter said, "Fine, I'm available at that time. Let's meet at the Fairmont Hotel at 3:00 p.m. When you arrive at the hotel, see the concierge. He will escort you to my suite."

At the next Easter, Langley, and Jackson staff meeting, Easter reported the status of his work on the search for a new AMSCO CEO: "Dr. Robert Drood's on top of the short list of candidates. I think we have a good chance to hook him. If we do, our fee will be a third of a million dollars plus expenses."

Easter used a mixture of his analytical and intuitive skills to ensure the first meeting with Drood would be positive. He had his assistant accumulate all of the available newspaper items, financial reports, and trade magazine articles on Drood, and he instructed their retained investigating agency to find out from waiters and doormen information about his personal tastes and habits.

Easter then decided how to bring up points about the AMSCO CEO position that would fulfill Drood's career objectives as well as indulge his personal interests and tastes. Many executives liked to have their mammoth egos stroked; Drood was not an exception.

Easter rented the Fairmont suite, room 2310, in the Fairmont Hotel atop Nob Hill. The suite, with its Persian rugs, contemporary and traditional wall hangings, and period English furniture had housed well-heeled patrons for decades. He promised a lavish tip for the senior hotel waiter and concierge to ensure they would be available on the day of his meeting with Drood.

When Drood and Easter met, Easter explained Dr. Stepanek's retirement and the board's decision to hire his successor from outside the company. He handed Drood a folder with additional information and said, "In order to conserve time, I've prepared this file for you. It contains the latest AMSCO financial reports, recent company newspaper clippings, and notice of the annual stockholders meeting." Easter included the last item because Drood could read Stepanek's compensation and assume he would receive a similar amount.

Easter knew the disadvantage of talking too much and finding later the candidate's interests and questions were not addressed. It took little encouragement for Robert to talk of his interests. Ever the negotiator, he said, "I'm happy with my current job. I returned your call out of curiosity about what the outside job market looks like." Easter knew this statement was malarkey; he had heard it many times before.

Easter picked up the ball again and moved on to what he thought would best feed Drood's ego. "AMSCO owns a small fleet of jets. Since the Gulfstream, the company's flagship plane, crashed killing Dr. Budak, they ordered a later model replacement Gulfstream. The plane assembly is nearing completion and the builder will soon need directions on the interior configuration and appointments. It will be available for the CEO's business and private use." From Drood's intent look, Easter knew he had hooked him when he told him a forty million dollar plane would be at his personal disposal. "The scarce availability of premium housing in San Francisco may delay the new CEO in finding living quarters. AMSCO owns a VIP condominium that will be available for his use until he establishes permanent living quarters."

Easter thought he had said enough to convince Robert his voracious appetite for high living would be indulged at AMSCO.

Robert asked, "What'll John Stepanek's role be in the future?"

"Dr. Stepanek will continue to be the nonexecutive Chairman until the new CEO is up to speed, and the stockholders have settled down. When the transition is complete—which I'd think would be in a short time—he will likely resign. Stepanek has lost his fire for running the company since he decided to retire, and he's still depressed about Dr. Budak's death; they were like brothers. The new CEO will undoubtedly be elected chairman when the transition to the new leadership is complete."

Robert hoped his meeting with Easter would be brief. He wanted to return to Paula Jefferson, who was waiting in his hotel suite. They planned to spend the rest of the weekend at an acquaintance's vineyard near Sonoma inspecting the fields and neighborhood estates on horseback followed by wine tasting in the vineyard cellars.

As the meeting approached its conclusion, Easter rang the suite kitchen for service. Oncidium orchids on side tables nodded while Robert ordered a Compari and soda and Easter a light Glenfidich with mineral water but no ice. The waiter moved serving tables, covered with crisp linen tablecloths, to each of them and served small plates of Beluga caviar, Greek olives, and Irish lox. When they finished snacking, he offered Robert a Cohiba cigar. Robert occasionally smoked, but he was uncertain of Paula's tolerance for the smell of tobacco so he tucked the cigar into his pocket.

When the waiter removed the serving tables, Robert said, "In a few minutes I must be on my way."

"I trust we've covered everything that's of interest to you today. If so, I suggest I call Justin Cairncross, the chairman of the nominating committee, to set up a meeting with the two of you. Justin will want to meet with you alone. He likes informal face-to-face meetings. Can you call me in a few days to tell me when your calendar is open for a meeting with Justin?"

Robert answered, "I'll be in New York next week. I'll call to let you know about scheduling the meeting."

The concierge returned to escort Robert out and whistle for his limo. Easter checked out of the hotel and took a redeye flight back to New York.

On the flight back home Easter wrote a note on his visit with Robert:

September 23, 2000

MEETING WITH DR. ROBERT DROOD

(1) Robert Drood was undaunted at the challenge of running AMSCO—especially the technical aspects.
(2) He agreed to a meeting with Justin Cairncross.
(3) It is apparent that he is receptive to an AMSCO offer.
(4) If the AMSCO position is offered to Drood, he is likely to accept it.

cc: Justin Cairncross
Partners—Easter, Langley, and Jackson

When Robert concluded his weekend dalliance with Paula Jefferson, he handed her a receipt for the delivery to her New York apartment of a case of wine she had admired—Maycamas Cabernet-Sauvignon priced at seventy dollars per bottle. She understood the weekend was a temporary diversion and had no expectations of further liaisons with Robert.

On the plane home, Robert read the file Easter gave him and considered the pros and cons of leaving his secure position at Union Electric. The AMSCO job would be an immense step upward. It would be a bird in the hand compared to one in the bush if he waited for the CEO position to open at Union Electric. If offered the AMSCO job, the decision to accept it was a no-brainer; he would take it in a heartbeat.

On Friday Robert shut his office door and used his secure line to call Easter. They set up a Saturday meeting in two weeks at Justin Cairncross's Wyoming ranch. It would serve the dual purpose of confidentiality and Cairncross's desire for informality. Easter arranged for a chartered Learjet to take Robert to Wyoming.

Cairncross had already interviewed three other candidates from Easter's list. None gave him the visceral feeling he liked to have before recommending executives for key positions.

Robert flew to Wyoming on Friday evening. Even though he gained two hours, it was too late to travel to Cairncross's ranch that evening so he checked into a hotel near Jackson.

The next morning, Eddie Tibbs, Cairncross's diminutive ranch foreman, picked Robert up at his hotel for the one-hour ride to the ranch.

Life in the sun and wind made Eddie look ten years older than his thirty-five-year age. If he were deprived of his go-to-town Stetson hat and tooled cowboy boots, he would look half his size. Eddie spoke only when necessary—mostly with monosyllabic words.

Eddie drove a well-maintained GMC pickup fitted for off-highway driving and equipped with a gun rack in the rear window. He knew what speed to travel on the washboard sections of the gravel roads so the pickup and its passengers would not shake to pieces. He also knew how to dodge the oblivious cattle wandering onto the roads from the unfenced range.

Five thousand acres of functioning ranch surrounded Cairncross's house. The living room windows faced a scattering of unpretentious ranch buildings, semi-arid prairie, and distant snow-crowned mountains. A double-strand barbed wire fence stapled to split-cedar posts kept the cattle and horses away from the house. Prairie grass grew up to the house foundations. At a distance from the buildings, the dark scar of a ploughed firebreak was visible. He used the ranch for relaxing and reading; non-family visitors were rare.

Cairncross, with college degrees and work experience in engineering, accounting, and marketing, was hard to fool. One of his standard remarks about people who presented their cases to him without adequate substantiating evidence was, "They're all hat but no cattle." He used the perquisites of his high position at Titan Motors as tools of convenience, not for garnishing glory. He did not place a high value on the acquisition of personal wealth beyond that needed for his family's modest comfort and security.

Cairncross did not think memberships on corporate boards were sinecures where the officers only needed to rubber stamp the operating management's recommendations to collect their generous fees. He believed boards should provide demanding oversight of the performance of company management. He called weak boards "pet rocks." Cairncross learned the basics of management when he was a boy by observing his father run his Missouri farm. If a farm boss did a good job, his father left him alone and paid him a bonus. If he did not, he counseled him, and if he still did not perform well, or if he cheated, he fired him.

CHAPTER SIXTEEN

Cairncross greeted Robert on his ranch house porch dressed in a checked flannel shirt, tan corduroy trousers, and scuffed cowboy boots. It was hard to believe this gray-haired man with a gentle stoop and stiff knees was the same person who arrived the night before on the majestic Titan Motors jet parked at the Jackson airport. Only Cairncross and his wife, who excused herself after a few minutes of social amenities, occupied the ranch house for the weekend. The housekeeper had prepared lunch early in the morning and placed it on a tray in the refrigerator before she departed. After Tibbs let Robert out of his pickup at the ranch house porch, he returned to his home in the rehabilitated bunkhouse located behind a nearby Russian olive tree windbreak.

Cairncross and Drood sat in the living room on rustic furniture arranged with a view of the mountains to the west. The light from the windows shone onto a brilliant Navajo rug. The setting was in a different universe from the sonic-speed business and industrial world Cairncross and Drood would return to after the weekend.

Cairncross talked for ten minutes about his uncomplicated boyhood on a Missouri farm twenty miles from the nearest town. He encouraged Robert to speak about himself. Robert responded by talking of his youth in Chicago but not of his miserable childhood in Ireland.

Cairncross abruptly shifted gears. "Robert, why are you considering walking away from your enviable career at Union Electric?"

"Because I wrote a career plan when I finished my university education that called for becoming the CEO of a major company by the time I was forty. That isn't in the cards at Union Electric; George Winthrop has seven more years to go before retirement. By then I'll be well-past forty."

Cairncross chuckled and said, "There's no ambiguity with that answer. I know George; you can count on him staying in harness until the company age limit forces him out." He then went on in another direction. "By now you have probably read the AMSCO files Ed Easter gave you. Can you share any observations with me?"

"Yes, Justin. I question why AMSCO's research budget isn't higher and more focused on theoretical work so the company will know in what direction to point when the silicon chip eventually hits its development limit. And I think AMSCO should have a heavier presence in the fast-growing Asia-Pacific markets. Lastly, I don't think their revenue and profit projections are aggressive enough."

"Robert, most of your observations are also the causes for concern by the AMSCO board. We want a new CEO who'll fire up the company and grow past the admirable, but a little dated, legacy of Stepanek and Budak. The board's instructions to the new CEO will be simple: increase the annual revenues by six percent and the profits by seven percent. If he or she can do that—and it's a tall order—the new CEO will have a board that purrs like a cat."

By lunch time Cairncross had the positive visceral feeling he liked to have when making executive decisions. He was confident Robert was the right man for the AMSCO CEO position and persuading the other members of the nominating committee and board would be a cinch.

He hobbled stiff-legged to the kitchen and brought back a tray with ham sandwiches, potato chips, a coffee thermos, a bottle of yellow mustard, and cold bottles of Coke and Coors.

After a lunch discussion on foreign trade policies, Cairncross said, "Well, Robert, I think we have the makings to move forward with this process. I'll brief Hank Carter and Louie Jordan, the other members of the nominating committee, of our discussion today. They may also want to talk to you themselves.

"Then AMSCO will want you to go through a pretty comprehensive session with a firm of psychological testers and interviewers. If the tests and interviews don't reveal anything too scary, I want you to meet the other board members the day before our next meeting in Dallas. We always have an informal get-together the evening before the board meets. The next day we'll bring your name before the board and, if everything looks okay, vote on electing you the new CEO.

"I know I'm being quite open on this, Robert, and going pretty fast, but I don't like to play a cat and mouse game and have you leave here in a state of uncertainty. Now, if I do start the ball rolling and everything falls in place, I need some indication you'd be receptive to the job."

Robert believed in rapid action, but this meeting was going faster than a bullet train. After a pause and a deep breath he replied, "Justin, I'm receptive to the actions you just outlined; let's keep the ball rolling."

"Now, Robert, let's take a ride around the ranch before Eddie takes you back to your plane. I call this ranching through the windshield."

The weathered, open-sided Jeep was accompanied by billowing dust and swarming flies. Cairncross still had the same love for white-face cattle he did in his youth on his father's farm. They stopped at a water-pumping windmill beside a round, galvanized stock tank to look at the gathered cattle and examine the condition of the grass and soil. The cattle formed an investigation circle around Cairncross and Drood, but they soon exhausted their curiosity and ambled away to more interesting quests.

Cairncross explained, "When I'm on the ranch, I tour the land every day—sometimes alone and sometimes with Eddie. We enjoy the silence of each other's company. Eddie has the authority to make most ranch operations decisions, but I like to be involved when I'm here. Sometimes, if my arthritis is not acting up, I help with the haying, fence repairing, and cattle herding. It helps me remember the realities of life."

While driving across the rolling prairie, Cairncross spied a distant calf separated from its mother. He turned off the engine and waited for the calf to come toward the Jeep while a coyote stalked it. He took a thirty-caliber rifle from the Jeep gun rack and winged the coyote with a single shot. It yelped and limped away. The calf's frenzied mother raced up from a draw and resumed her protective duties. When the ranch tour ended, they returned to the graveled parking space beside Tibb's little house. Eddie was working in an open-sided machine shed near his house replacing worn tines on a John Deere hay rake.

Tibbs drove Robert back to the waiting plane for the trip home to New York. When he handed Robert his overnight bag from the back of the pickup, Robert said, "Thanks for the ride, Eddie."

Tibbs touched his hat brim with two fingers and drawled, "Yup, you betcha." He slammed the pickup door and eased out the clutch. From overhearing a discussion between Cairncross and Tibbs, Robert knew he would now stop at the implement dealer to buy replacement tines for the hay rake before returning to the ranch.

Tibbs had no curiosity whatsoever about the world of the people who came and went in private jets. His world existed within the fifty-mile radius around the Cairncross ranch. He lived his life according to the precept he learned in his childhood from his Lakota Indian mother: Life should be in balance and at peace with the natural environment, all according to the will of the spirits that lived in the sacred Paha Sapa to the east—the white man's Black Hills.

When the plane was airborne, the pilot announced, "We'll have to vector south to avoid a thunderstorm, but the headwinds are minimal today so we should arrive at Teterboro at our scheduled arrival time."

Robert slept during most of the four-hour flight home to New York. While sleeping, his subconscious mind properly arranged the remaining loose ends about his potential offer to be the CEO of AMSCO. It would be after midnight, with the time zone changes, when he arrived at his condominium.

The next morning over a brief cup of coffee with Sarah, Robert cleared his throat and said, "Sarah, I'll likely be offered the AMSCO CEO job. The interview process isn't over yet, but my assessment after my meeting with Justin Cairncross is its board will vote to elect me. Cairncross has the dominant voice on the nominating committee and the board will probably follow his lead. The job will require residency in San Francisco."

Sarah knew if Robert said something was likely to happen, she could take it to the bank. "Congratulations," she said. "This will allow you to reach your objective of becoming a CEO several years earlier than you planned. What a day when an Irish peat digger like you takes over such a prestigious company. Of course, because of my job, I must remain in New York. I guess we'll have to get used to commuting between coasts on weekends."

They both refrained from saying what they were thinking: Their marriage was only an arrangement of convenience. Living three thousand miles apart would not be a hardship for either of them. The only reason they stayed together was because marriage was the accepted norm for big league executives. They were both relieved the subject of Sarah quitting her job and moving to San Francisco did not come up.

Easter called Drood a few days later to arrange for the required eight-hour session with the psychological testing and interviewing firm. "Tell me more about this session," Robert said. "I have an aversion to the involvement of psychologists. I can't see why a board doesn't make such an important decision on its own. Is AMSCO really committed to this part of their hiring procedure?"

"Yes, Robert, I'm afraid it's locked in on it. Justin once tried to scrap this part of the hiring procedure, but the company wouldn't budge. They think it gets problems out in the open before hiring. It helps identify potential cultural or personality conflicts. The testing and interviewing helps ensure there will be a good fit among all of the players. If the job does not work out, fixing it is such a messy business."

Robert sighed and stared out his window at the sky for a long time before he agreed on a date and location for the session.

The written portion of the test took four hours followed by four more hours of role-playing with an experienced psychologist. The testing firm submitted its report on the results in a week. The summary read:

> Dr. Robert Drood is a strong leader who effectively manages executives if they can keep up with his demanding expectations. Although he is confident of his intellectual and executive skills, his psyche seems to be adversely influenced by a traumatic undisclosed event from his past. There are indications Dr. Drood is weak at developing personal relationships with others and the potential exists that he may sometimes disregard ethical standards in order to achieve his objectives.

Cairncross believed he was an expert at judging and selecting executives and did not need help from psychologists and psychiatrists. He thought Robert's high intelligence combined with his deep understanding of technology and successful business experience was all he needed to know. He once said to the human resources director of Titan Motors, "Most psychological testing is psycho-babble created by overeducated people who wouldn't succeed if they had serious professions."

When Cairncross read the report on Robert, it confirmed his skepticism. He said to Carter and Jordan, "The psychological report is waffling mush. They didn't even make an unqualified hiring recommendation. If I ran my business with that kind of indecisiveness, my board would hire a new CEO." Carter and Jordan followed Cairncross's lead to recommend Drood to the AMSCO board for the CEO position.

Robert met with Carter and Jordan and the other board members the day before the next AMSCO board meeting in Dallas. When he met Stepanek, he was at his best.

Stepanek mentioned future technology to test Robert's technical knowledge. Robert launched into an esoteric area of science related to the ultimate limit for silicon chip development. "As you know, for the foreseeable future, Dr. Stepanek, Moore's Law can be accommodated by manufacturing silicon chips with ever more densely packed transistors, but eventually the development limit will be reached. The limit may come within ten-to-fifteen years." Robert continued for fifteen minutes giving a theoretical analysis of the materials and technology that might replace silicon. His lucid observations impressed Stepanek.

The next day at the board meeting, the nominating committee, with Cairncross as its spokesman, reported on the three candidates remaining on the short list for the CEO position. He dismissed two of them out of hand and focused on Drood after brushing aside the psychologist's concerns. During the board discussion, Stepanek endorsed Cairncross's recommendation. "I talked to Dr. Drood last evening. He has the communication skills of Ronald Reagan, the management experience of a seasoned industrial executive, and the scientific knowledge of a physics professor. I have no problem voting for him for my successor." Stepanek's opinion clinched it for several of the board members who were on the fence.

The AMSCO board unanimously elected Drood for its new CEO.

George Winthrop accepted Robert's resignation from Union Electric with equanimity. Union Electric always had several people in the wings for every executive position. Winthrop did not expect talented people to wait around for promotions. He prided himself because the executive suites of so many major firms were occupied by former Union Electric personnel.

CHAPTER SEVENTEEN

A posting on AMSCO bulletin boards around the world announced Robert Drood's appointment as the new CEO:

Bulletin No. C- 7850

AMERICAN SEMICONDUCTOR CORPORATION
AMSCO Plaza
671 Golden Street
San Francisco, CA 67050 USA

July 18, 2000

Election: Dr. Robert Garrity Drood
Chief Executive Officer

    The American Semiconductor Corporation Board of Directors elected Dr. Robert Garrity Drood to the position of Chief Executive Officer to succeed Dr. John Stepanek. Dr. Stepanek will continue to serve as nonexecutive Chairman and member of the board.
    Dr. Drood's executive experience and capability well qualify him for the task of leading the remarkably talented American Semiconductor Corporation workforce while the company continues to introduce innovative products and to grow.
    Since receiving his Ph.D. from MIT and his M.B.A. from Harvard University, Dr. Drood has competently performed in a number of senior executive positions at Union Electric Corporation. While serving in these positions, Dr. Drood distinguished himself by exhibiting strong technical leadership, business acumen, and strategic vision.
    We are confident the men and women of American Semiconductor Corporation from around the world will welcome and support Dr. Drood as he undertakes the demanding responsibilities of the Chief Executive Officer.

THE BOARD OF DIRECTORS

Business reporters had a field day writing headlines such as: "Can Robert Drood Shoulder the Mantles of John Stepanek and Adam Budak?"

Because of Robert's failure to bond with anyone, he had no close friends either within or outside Union Electric. He told his secretary, "Do not allow anyone to organize a departure party for me."

Stepanek called Robert and said, "I'll set up a round of introductions to the AMSCO executives who will report to you when you arrive Monday morning. And I'll send an AMSCO plane to New York to pick you up; let my secretary know the time and place. She'll also give the pilots keys to the AMSCO guest condominium."

Sarah was in Paris for the weekend. She would arrive home on a four-hour Concorde flight on Sunday evening. By then Robert would be on his way to San Francisco. The maid did not work on weekends so he was alone in their New York condominium.

Robert thought about how to handle the transition to his new job. He must bank his aggressive fires until he firmly settled in and confirmed John Stepanek's faith in him. He didn't want to move too fast like the hired guns at several other companies who had earned crippling nicknames: "Chainsaw Augie," "Buzz Saw Bill," and "Charlie the Chopper." He'd start with an icebreaker round of one-on-one meetings with each company executive and ask them about their career histories, families, and nonbusiness interests. He would facetiously call himself "The New Boy" for the first several weeks.

Late on Saturday evening, Robert prepared for bed. Before going to sleep he was again visited by the gaunt and terrible specter that recounted the memories of his wretched youth in Ireland and McClellan's sexual assaults on his sister and mother. He tried to ignore its baneful presence by savoring his professional successes and the deserved thrill of his new job, but the demon was immune to his determined resistance. It churned the disturbing memories in the dark chamber of his mind and intensified his cleaving guilt for not defending his mother and sister from McClellan's evil attacks. The demon huddled around him for hours wailing at him in his troubled sleep. At 5:00 a.m. he called a taxi to take him to his gym for a vigorous physical workout.

During his session at the gym, the demon ended its tormenting dance, unfolded its sooty wings, and flapped away to rejoin the other demons and harpies in their gloomy crags. But Robert knew it would return to torment him at a time of its own choosing. He again thought about seeking psychological counsel, but he still could not accept that another person could solve his problem any better than he, with his superior mind and discipline, could solve it himself.

Sunday afternoon Robert packed his suitcases and placed a copy of the AMSCO announcement by the kitchen telephone with a note for Sarah to read when she returned from her Paris trip. His note read, "Call me sometime so we can discuss when we might get together for a weekend." He called a limousine to take him to Teterboro Airport where an AMSCO jet waited for him.

Monday morning Robert and Stepanek met at the Fairmont Hotel coffee shop. Stepanek did not want to meet at Mother Garvey's where he and Budak regularly met. The café was a hallowed place for him because of the many fraternal meetings they held there. Stepanek still could not speak of Budak without his eyes moistening and his chin quivering.

By evening Stepanek had introduced Robert to his executive staff and briefly reviewed key company issues. When he departed he said, "I'll now leave the building, I will return at your invitation and for board meetings. The AMSCO Foundation director has agreed to provide me with a cubicle and a secretary at his offices over in Oakland. This will give you space to take over your management responsibilities without me in your hair. Goodbye and good luck to you, Robert. I know you will take good care of my company."

That evening when Robert reviewed his first day on his new job at AMSCO, he thought about the tears on Stepanek's cheeks when Budak's name came up: How could a grown man have such feelings toward another person? In all the days since my early youth when my sister was raped and my mother violated, I have not felt an emotional attachment to anyone. I can't fathom why a person would feel this way. Am I lucky not to be burdened with such emotions—or am I unlucky because I don't have them? Do emotional attachments add to or detract from other people's quality of life? And yet a shadowy memory still flickers in my mind of the wonderful love I once had for my mother and sister before McClellan slithered into—and shattered—our lives.

Stepanek and Budak wrote the criteria for the architect to design the recently built AMSCO high-rise headquarters building in the Financial District of San Francisco. Functionality was the key criterion; architectural grandeur was not on the list. The interior layout fostered the egalitarian culture advocated by Stepanek and Budak. All employees, including Stepanek and Budak, worked in standard-size cubicles. After Robert occupied Stepanek's cubicle a few days, he ordered an adjacent conference room redecorated and furnished for his office. He maintained his cubicle, however, for press interviews, photo ops, and infrequent visits by Stepanek.

AMSCO leased a Gulfstream V from an aircraft charter service while its new plane was under construction in Savannah, Georgia. Robert set up an arduous forty thousand-mile world odyssey to visit company facilities and major clients around the world. Ahead of the visits, he sent word he had read the reports on each company unit scheduled for a visit, and he did not want presentations telling him what he already had read. He wanted to have casual meetings so he could informally discuss crucial business subjects and gain a first-hand impression of the visited executives. He throttled his habit of turning the meetings into grilling sessions when he did not like what he heard. Nevertheless, the visited executives instinctively understood there was a new boss in charge with aggressive new demands.

During his world tour, Robert visited Hong Kong where he had happy memories of his many visits during the time he lived in Tokyo. He renewed his relationship with Chen Li Maharanes who had just been promoted to a management position for Cathay Airlines at the just-completed Chek Lap Kok airport on Lantau Island. Li Chen still had her exotic beauty. Robert pulled out all the stops on a spending spree by renting a helicopter, a Rolls Royce limo, a yacht, and a suite at the Peninsula Hotel luxurious enough for a Turkish caliph. The weekend with Li Chen invigorated him and stimulated his growing appetite for the privileges of the wealthy.

After Robert completed his visit to the AMSCO office in Singapore and boarded his plane for the long flight back to California, he motioned Howard Hanson, the senior overseas vice president, to sit across from him at the fold-out conference table in the rear of the plane. "Howard, I want you to organize an Asian marketing study with the objective of tripling revenues in three years. Our current Asian sales are no more than a ripple on the surface." Hanson, who did not yet know Robert very well, thought his sales objective was so optimistic he must be pulling his leg.

When he realized Robert was serious, he gulped and replied, "We've recently reviewed the Asian markets and concluded our sales are already at the upper limit. To maintain them, we're installing a new organizational structure modeled after our European business."

Robert said, "Howard, I've worked all over Asia, and I can tell you from my playbook, copying a western business model is not the way to go. You need a radically different plan for Asia."

Hanson was still smarting that he had not been selected to replace John Stepanek. It galled him to have Robert, a younger man, tell him what to do. And it humiliated him that he did not have the gumption to resign and move to a new company as people at his level often did when passed over for promotion to the top.

Robert decided to replace Hanson, but he would wait until he was better entrenched in his new job.

When the world tour was over, Robert believed he had a comprehensive knowledge of AMSCO's physical facilities, its executives, and its major clients. It was now time for him to launch his "carpet bombing" management style.

Robert's first demand for changes by his executives was to improve their sloppy habits during his weekly staff meetings. He demanded they attend his meetings unless he excused them beforehand for an urgent reason. He told his secretary, "Lock the conference room door at the scheduled meeting time, and do not let anyone in who arrives late."

The first time he saw executives working on Palm Pilots or non-related files during his meetings he said, "Please present to all of us the information you apparently think is more important than my agenda."

After Howard Hanson set up Robert's requested Asian study, it became obvious his negative attitude was dampening the objectivity of the study. Robert said, "Howard, hire a consulting firm with Asian experience to assist your team. They need an outside voice to stir them up."

"Robert, I don't know of any consultant that would be any good at helping us. I think we already know the Asian market well enough to make our own study."

Robert said, "Hire Asian Marketing Associates. Okiko Ogata, who used to work with me before she left Union Electric, owns the company. She knows the Asian culture and marketing conditions better than anyone I know. Okiko will stir the study to a fever pitch, and her recommendations won't be qualified with the kind of weasel clauses often found in consultants' reports. It'll have a solid basis for its recommendations and action plans. It'll be a plan that we can execute with confidence."

As Howard departed, Robert smiled and thought: If anyone fails to cooperate with Okiko, they'll learn what it is like to be dropped into a velvet-lined viper pit.

When Stepanek and Budak ran AMSCO, for many years they insisted that all company employees fly in the coach section of commercial airlines when they travelled. As the company grew and the travel demands increased, they finally accepted the fact that the company needed to buy its own corporate planes for efficiently transporting its employees and its customers. Stepanek and Budak set a strict policy on the use of the planes. The principle point in the policy was that the planes would not be considered prestigious perks for the senior executives. They regarded AMSCO planes as airborne taxis.

When Drood became CEO of AMSCO, the corporate plane policies remained in place, but he totally disregarded them. The largest plane in the AMSCO fleet would become "AMSCO One" with control and usage Drood's exclusive privilege.

When AMSCO took delivery of its new Gulfstream plane to replace the one that was destroyed at the time of Budak's death, Robert was like a boy with his first bicycle. When he took guests on trips, he liked to hand them a printed card extolling the plane's grand features:

AMERICAN SEMICONDUCTOR CORPORATION GULFSTREAM

- This Gulfsteam plane is powered by a pair of Rolls Royce engines that propel it at Mach .88—more than five hundred miles per hour—at an altitude of fifty-one thousand feet.
- The wingspan is ninety-three feet.
- The ten passenger seats are designed to convert into sleeping berths. They are fitted with a telecommunication system connected to anywhere in the world.
- When loaded with twenty tons of fuel, the plane can travel 6,500 nautical miles and stay airborne for up to twelve hours.
- The plane is equipped with a shower and a full service cooking galley.

One of Robert's rich, irreverent guests observed while flying with him on the plane to a weekend golf outing, "This is one honking fine bird to haul us pampered nabobs to our weekend watering holes."

Robert told his senior executive staff, "The plane is also for your use." But there was seldom a time when it was not reserved for his purposes.

CHAPTER EIGHTEEN

Robert took the Gulfstream to Germany on its first overseas trip. Sarah accompanied him because of the potential business benefit to her bank. During her preparation for the trip, she remembered her refugee grandparents' stories, told to her in Yiddish-accented German, about the shameless treatment and savage slaughter of their relatives by the Nazis in World War II. Although she knew most of the Nazis who committed the atrocities were dead, she detested the idea of even walking on the soil where they committed their savagery.

Robert and Sarah were weekend guests of Karl von Kleinschmidt, the wealthy owner of a German firm that builds devilishly-complicated chip-manufacturing equipment. Only a few companies in the world have such capability. Von Kleinschmidt invited the Droods for the weekend so he could develop an inside track for future AMSCO business. The subject of business, however, did not arise during the visit. Von Kleinschmidt used the time to size up Robert and gain insight for a sales campaign to land the huge orders that AMSCO would place for its next new fab.

Von Kleinschmidt owned an eight-hundred-year-old castle on the forbidding bluffs of the Rhine River near Koblenz. According to ancient legends, the sirens of Lorelei once resided in the castle towers and beckoned boatmen from passing vessels for their nefarious purposes. The von Kleinschmidts occupied the castle on most weekends and holidays.

Sharing opulent playgrounds with those who occupied the pinnacles of power was enjoyable to Sarah, but it was not a new experience for her. Since childhood she was accustomed to the luxuries surrounding her affluent parents and their friends. For Robert, it was different; contrasting the luxurious von Kleinschmidt castle to his family's hovel in Ireland brought troubled memories.

Von Kleinschmidt's driver picked up Robert and Sarah at their Frankfurt hotel and drove them to the castle in the lush comfort of a twelve-cylinder Maybach limousine.

The car halted on the cobblestone courtyard in front of the castle's massive, wisteria-surrounded doorway. Von Kleinschmidt and his wife greeted Robert and Sarah in the cavernous reception hall. The cathedral-like hall was decorated with shined and waxed knight's armor, polished antique weapons, and centuries-old ancestral paintings. Von Kleinschmidt was too steeped in formal German culture to call Robert and Sarah by their first names even though he spoke fluent English.

After a welcoming glass of wine and a tray of canapés, von Kleinschmidt said, "We will dine at eight this evening, and tomorrow morning we'll tour local places of historical interest. In the afternoon we'll attend the dedication of the new Save the World Rainforests headquarters; I'm chairman of the foundation. With your knowledge of science, Dr. Drood, I believe you'll find it interesting. I've also invited Herr Dr. Horstmann, the managing director of the foundation, to dine with us this evening. I hope this is satisfactory to you."

A servant escorted Sarah and Robert to an enormous bedroom suite with a sparkling spa-like bath. The view across the Rhine, which bustled with cruise ships and barge traffic, was toward the steep, shadowy bluffs on the far side of the river. It looked like a picture on the cover of a coffee table travel book.

The guests sat down for an elaborate wild-game dinner precisely at eight After the meal, the dinner party moved to the wood-paneled parlor, heated by a fireplace, for coffee and a warmed snifter of Asbach Uralt brandy. The men and women sat apart.

The ladies, thinking Sarah was listening to the men, switched from English to German. They discussed a recent incident where a U.S soldier who was stationed in the area had been rowdy in a restaurant. Mrs. von Kleinschmidt huffed, "It's incredible our government still tolerates the unwelcome presence of the U.S. military. It is unimaginable that soldiers of every odd ethnic origin are allowed to come here to misbehave and defile our young women. It is humiliating for us to have those dumbheads residing on our soil. Since our military has regained most of its past glory, we don't want or need them any more." Mrs. Horstmann rolled her eyes, but in deference to her hostess, remained silent.

Sarah took a deep breath to control her fury while she caved in on her resolution to stay out of antagonistic conversations during the weekend. She switched to the German she had learned from her grandmother and with difficulty controlled the intensity of her feelings before she said, "I think you'll find American soldiers behave in an exemplary manner when contrasted to the savagery of the German armies in the middle of the twentieth century. Their treatment of people from 'odd ethnic origins' was so flagrant that books about it are still being written and read in disbelief. And if you don't know why the American soldiers are still on German soil, someone needs to give you a Realpolitik lesson—especially with the threat hovering over Germany from the resurgent Russian military. I had hoped my first visit to Germany would reveal more enlightenment."

When Sarah finished her outburst, the embarrassed ladies sat in silence. She turned away from them when she heard Dr. Horstmann expressing uncertainty about a complex technical point relative to the new European currency and international trade. She switched to English and clarified the question that was stumping him based on her experience with international banking. She kept her back turned to the other ladies for the remainder of the evening.

Mrs. von Kleinschmidt received a severe drubbing from her husband when they retired for the night. "I told you the business importance of Dr. Drood's visit and to lay off spouting the drivel promulgated by the idiotic neo-Nazi movement that you support. After your tirade, Mrs. Drood is certainly not going to ever have anything good to say about her visit here. You're a first class dumbhead."

The next day Sarah and Robert accompanied the von Kleinschmidts and Horstmanns to the new Save the World Rainforests headquarters dedication. Von Kleinschmidt said, "Dr. Drood, our company supports the foundation by donating a small percentage of our revenue. Incidentally, we have a foundation board position open at the moment. Perhaps AMSCO would have a candidate to fill it."

Robert responded, "It sounds like a worthwhile cause. We're re-evaluating our company personnel at this time so I don't think we can offer a candidate, but in the future when another opening occurs, perhaps we can positively respond to your request."

After the long and dull dedication, Reuters, Associated Press, and CNN photographed and interviewed the Droods and von Kleinschmidts. Robert and Sarah were still young, attractive, and in demand for photo ops.

During the day, Mrs. Horstmann drew Sarah aside and said, "I disagree with the opinions stated by Mrs. von Kleinschmidt last evening. I think the presence of the U.S. military on our soil is good for Germany and for Europe. We hope they continue to support us as we go about finally achieving our long-pursued goal of reuniting West Germany and East Germany."

Sarah was still seething from the evening before. She said, "But when Mrs. von Kleinschmidt presented her warped viewpoint on 'odd ethnicities,' you remained silent. I think the German mentality has advanced little for the last seventy years."

Mrs. von Kleinschmidt tried to pacify Sarah after the dust-up the evening before. "Mrs. Drood, I did so enjoy my last trip to California.

The Americans treated us like we were cousins." Sarah responded with a frosty nod and a tight-lipped smile. She let Robert deal with their departure amenities. When she entered the stately Maybach for the ride back to Frankfurt, she did not wait for the driver to close the door; she insulted both Mrs. von Kleinschmidt and the $400,000 Maybach by slamming the door hard enough to rattle the double-pane, sound-insulated window glass.

When Robert got into the car, Sarah said, "Thank God this miserable weekend is over. It'll be a cold day in hell before I ever set foot on the soil of this obscene country again."

Robert received an adrenaline rush when he peered into von Kleinschmidt's private world during the weekend. He dreamed of living in similar opulence himself. His problem was he only had limited assets whereas people like von Kleinschmidt had millions of dollars—or maybe even billions—on their balance sheets.

Stepanek said to his wife, a management professor and consultant, while they shared their customary evening drink, "I'm going to resign my AMSCO board position. I'm satisfied Robert Drood is now in full command and does not need any further mentoring from me."

His wife said, "For some reason, I feel in my bones Drood needs to be watched. I suspect ethics is a *terra incognita* subject to him. When I give my seminars to senior corporate executives, I quote from *Satires* by Juvenal to warn them of the greed that can accompany power: '*Quis custodiet ipsos custodies?*' (Who will guard the guards?) Without your steadying hand on the AMSCO board, I'll be nervous."

Stepanek said, "Maybe that's a perceptive observation, dear, but with Justin Cairncross on the board, there'll still be a guard present. There's little that escapes him. But I don't really think you need to worry about Robert."

"I hope you're right, but you've always been far too trusting of people. You think they're all full of goodness like you are."

Although Robert now directed every aspect of AMSCO, he recognized Stepanek's latent power because of his enormous stock voting rights. He invited him to monthly lunches to ensure his support when he submitted his annual voting proxies.

Robert chaired his first board meeting at the AMSCO European headquarters in London. He also invited thirty senior company executives for a round of information meetings and discussions after the board meeting. A refurbished castle in Kent, an hour drive from London, housed the AMSCO delegation.

Robert's simplified presentation of complex information and articulate answers to questions were in sharp contrast to the stiff, formal presentations in many board meetings. The AMSCO board members were impressed.

In the separate round of meetings that followed the board meeting, Robert showed the thirty attending company executives an introductory slide on an oversized screen of a breathtaking herd of wildebeests sweeping across the African Serengeti in an enveloping swirl of dust. After a long pause he said, "This awesome and majestic herd, seemingly in total control of its fate, appears to be invincible. This is how many of you perceive AMSCO."

He then showed another slide of the flanks and rear of the wildebeest herd with vigilant predators eyeing and stalking any animal that was old or injured or that lagged or strayed. "But this is how I view our company," Robert said. "The cunning predators are moving in to snatch their meal from the first animal that falters or fails to follow the herd leadership.

"It's your obligation to see that your sector of AMSCO's business is not assailed by its predators. And it is my responsibility to monitor each sector and bench any faltering executive at the first sign a competitor's attack is not being successfully countered."

The room was hushed. The executives were used to accolades from Stepanek and Budak for superior performance and promises for a rosy future. Robert's grim representation of the AMSCO business climate and the threat to their careers if they did not perform well was an unnerving experience.

For some of the executives invited to the Kent Castle, it was the first time they had seen Robert conduct a meeting. He spoke with the measured words of an English professor while wielding a pointer like a field marshal's baton. While others talked, he tapped his steepled fingers together. His intensity when he spoke was understood to mean they were receiving marching orders—not just ideas offered for consideration.

When Robert met with his assistant in the late afternoon to discuss administrative matters he said, "I had to find a way to put the fear of God into them and make them understand our competitors are like ferocious, wild animal predators. I hope my wildebeest parable gained their attention."

"According to the comments I overheard, I think your message hit them hard—in fact it scared a couple of them half to death."

After the first day of meetings, and over a whiskey and soda, one of the executives muttered to a friend, "When I sit in a meeting with

Drood, I feel like a beetle under a microscope being probed with a needle."

"And I feel like a wildebeest with an exploding bladder because it is afraid to slow down to take a leak," his irreverent friend responded.

Sarah, who was in London on business, spent her last night in England with Robert. While they were in their suite preparing for bed, Sarah tearfully said, "Robert, our marriage has been hollow almost from the beginning. It's only a marriage of convenience. There's something fundamentally missing, and I see no way to get it on track. I can't go on this way any longer. I've told my lawyer to start divorce proceedings when I return to New York. This decision has given me more distress and heartbreak than any I ever made before." Sarah wiped her eyes and continued, "And I have something else to tell you; I've been seeing another man for several months, and we've decided to marry. He's an investment banker whom I have known for some time."

Robert hesitated for a long time and said, "Well Sarah, I'm not surprised. For whatever reasons, we've always had a rocky marriage. The fault is probably with me. For some reason I was never able to acquire the emotions that should go with a marriage. Your lawyer can speak to mine anytime. Since I moved to San Francisco, Martin Blanski is my attorney. I'll cooperate any way I can. I regret we didn't make a good match. I wish you all the best in your new marriage. I'll always remember you for the good person you are and for the pleasures we had together."

Sarah paused and said, "Based on the terms of our pre-nuptial agreement, I don't see any complications relative to our property distribution. The only things we own in common are the Bentley and our condo. Any offer you make for buying out my share of the Bentley will be okay with me, and I'll pay you the market price for your share of the condo." Sarah was a good investor of her considerable income and substantial inherited money. Robert's finances were in shambles as usual from his compulsive spending.

Although Robert expressed remorse to Sarah about the end of their marriage, he felt no more emotions than he would if a valued employee resigned.

A few weeks after the board meeting in England, Robert met with security analysts in New York—a group legendary for their skepticism—to explain the status of AMSCO's business. The bright, cocky young analysts liked to amuse themselves by asking impudent questions hoping the featured executive would lose his or her equilibrium and blurt out unintended remarks. Robert overwhelmed them with his studied charm and convinced them all was well at AMSCO. He did not mention that storm clouds, due to a fall-off in sales, were gathering over the horizon. The stock price rose several points the next day.

Robert participated in a series of discussions with the AMSCO advanced products group. The scientists and engineers in the group were his intellectual peers on technical matters. They could endlessly expound on the intricacies of chip designs and the fiendish complexities of manufacturing them. The only way to challenge this group was on an intellectual basis. Appealing to them on the grounds that profit margins would improve if they conceived successful new products was like promising gold stars to a dog if it performed tricks. He earned their attention in his first meeting by speaking about an arcane technical article he had read in a recent issue of the *Journal of the Babbage Society*.

The further Robert delved into the outer boundaries of technology, the more they enjoyed it. They liked discussing how Moore's Law (transistors in computer chips will double every two years) could go on indefinitely or even accelerate if the technology for quantum computing ever became practical. Robert challenged them by asking, "What about biotechnology to replace the current designs of silicon chips. Within living creatures, computer-like processes are constantly making billions of decisions. Perhaps DNA molecules could be used as a silicon chip alternative. We might think of DNA molecules as software and enzymes as bits of hardware." This opened floodgates of speculation about neurons in living bodies that function as tiny hybrid computers and the complex calculations performed by a combination of digital pulses between the neurons and analog computations within them. The engineers and scientists loved this kind of far-out techie talk. They liked it even better if a note of science fiction weirdness was added to the discussions.

Nathan Veldthoff was the most creative scientist in the advanced products group. He said, "Someday we'll understand the nanotechnology of neurons enough to imitate them and manufacture apparatus that will make today's computers look like primitive abacuses or slide rules. I'm betting my pad and pickup on future quantum computers that'll harness atoms and molecules to perform memory and processing tasks. Theoretically, quantum computers have the potential to perform calculations billions of times faster than our current silicon chip-based computers."

With Veldthoff, Robert could indulge in bare-knuckled give and take. Nathan was oblivious to rank and could not be intimidated. Employment by competitive companies was open to him any time he made a phone call. Having a CEO who talked his language and contributed to rowdy creativity sessions was as enjoyable to him as a midnight delivery of pizza and beer.

When Veldthoff was sixteen, he enrolled in the University of California, Berkeley and immersed himself in the school's computer science courses and laboratories to the exclusion of sleeping, eating, and attending required noncomputer-related classes. His professors, recognizing he possessed a brilliant mind, made every allowance for his eccentricities, but they finally expelled him from the university because of nonparticipation in required classes. They saw to it, however, that he had the opportunity for continuing his technical development by giving him projects to work on from their corporate client assignments and by allowing him access to the university computers. One of the corporate clients was AMSCO. When its scientists saw Nathan's work, they hired him.

When Nathan started on a creative roll, he went into a trance that could not be penetrated by any normal exterior stimulus. When his colleagues saw a trance coming on they said, "He's packing up for a trip to Nathanland." The trances could last for minutes, hours, or even days. When Nathan returned from a trance, he often revealed a technical fantasy worthy of a plot for a science fiction book or a practical design breakthrough that would allow AMSCO to introduce another blockbuster product.

Nathan often slept on a cot in a walk-in closet behind the laboratories when his body shut down from sleep deprivation. Other times he drove to a remote grove of trees and slept in the back of his pickup or in his modest apartment. He liked to work with the blinds drawn in his laboratory and office so his personal circadian rhythm functioned without the influence of the normal twenty-four-hour schedule of the rest of the world.

Dressing and grooming did not appear on Nathan's radar screen. He favored oversized tan pants held up with wide green suspenders, dark T-shirts, a brown knit cap, and sandals—all from the Farm and Fleet store—to clothe his pudgy body. He groomed his hair only when it restricted his head movement or vision. His facial hair was nonexistent except for kinky sprouts of chin hair that looked like transplants from his ears. When Nathan occasionally emerged from his cerebral fog bank and recognized someone, he blinked through his bottle-bottom glasses, mumbled, "Yo," and shook their hand like it was a bulky uncapped ketchup bottle.

Several years earlier Nathan took his girlfriend on a camping trip to a remote mountain area. He went into a thinking frenzy that turned into a trip to Nathanland. He required computer access, so he drove trance-like back to his office. Three days later when he returned from Nathanland, he explained to his peers and awed management an ingenious answer to a problem that had always before appeared unsolvable.

When Nathan finished explaining his solution, he banged his palm on the side of his head and said, "Oh, my Lord, I left my girlfriend alone at our campsite." When a forest ranger located her, she was famished, dehydrated, and as riled as an agitated rattlesnake. Her relationship with Nathan did not continue.

Nathan never attended administrative meetings or opened mail and seldom answered his telephone. After a secretary found three months of unopened paychecks and a year's worth of stock options in a paper bag stuffed behind his desk, she handled his financial affairs for him. Nathan owned stock options worth more than ten million dollars, but he lived a life he could sustain on little more than a minimum wage income. His physical appearance was similar to the homeless people who resided under Interstate overpasses. A few years earlier he slept with them for several weeks after he was evicted from his apartment because he forgot to pay his rent. He was oblivious to company politics, administrative rules, money, and time. Nathan's presence was a constant irritant to administrators who sought more orderliness than was of any interest to him.

Veldthoff was the crown jewel of the AMSCO advanced products group. His name appeared on dozens of the most valuable company patents. For years technical societies awarded him their highest honors, but he never had any interest in attending the award ceremonies.

A technical journalist concluded an article on Nathan by writing, "If Nathan Veldthoff was asked to point to true north on a map, and he pointed in another direction, it would probably be because true north was not where everyone always thought it was."

Most company employees, from the senior officers to the janitorial staff, took pride in Nathan's singular creativity, off-the-wall wit, and exquisite weirdness. A colleague said, "A conversation with Nathan is better than watching *Saturday Night Live.*" Employees developed a protective cocoon around him out of personal affection and admiration for his unfathomable intellect. They thought of him as their very own mad scientist.

CHAPTER NINETEEN

Since Drood became the CEO of AMSCO, doors opened for him to many of the world's most elite and exclusive haunts. They were often family *sancta sanctorum* in remote and secure locations that had existed for generations. They were designed to provide unbounded comfort, pleasure, safety, and anonymity to the owners, their families, and selected guests. The need had long since passed for the key holders to the haunts to impress anyone; they were born with wealth and its privileges embedded in their DNA.

Servants, pilots, nannies, chauffeurs, gardeners, administrators, guards, and cooks were only employed by the super-rich after an apprenticeship where the most important factor was sealed lips. They were trained to plead ignorance when asked questions about the homes, offices, planes, and yachts of the people they served. The penalty for the mortal sin of talking to outsiders about their employers was summary dismissal.

Hans Bartoluzzi headed an ancient Swiss family with a prominent but secretive history extending back centuries. He directed Bartoluzzi Enterprises from an unpretentious bank building on Bahnhofstrasse in Zurich. The building appeared to be a commercial bank, but executives, who managed the family's enormous wealth, occupied the highly-secure upper floors. Even the families of the company executives did not know exactly how they earned their livings. Bartoluzzi Enterprises functioned within a Byzantine corporate structure designed to shield it from public view. Its internal corporate structure was the model for the other "Gnomes of Zurich" who quietly went about their investment and wealth accumulation businesses.

Bartoluzzi was interested in AMSCO because of his expanding Asian electronics businesses and comprehensive stock investments. He was fascinated with the fast-growing information technology industry centered in Silicon Valley, California. In order to become acquainted with an American executive in the silicon chip industry, Bartoluzzi invited Robert for a visit to his winter estate in the high Swiss Alps near San Moritz.

Robert called Nathan Norton, AMSCO's Chief Financial Officer, and asked, "How much AMSCO stock does Bartoluzzi Enterprises own?"

Norton checked it out and reported, "They own about two million shares although it was difficult to penetrate the obscure Swiss maze to the ultimate stock owner. And I checked the value of AMSCO annual orders to Bartoluzzi's Asian factories. It's nearly thirty million dollars."

The Bartoluzzi helicopter met Robert in Zurich for the flight to the sunlit courtyard overlooking the foreboding Alps behind the family aerie. Winter access was only by helicopter or a narrow, private road plowed free of snow during stretches of clear weather.

The Bartoluzzi complex, surrounded by snow-laden trees and brooding mountains, was domed with azure skies. It stood in magnificent solitude as if nothing else existed on the planet. The wooden main residence was built in the traditional Swiss style with surrounding balconies protected by broad overhanging roofs. The house could be the inspiration for a Swiss tourist brochure.

After lunch and conversation confined to light social subjects, Bartoluzzi said, "Unfortunately, due to the flare-up of an old ski injury, I can't accompany you while you ski. Some of the slopes are quite unsafe for skiing alone so I've engaged a guide for you. I suggest you enjoy your skiing, and tomorrow evening return here for dinner with me. Perhaps while we're taking our after-dinner coffee, you can tell me something about your remarkable company. My pilot will return you to Zurich on Monday morning."

Bartoluzzi ushered in the guide. She was a willowy snow goddess who moved with the grace of a gazelle. Bartoluzzi said, using the American informality of first names, "Robert, this is Ursula. She will ski with you and guide you down the unfamiliar slopes. In case of accident or difficulties, she can summon the authorities on her mobile telephone. She has a Sno-cat for transportation to the best ski areas."

They skied for the afternoon on pristine powder snow. When the late afternoon sun descended and the temperature dipped, Ursula and Robert returned to the guesthouse. She parked the Sno-cat in an open-sided shed and came into the house with Robert. By this time they had developed an amicable relationship.

Two middle-aged women were at work in the house. They spoke Romansch, the ancient Latin-like language of the region, but switched to French when Robert and Ursula entered, assuming they both spoke it. They had heated the sauna cabinet, lit the fireplace, turned back the goose-down bed cover, and laid out a bountiful cold supper and bottles of local drinks on the sideboard of the dining room. They said they would return late in the morning to prepare a mountaineer breakfast. Bartoluzzi had obviously engaged Ursula for more than ski guide services; she remained with Robert until they finished skiing in late afternoon of the following day when she discretely departed.

For dinner on Sunday evening with Bartoluzzi, a younger man was present. "May I introduce my brother, Alfredo?" Bartoluzzi said. "He assists us with our investment decisions."

After dinner, they moved to the library for coffee and liqueur. The Bartoluzzi brothers directed the conversation to the future outlook for the information technology industry. Alfredo, in his polished London Threadneedle Street accent, explained, "We favor investments with long-term, sustainable growth potential and consistent earnings. Because of the uncertainties with computer and information technology companies, we have, until now, shied away from investing much in them. Perhaps we were influenced by your Mr. Warren Buffet who also shied away from IT investments. However, AMSCO is an exception. We maintain a nominal position in AMSCO stock. And of course we also have beneficial relationships with AMSCO through our Asian factories."

"We're conservative here in Switzerland," Hans interrupted. "It is amazing to us the U.S. information technology industry is directed by such young people. In Swiss corporations, it would be considered irresponsible to give significant authority to young, inexperienced people."

"The experienced people were the ones who failed to foresee the new information technology industry," Robert responded. "So from our viewpoint, it's illogical for them to lead the new high-tech companies."

"Your point's well taken," Bartoluzzi said. "We can now see the American computer and information technology industry has been a colossal success—especially AMSCO."

Robert said, "We think in spite of the growth in the industry until now, it's still in its infancy."

Bartoluzzi said, "Alfredo, please develop a new investment authorization file on AMSCO so our review committee and I can consider expanding our current holdings."

Robert thought about the Bartoluzzi bank's current ownership of two million shares of AMSCO. Hans apparently considered investments to be nominal if they were valued at less than forty million dollars.

After Robert tried to conceal a stifled yawn induced by a hard day of skiing in the cold air, Hans said, "Alfredo and I will be engaged tomorrow when you leave, so we now wish you good evening and goodbye. The snow will be cleared early from the helicopter landing pad. Our pilot will be here at 8:30 to take you back to Zurich. We hope your weekend was enjoyable and you'll soon visit us again. It was an honor for us to have you for our guest and to allow us to learn more from you about your remarkable firm. Please call me any time I can be of professional or personal service."

Robert mused while he walked back down the snowy, moonlit path to the guesthouse: How blessed and lucky are the select few who are born into such privileged circumstances as the Bartoluzzis and who have the intellect and sensitivity to enjoy it. When the performance goals set by the AMSCO board are met for the year, a substantial bonus will be paid and stock options will be granted to me. This should be enough for me to make a down payment on an estate similar to Bartoluzzi's or von Kleinschmidt's. But why wait? The bonus and options will soon be in hand. Why not start looking around now for an estate even if bridge financing is needed? Hans Bartoluzzi appears to walk on the high ground, but the words "Discreet Financial Services" are written on his business card implying wide flexibility to accept any proposition that can aid in feeding the money chutes into the Bartoluzzi bank vaults. He could be my source for bridge financing if I buy an estate soon.

Robert's compulsive spending accelerated. He could not visit an art gallery or an antique Persian rug store without making costly purchases. His buying splurges were as undisciplined as a crow collecting baubles. He seldom distinguished between tasteful and expensive. He was not a connoisseur; he soon lost interest in what he bought. Some of his purchases remained packed and forgotten when he took them home.

Robert harvested prestigious golf club memberships like Boy Scouts collect badges. Although he belonged to the Olympic Club in San Francisco, he favored playing at Pebble Beach Golf Links where he could associate with celebrities and Fortune 500 CEOs. He also belonged to other "sniffy" golf clubs and wore their paraphernalia whenever possible: a belt showing the lone cypress tree of Cypress Point, a jacket with the Indian chief of Seminole, and a tie sporting the striped shield of Pine Valley. But he broke the established code of conduct at ultra-exclusive and elite Augusta National by personally lobbying for membership; his membership application was rejected.

Robert's unthrottled high living was becoming ever more difficult to sustain even on his princely salary and bloated expense accounts.

Robert had an aversion for the detailed AMSCO procedure manuals. He called them "Mao's Little Red Books." An executive excused his slowness in grasping an urgent business opportunity by saying, "I can't go ahead until we've completed the risk analysis and financial reviews specified in the procedure manual." After this remark, Robert had his copies of the manuals stacked in the hall outside his office for several weeks with a conspicuous note to the janitors to haul them to a dumpster. He wanted to imbue a much faster decision-making culture into AMSCO.

His administrative assistant understood Robert wanted to hold his time for company work to fewer than fifty hours a week. With his blinding speed and intensity, he could manage the company in that time. He wanted the rest of his time to be available for his expanding personal pursuits. She, with the assistance of several secretaries, streamlined Robert's immense paper flow so he could administer it in short order.

After the board meeting in England, Robert ratcheted up the pressure on his executive group. He reverted to his old style from Union Electric of keeping a dozen balls in the air at the same time. An executive grumbled to his assistant, "How the hell does Drood do it? When I was in his office yesterday, he talked to me about my division performance while he simultaneously read a report in Japanese on Asian sales. He must have a pair of independent brains in his head. A conversation with him is like trying to sip water from a fire hose."

Drood's executives became used to remarks such as, "How can you run your business without knowing that?" or "You better hard-wire that promise because if you don't deliver on it, you can count on some serious unpleasantness."

Ken Yee, senior vice president of manufacturing, was one of the few executives whom Robert considered his intellectual equal and whom he treated like a peer. He expanded Yee's work responsibilities to broaden his executive experience.

By now, Robert had sized up the executives of the company and decided who was not up to his standards of competence or not supportive of his leadership. Howard Hanson and Nicolas Swopes, the senior vice presidents who resented Robert, had not come around to accepting him. They were indifferent to his directions and critical of his leadership. Robert could not let their challenges go unchecked. They had to go.

He did not think Hanson could stand up to the stress of vigorously applied pressure. He summoned him to his office. "Howie, tell me about your progress in achieving our sales objectives in the Asia-Pacific market."

"You know, I never was much impressed with that Asian study group that you set up and that fancy Japanese girl we hired to facilitate it. I didn't agree with the team's recommendations. I think the annual two to three percent growth we've been getting for the last few years is about all we can squeeze out of that market. I don't have the latest figures at my fingertips, but I'd guess we aren't beating my forecasts by very much. I can check out the figures for you and let you know."

Robert said, "It is three months since the Asian study group set new objectives. You should be executing the group's recommendations and showing results by now. Your Asian sales are flat in a growing market and your profits are off. With the burgeoning markets of China, you should be spending the bulk of your time there. You've only been there for short visits twice during the last year. Our competitors are not sitting around sucking their thumbs when they see you faltering in Asia. And you should check the Asian sales figures for yourself—not for me; I already know how bad they are. Howie, let's cut to the chase; your marketing leadership in Asia isn't cutting it."

Howard turned beet red as his resentment of Robert spewed out. He sputtered in a rising voice, "Bob, you came here like a bright flashing star from the east." He knew Robert hated being called Bob. "You use your trick memory to rattle off a bunch of numbers as if I'm a slow-witted boob. You expect me to sign on to your unsubstantiated sales objectives and disregard my thirty years of sales experience. One of these days you'll find AMSCO, which was built by John Stepanek and Adam Budak and some of the rest of us, is not a Disneyland toy for a whiz kid like you to use for your self-indulgence. Some day the board is going to wake up and see how you're hoodwinking them."

Robert was satisfied he had provoked Hanson enough so he cut in, "Howie, I have no intention of reporting to the board and stockholders that any division of AMSCO is not achieving its objectives. If I leave you in your position, I'll need to give my personal attention to your division's lagging performance. I don't think you are up to the intensity that I'd bring to bear. I'm going to appoint someone else to take over your job. I think you'll be happier if you consider retirement or a career at another company. See Jack Hamilton in human resources; he'll show you a generous early retirement package."

Hanson left Robert's office knowing he had launched his verbal missiles, and they were irretrievable. His career at AMSCO was over.

Word of Hanson's departure spread throughout the company like a shock wave. In the past, if anyone missed objectives, forgiveness was usually granted. It was now evident Robert Drood was running

AMSCO with a hefty club instead of the gentle switch wielded by Stepanek and Budak.

Ridding the company of Swopes would require a different tack. Swopes had the ear of Stepanek and several board members. He devoted his spare time to state Republican politics. For a long time, he had political ambitions but did not pursue them due to Stepanek's insistence that his employees focus their energy only on AMSCO. Although Swopes was disappointed at not being selected for the AMSCO CEO position, it did not consume him as it did Hanson. He knew he would never be CEO, so he throttled back on his previous energetic management style.

Robert called Marco Ruiz-Jones, chairman of the California Republican Party, for a lunch meeting. They met in a small private dining room at the Mark Hopkins Hotel. After coffee Robert asked, "Marco, do you have your gubernatorial candidates list completed for the next election?"

"Yes, and we're now whittling it down to a short list."

"Nicolas Swopes seems to have good political skills and has been active in the Republican Party for years. Is he on your list?"

"No. He told us if he ran for political office, it would jeopardize his AMSCO career. However, we have discussed Nicolas; we would likely put him on our list if he's ever available."

"That presents no problem now. If you select him for your candidate for governor, we'll give him a paid leave of absence."

"I'm confident, based on this information, the party will give strong consideration to Nicolas as its candidate for governor," Ruiz-Jones said.

After Swopes was selected for the Republican candidate, Robert said, "Nicolas, you have my endorsement for the governorship. No doubt it will be a full time job for a while so we will place you on administrative leave. I assure you the door here at AMSCO shall always be open for your return."

After the campaign for governor started, Robert put into motion a complete reorganization and reassignment of personnel in Swope's division to ensure he would never want to return.

Swopes lost the gubernatorial election, but gained enough national recognition during the campaign to earn a sub-cabinet post in Washington. He and his wife became intoxicated with Washington politics and the high-octane Georgetown social whirl. They never returned to California.

Robert now had unchallenged control of all of the AMSCO executives.

CHAPTER TWENTY

AMSCO periodically forecast the worldwide silicon chip markets to determine when a new chip fab needed to be planned and built. A company planner said, "Building a new fab at the right time is like a hunter trying to lead his aim so the bird and the buckshot simultaneously converge at the same point in the air."

Augie Harrison, head of the chip market-forecasting group, sent the latest chip forecast to Drood who called a meeting to discuss and challenge it. Harrison kicked off the meeting by showing a PowerPoint slide of the meeting agenda. Robert said, "Augie, turn off that projector. You already gave me a copy of your bloated forecast and I read it. I don't need to see it again. Can you tell me why you included low-profit products that are not included in the strategic markets approved by the board?"

Harrison's neck reddened and his mouth turned dry; senior executives always intimidated him. He answered, "The individual divisions did not all agree with the approved strategic markets." He again turned on the projector and tried to locate a slide to clarify his point. Robert pulled the projector plug and tossed it aside. Harrison put his hands under the table to hide the trembling.

"Augie, your job description says you're to forecast our chip requirements based on board-approved strategic markets. This doesn't mean you're to willy-nilly add up the forecasts of all the divisions for any markets they personally choose to enter. The board still gives us our marching orders. Why do you think your criteria are superior to those of the board?"

Harrison was in acute discomfort as he attempted to wriggle out from under the spotlight. While he tried to think of a suitable answer to Robert's question, his bright, young assistant, Billy Jordan, brashly jumped into the conversation and said, "Dr. Drood, we actually did rough out an alternative forecast that lines up with the board's direction. We can finalize it in short order." The dirty look from Harrison to Jordan could have decked a charging elephant.

"I'm being urged to okay the design of an enormously costly new chip fab," Robert said as he scowled at Harrison, "Do you now understand my reluctance to give the go-ahead? The forecast you just suggested as the basis for the new fab capacity looks like something concocted by the pointy-haired character in a Dilbert comic. Billy, when can you have your new forecast wrapped up?"

"Sir, we can have it fully detailed and complete in two weeks or sooner."

"Call me when it's ready."

As Robert stood to leave the conference room, he asked Harrison to follow him to his office. "Augie, I want you to go to Singapore for a couple weeks to see if you can locate other companies that have excess capacity and would be willing to supply chips to us. This could allow us to delay building our new fab. In the meantime Billy Jordan can finish up the chip forecast based on the markets agreed to by our board."

"I've just been shipped off to Siberia on a wild-goose chase," Harrison grumbled to a trusted assistant. "Everyone knows all Singapore chip fabs have full order books and are running flat out."

Jordan refined his forecast and took it to Drood. After he read it, he made a few minor adjustments and wrote a note to his staff:

> The chip forecasts now look okay. Let's proceed with the design of the new fab. When the design criteria and fab location are determined, I want to see another project review.
>
> RGD

Although Drood always asked all of his executive staff for their comments on important decisions, he valued those of Yee the most. Drood and Yee, when in private, had a jocular way of addressing each other. Robert called Yee "Inscrutable One" and Yee called Robert "Maximum Bossman." Their sophomoric silliness with each other allowed them to work together in relaxed harmony.

"Inscrutable One, some of our board members will contract a bad case of hand wringing when they see nine zeros on the capital estimate for our new fab," Robert said. "They'll not be comfortable until we can demonstrate we have examined every alternative to investing in a new fab. Set up a team to investigate the Somita Company in Japan as a supplier for some of our chips. Somita's the only major silicon chip manufacturer in the world with excess capacity due to their overly optimistic sales forecasts that have not yet materialized."

"Okay, Maximum Bossman. Inscrutable One do chop-chop. Belly good idea."

"You wily chopstick clacker. You sure know how to read the fortune cookies and suck up to the honorable boss," Robert chuckled.

Robert and Yee never failed to laugh together at their banter. They sounded like a parody of an old Charlie Chan detective movie. They sometimes used lines from the old movies when they conducted AMSCO business. Robert tried out a flawed idea on Yee. Yee said, "Honorable Maximum Bossman, that idea not have a Chinaman's chance; it have as much likelihood of success as man trying to bounce egg off sidewalk."

Yee assembled a small group to work with him for the Somita investigation. The financial representative he wanted was unavailable so he picked Jan Van Hook from the European division. Van Hook was a financial wizard, but his toadying behavior in front of managers and craving for promotion turned off many people.

The team negotiated with Somita, but could not reach a satisfactory agreement on price and quality objectives. Robert asked the negotiating team for a briefing in the hope he could find something they might have overlooked. Every time Robert challenged the financial figures, Van Hook changed them to whatever he sensed Robert wanted to hear. In exasperation Robert said, "Jan, if you don't have enough confidence in your numbers to defend them, then I don't have confidence in them either." Robert was inclined to dismiss Van Hook from the team.

Yee slipped Robert a note that read: "Van Hook's figures are okay; he just loses the starch in his sails when he is in front of senior management." Because of Robert's high confidence in Yee, he accepted his assurance.

Robert said, "Ken, sometimes the Japanese hold back their final position until they face the highest-level negotiating official. Set up a meeting for you, our best Japanese interpreter, and me to meet with Isoroku Somita at a neutral location."

They met in a conference room of the Marriott Waikiki Hotel near the Honolulu International Airport. After the meeting went on for several hours with no progress, Drood called a break for private consultations. Drood and Yee decided to terminate the negotiations if Somita did not offer concessions when they reconvened. Drood returned to the conference room a few minutes early to wait for the meeting to resume. Through the open side door he overheard the Somita officials still conferring in the adjacent room.

"We'll give no concessions," Mr. Somita said. "That snooty fellow, Drood, appears to be a university student and Yee could be a coolie who just clomped out of a rice paddy. I don't want to deal with them. Let's terminate this meeting and fly back to Tokyo this evening."

As Somita returned to the conference room with his assistant and interpreter, they were startled to notice the door had been left open, and Drood was quietly waiting in the room. However, they did not think any harm had been done because they assumed Drood did not understand Japanese.

They were stunned when Drood who had learned the language during the time he lived in Japan, said, "I want to speak to you alone, Somita-san." Somita realized with horror Drood may have heard and understood their discussion in the adjacent room.

When Somita's staff left the room and closed the door, Drood said in Japanese, "Somita-san, we have decided not to continue considering your firm for supplying AMSCO chips. I don't need to hear your final position because I already heard you clearly state it to your staff in the next room. With lack of mutual respect between us, it is futile to go on with this meeting."

Drood's abrupt words were like salt rubbed into an open wound. When they parted, Drood added to his violation of Japanese etiquette and respect by giving Somita an inadequate bow for a man of his age and stature.

Drood called Yee in his hotel room and said, "Inscrutable One, let's hightail it for home. I just peed in Somita-san's rice bowl.

"I can now assure our board we left no stone unturned for finding an alternative to investment in a new fab. Call the pilots and have them rev up the plane. I'll meet you in the lobby in fifteen minutes."

Yee said, "Okay, Maximum Bossman; you made a good decision. I didn't like the attitude of Somita's staff and the prospect of working with those shirty chaps whose countrymen used the decapitated heads of my ancestors for bowling balls when they occupied Manchuria before World War II." A few British expressions still remained with Yee since his boyhood when he learned English from Hong Kong BBC radio broadcasts.

When the Gulfstream gained cruising altitude, Robert ordered a rare roast beef sandwich and a light beer from the flight attendant and slept the rest of the way home.

On the trip back to Tokyo on the Somita company jet, Mr. Somita shed his normal polite manners and gave his staff the worst drubbing they ever had to endure for not securing their conference room and not knowing Robert Drood spoke Japanese.

When the lineman flagged the AMSCO plane to a stop in San Francisco on the wet slippery apron in front of its hanger, Robert's detailed and fueled Bentley was parked near the plane wingtip with the driver's door and trunk lid open. Robert's assistant had sent his leather mail pouch to be placed on the passenger's seat. The flight attendant put his briefcase and laptop computer in the trunk and clicked the lid shut. The afternoon rain stopped long enough for Robert to remain dry while he walked the few paces from the plane steps to his car.

The Bentley purred away from the plane with its oversized Dunlop tires squeaking on the wet concrete. Robert felt a surge of satisfaction as he savored the conclusion of the meeting with Mr. Somita, although he knew he must take the edge off the harshness of his closing remarks and departure. In the morning he'd call in a Japanese-speaking secretary from the international sales division and dictate a short, respectful courtesy letter to Somita in Japanese rather than the customary English of international business.

Robert stopped at the venerable Olympic Club for a workout and steam bath on his way home from the airport. While still on the plane, he had called ahead to ask his favorite Russian masseuse to be there to assist with his steam bath after his gym workout. Her beautiful, exotic face, with its hint of eye folds and broad cheekbones, recalled the Mongolian presence on the Russian steppes eight hundred years earlier. She brought with her an oak leaf broom, birch switch, wooden bucket, soap, and thick, heavy towels to perform the traditional rituals of a Russian steam bath. The vigorous rubbing and invigorating pummeling during the steam bath were like an out of body experience. After Robert left, the masseuse gasped when she looked at the lavish cash tip he had folded into her hand.

After Robert authorized the initiation of design of the new chip fab, it became the responsibility of Jerry Colson, vice president of facilities engineering, to organize and execute the project. Colson had extensive experience handling large engineering and construction projects in the Navy and at AMSCO. He was good at hammering contractors and equipment suppliers into submission and ruling his staff of two hundred engineers and architects with a beefy fist. His technical and creative capabilities were mediocre, but his organizational skills and political instincts were usually good. He wore short-sleeved shirts to display his well-formed biceps—from daily weight lifting—and to enhance his threatening image. His employees called him "The Intimidator."

Senior AMSCO officials periodically reviewed important capital projects. If they were satisfied with the reviews, Colson was front-and-center to receive credit. If they went poorly, he typically whispered to a senior officer, "I just got in last night from a trip and didn't have time to review this presentation. I'm sure going to do some butt-kicking until I straighten this mess out." He never defended his engineers' work even if the unacceptable parts were because of his specific direction. His engineers expected an undeserved chewing-out when their presentations did not satisfy the senior officers.

After Robert read a status report on the new fab project, he asked Colson to come to his office. He motioned him to sit at the small glass-topped table in a corner of his office. Robert believed eighty percent of communications occurred through nonverbal body signals. He liked to watch people from head to toe when he talked with them.

"I've read the fab status report," he said. "I want three things changed: First, the report says the new fab will be a clone of the last one we built. That strategy may have been okay a few years ago when our fabs led those of our competitors by a wide margin, but if we clone fabs now, we'll have an out-of-date fab the day it starts up. Second, your preliminary recommendation is to build the fab in Arizona. Analyze locations all over the world with the main criteria being customer convenience and availability of talented people. Third, the project manager whom you selected from your engineering staff has no fab management experience. I once managed a fab designed without an operating management voice in the planning and design; it was difficult to manage. Use your engineers for technology, but transfer a chip fab manager with strategic planning experience into your department to be the project manager."

"I'll get right on those points, Robert. I've been traveling a lot lately and have not had time to watch the project closely."

Robert had not had many opportunities to work closely with Colson, whose tail-wagging gave Robert the uneasy feeling Colson was a toady with a narrow-gauge mind. The new fab would cost more than two billion dollars; it must significantly contribute to the competitive advantage of AMSCO. Robert decided for such a crucial investment, he would keep close watch on it—and on Colson.

Promising young executives attended advanced management development seminars at the AMSCO Training Center. Robert told his assistant to place him on the training lecture agenda at least once a month. The course participants were always surprised when he courteously answered their questions and encouraged free-ranging discussions. Those who had seen his acerbic behavior in other meetings called him Dr. Jekyll and Mr. Hyde. When they filled out their anonymous teacher evaluation forms at the end of the seminars, they usually gave him high marks for effective teaching.

Robert started to accept elections to the boards of prestigious charitable and academic institutions. The board memberships gained him entrée to stratospheric social life. With his confident manners and good looks, he became a sought-after guest at grand affairs, always in the company of attractive women. A national newspaper named him San Francisco's Most Eligible Bachelor.

The exposure to wealth and affluence spurred Robert on to an increasingly lavish lifestyle. He coveted the luxurious possessions and social positions of wealthy people. He aped them by chartering yachts, renting villas for extravagant parties, playing golf at posh clubs, pledging donations for high profile charities, and leasing luxurious boxes at sports arenas.

Robert's precarious financial situation worsened because of his out-of-control spending. His banker said to a colleague, "Robert Drood is like an irresponsible heir who comes into an inheritance and throws it to the wind. If it were not for AMSCO's business, I'd have denied his last personal loan request. I advised him we would require a stringent personal budget the next time he requested a loan. He huffed and said he'd seek another source for money the next time."

A small number of greedy corporate CEOs manipulated their compensation to levels far beyond the value of their services. Although their boards had the duty to set corporate officer compensation, they were sometimes lap dogs who rubber stamped whatever the company officers decided they wanted to be paid.

Robert followed their lead by investigating ways to bloat his compensation to cover his burgeoning expenses and losses from poor investments. When Cairncross heard rumors of Robert's attempt to manipulate his compensation, he requested an audit of AMSCO executive pay. The audit revealed that total compensation was in line with the amounts authorized by the compensation committee, but the auditors found evidence of sub-rosa plans under development for substantial increases.

Cairncross took Robert aside after a board meeting and talked to him like a Dutch uncle about the virtues of personal spending restraints as he learned them from his Scottish ancestors. While he tenderly massaged his arthritic fingers, he said, "Robert, you don't need that stuff you buy and all of that high living; it's a useless distraction. The auditors say you're fiddling around with your compensation—stop it! Your compensation is the sole responsibility of the compensation committee and the board. The way for you to increase your pay is for you to manage the company so it will increase in value; then you'll be paid more. I want you to follow the ethics standards set by Stepanek and Budak. If it comes to my attention again that you're attempting to manipulate your compensation, I'll deal with you as harshly as I did with that coyote I winged when we toured my ranch together a few years back."

Robert was embarrassed that he had to be taken to the woodshed by Cairncross. Even though he had always failed on his past resolutions to tame his compulsive spending, he again resolved to curb his expenditures. With a salary that was beyond his imagination a few years ago, it shouldn't be that hard.

To the people who knew of Drood's drunken-sailor spending habits and unmanageable personal debts it seemed inconceivable he could live in two such disparate financial worlds; he ran AMSCO with exemplary financial discipline, but simultaneously allowed his personal finances to become ever more chaotic.

CHAPTER TWENTY-ONE

Soon after Colson and Drood discussed the fab project, Colson sent out an appointment announcement:

Bulletin No: C-7879

AMERICAN SEMICONDUCTOR CORPORATION

AMSCO Place
671 Golden Street
San Francisco, CA 67305 U.S.A.

June 5, 2003

Appointment: Dennis Curran
Project Manager, New Chip Manufacturing Fab

Effective immediately, Dennis Curran is appointed to the position of Project Manager for the new silicon chip manufacturing fab now being planned.

Dennis will be responsible for site selection, design, and building the new fab.

Dennis's most recent position was Manager of the Phoenix Special Chips fab. Previously he managed various manufacturing and quality improvement projects throughout North America, Europe, Latin America, and Asia. Before coming to AMSCO, Dennis was a U.S Air Force pilot and strategic planner. He holds an Electrical Engineering degree from the U.S. Air Force Academy and a Master of Computer Science Degree from Purdue University. He recently earned his MBA degree from the Kellogg Graduate School of Management.

Dennis's experience and record for achieving objectives well qualify him for his new position.

Dennis will report to the writer.

Gerald Colson
Vice President, Facilities Engineering

After Currans's appointment to head the fab project team, he spent the next several months organizing the project and securing the required resources. He then traveled the world with part of his team to evaluate potential locations for the new fab.

Dennis's team found the Republic of Ireland—for the first time in its history—was firmly planted in the modern world, having entered the European Economic Community and liberalized its business laws. Fifty thousand people worked in the electronic industry in Ireland, and annual exports exceeded twenty billion dollars. The Irish work force was young, motivated, and educated in new technology. Ireland was well situated to serve the AMSCO European market. The project team recommended Ireland for the site of the new fab.

Dennis directed his team to read and study a book entitled *The Machine That Changed the World*. The authors had singled out Toyota as the benchmark company for world-class manufacturing practices. The team was influenced by the innovative Toyota concepts and adapted many of them for the new fab plan.

They faced heavy headwinds of opposition to their imaginative fab plans from some of the company executives. "If you give us a cookie-cutter copy of our current fabs and you build it in the U.S., it will make the start-up and management a lot easier," they reasoned.

"But if we make no improvements we'll lose our competitive edge and no longer be the leader for our industry. And a U.S. location may not best suit our customers' needs," Dennis argued.

The marketing group was an ally of the planning team. They said, "The efficiency improvements of the new plan will allow us to set more competitive chip prices and the Irish location will better serve our growing European markets."

Colson was aligned with the executives who wanted a cookie-cutter fab design and a U.S. location. After a fiery argument with the fab team, Colson directed Curran to ignore what they had learned from their studies and travels and to water down the plan by stripping it of most of its innovations. Colson said, "The proposed changes in the plan involve too many risks." One of Dennis's aggressive engineers vehemently opposed Colson's direction. Curran sent him out of the conference room to cool off after he blurted out, "Jerry, maybe you'd like us to draw our inspirations for the new fab from the Dead Sea scrolls instead of the recognized state-of-the-art models we chose."

Colson knew his orders to the new fab team countered some of Drood's directions, but he thought selecting Dennis Curran for the project manager would be enough to mollify him and he counted on the support of the other executives who opposed the innovations.

Dennis reluctantly told his team to emasculate their fab plan as ordered by Colson. Dennis felt compelled to follow Colson's direction and override the team's recommendations because he was accustomed to the command environment of the military. The team revised their plan to satisfy Colson but with serious misgivings.

When Dennis presented the watered down fab plan to Drood, he listened with half-closed eyes and pursed lips. At the end of the presentation, he blasted it. "We spend millions of dollars each year for our people to attend seminars and travel the world to gain knowledge, and we pay for their advanced education. We tell our investors we're the leading silicon chip maker in the world. And what happens? You come to me with this musty plan that looks like a museum exhibit for yesterday's technology. The leading fabs and electronic factories of Asia abandoned most of what you have in your plan five years ago."

Robert paused for his remarks to sink in and went on. "Our marketing people tell me every day we need to reduce our prices and improve our quality to stem the erosion of our competitive position. Your argument that a cookie cutter fab design will allow for an easier start-up does not hold water. What good does it do to have an easy start-up if we don't improve our competitive position? And your Arizona fab location doesn't best satisfy the growing needs of our international clients."

Robert turned to face Jerry and Dennis. "Jerry, I see only a little evidence of the direction I already gave you. And Dennis, you're not providing the leadership for this project we expected from you." Robert noticed Dennis's face when he stared daggers at Colson and a red spot shone on his forehead. He guessed it was really Colson's plan.

When Colson saw he was not going to receive any support from other executives, he gave his normal, suck-up response. "Yes, Robert, you did give direction earlier and I agreed with it. Somehow this plan slipped by me before I had time to catch the points you just mentioned."

Before Robert slammed out of the room, he turned to Colson and snorted, "Do you have flash cards with your B.S. excuses written on them, Jerry? That's almost the same hooey you gave me the last time we discussed the project."

When Robert returned to his office, he called Jack Hamilton in human resources. "Jack, look at Dennis Curran's performance reviews, and let me know if he's a good performer and a strategic planner. I suspect he's better than indicated by the crummy fab plan he just showed me. Also let me know what that dolt Colson's performance reviews look like. I'll bet you a bottle of beer his reviews show he bullies his people, and I'll bet another one he crammed that unimaginative fab plan down Curran's throat. When I see him with his cropped military haircut and short-sleeved shirt showing off his biceps, I think he has seen too many Arnold Schwarzenegger movies."

Curran stomped back to his cubicle. After fuming for fifteen minutes, he called Colson. "This is Dennis; when can I meet with you?"

Colson said, "Come on over right now, Dennis."

When Dennis barged into Jerry's office, he said, "Jerry, a meeting like the one we just had with Dr. Drood will never happen again. My team and I got the crap beat out of us, because I had them rewrite the new fab plan based on your directions on fab technology and location. Dr. Drood told us to do exactly what my team had already recommended before you insisted we gut it of its innovations. You sat there during the meeting without a word of explanation as to why the team turned their logical plan into that relic of yesterday's technology. I bit my tongue half through when I held back from telling Drood how my team really thought the fab should be planned."

Colson glowered at Dennis but he remained silent. "From now on, Jerry, my planning team will listen to your input into the plan, but they will use it only if they think it's best for the project. During any future senior executive presentations, you can give an independent rebuttal of the plan if you want, but it'll be over your name. If this is not acceptable to you, I request a job transfer."

"Dennis, you're getting yourself all lathered up. This is corporate life; it gets gritty once in a while. A slap now and then won't kill you. The old man was probably just having a bad day, and he took it out on you."

Dennis, with a red spot on his forehead and in tight-lipped silence, glared at Colson. Colson considered his choices. He would like to take Dennis down a peg, but Drood could hear of it. Butting heads with Dennis would probably not be wise.

Colson conceded. "Okay, Dennis, do it your way, but you better not screw up this project."

"I'm blessed with the most capable team of people I've ever managed. I have high confidence they will create the best fab in the world if I don't make a damn fool of myself again by overriding their recommendations."

Dennis stomped out of Colson's cubicle and called an impromptu meeting with his team. He said, "In the future we'll only submit our plans to management after we've reached team consensus. In the process of reaching consensus, we'll solicit and evaluate the input of others, including Jerry Colson, but the team will decide what input to use and what to reject. I solemnly promise you my resignation from this team if I ever again lead you into a meat grinder like I did today. Now, let's resurrect our original plan."

Hamilton reported to Robert, "Dennis Curran has a good performance record and promise as a strategic planner. I talked to one of his team members who was my college classmate. Colson is the one who demanded the cookie cutter criteria for the fab plan and the Arizona location. Curran accepted Colson's demands, probably based on his background in an authoritarian military atmosphere. After the meeting with you, I hear Curran cleared the air in a dust-up with Colson. He told Colson he would only accept his advice if his team concurred with it. Curran will no longer tolerate Colson's bullying. And as for Colson, he has limited creativity and he rules by intimidation, but he's a good organizer and a tiger for completing projects on-schedule and within budgets."

When the fab planning team revised the plan, Dennis and his staff reviewed it again with Drood. He listened until near the end of the presentation when Dennis mentioned the Republic of Ireland for the recommended fab location. Drood inhaled sharply and paled. He was overcome when memories of his dreadful Irish childhood flooded over him. He had not been in Ireland since he was a child. When he recovered, he turned to Colson. "Jerry, what is your assessment of the revised plan?"

Colson hated to give his opinions to senior executives before they indicated what direction they were leaning. "Well, Robert, it has a lot of new ideas that could be risky. On the other hand if you want an aggressive plan, this one might not be bad."

Robert said, "Considering that valueless answer, I apparently must decide on my own what direction to give. Dennis, I think you and your team have created a splendid plan. Go ahead and develop it in detail. Of course, we'll need the board's approval before we invest any money in it. When you're solid on the capital cost estimate and secure on the details of the site, prepare a presentation for board approval and a formal request for the required capital."

Colson cut in, "Robert, let me clarify my earlier comments."

"Jerry, your *post factuum* observations are too late to be useful. The purpose of this meeting was to approve or reject the revised fab plan. I just approved it. This meeting is adjourned."

That night, Drood's mind reeled with uncontrollable and disturbing memories of his Irish youth. He thought: Maybe I should have rejected Ireland for the fab location so it won't remind me of my horrible childhood. On the other hand, maybe it is an opportunity to confront and bring to justice the despicable people who abused my family more than thirty years ago. Maybe if I take action against them, it will help bring an end to my never-ending torments. Besides, my personal problems aren't a valid reason for interfering with the decision to build the fab in Ireland. I guess I should let the Irish site stand for the new fab.

Even though the fab appropriation was enormous, it only took two minutes for the board to approve it. The single question asked was if an alternative chip source had been investigated. Robert easily answered the question based on his meeting in Hawaii with Somito.

Because of thorough screening processes, corporate boards almost never reject proposals presented to them. Nevertheless, the team waited with clammy hands for a formal approval on the day the Irish fab project was presented to the board.

Late in the day, Dennis called an impromptu team meeting. With a grin he announced to his team, "Good news! We now have more than two billion dollars in the till for our project. Now we can shift into high gear.

"Maybe it's also a good time to mention this to you: With such an enormous sum of money to spend, we'll be stormed as if we were the executors of an estate when a rich inheritance is about to be divided up. Contractors will offer us free weekends in posh resorts, boat and airplane trips, and valuable gifts. We'll be assaulted by salesmen who are so persuasive they can almost convince us there really is a tooth fairy. We must stick to an ironclad rule to make sourcing decisions based only on the merits of the supplier proposals. 'Free goodies' of any kind from suppliers are unacceptable."

Dennis poured himself a glass of diet coke and continued, "If anyone accepts something of value from contractors, he or she will be removed from the project, subjected to severe disciplinary action, or even fired. I know none of us is likely to succumb to the temptations, but I want to forewarn you of the cleverly concealed bait that will be cast in front of us to influence our supplier selection decisions."

Until the appropriation approval, the fab team worked in the AMSCO engineering offices in San Francisco. The project now advanced to the execution stage with the bulk of the work switching to Ireland. Dennis and part of his team prepared to move to Dublin so they could continue their work near the new fab site.

CHAPTER TWENTY-TWO

Dennis wanted his wife, Mary Catherine, and their two young daughters to be contented living in Ireland. He identified several affordable houses to rent and took Mary Catherine with him to Ireland to visit them and select one to live in.

Dennis still adored Mary Catherine as much as he did when they married after he resigned from the Air Force and was able to pry her away from the school where she taught first graders whom she loved as if they were her little brothers and sisters. For the first time in Dennis's life, he met a woman who did not fall in love with him on their first date; but a close and lasting relationship soon developed. They were proud and respectful of each other. At social gatherings they positioned themselves so they could share nods of assurance and admiration.

After several days inspecting the Dublin houses Dennis had selected for consideration, Mary Catherine said, "Dennis, they're all nice houses, but they're just lodgings; they've no character."

Without his knowledge, she called the property agent and asked, "Are there any other choices?"

The agent replied, "The fact of the matter is a delightful house with a lovely garden just came on the market. A diplomat, who has accepted an appointment to be the Irish Ambassador to Australia, owns it. It is available for a three-year lease. Now, what would be the harm in taking a look? I'll be around for you tomorrow at ten." Even though the rental price was more than Dennis's budget limit, the agent did not mention it to Mary Catherine.

The two-story stone house, built in 1830, was recently modernized and refurbished. It had nine rooms, an independent three-car garage, garden shed, and a half-acre terraced garden. It was surrounded on two sides by high boxwood hedges and on the back by a "ha-ha," a trench that acts as a barrier designed to give an unobstructed view of the sheep in the adjacent meadow but deny them access to the temptations in the garden. Mary Catherine was overjoyed at the prospect of living in the house. She wheedled the rental price out of the agent.

After Dennis looked at the house, he said, "Mary Catherine, the house is wonderful, but the rental price is over our budget, and we'd need to hire gardening and housekeeping help."

Mary Catherine had reasoned it all out and was ready with a solution. "I can use the income from the money I inherited from Auntie for the rent shortfall and staff cost."

"But, Mary Catherine, we already decided to live on my income and use yours for your personal extravagances and the children's education."

Mary Catherine knew Dennis would cave in to her wishes if she moped around for a few days, although moping was hard for her to do. It required her to suppress her sunny disposition, but for such a good purpose she could do it. After two days of moping and two more for negotiating the price, they rented the house. They moved in after they settled their affairs in California, and their children completed their school terms.

Dennis developed a trustful relationship with Paul Mason, the resident Marketing and Sales Manager who had lived in Ireland since AMSCO received its first major chip order from a computer company with Irish manufacturing operations. Dennis depended on Mason for administrative services, knowledge of local business culture, and contacts with community and government officials. Mason's office suite had unoccupied space, so Dennis's small staff moved into it.

He continued to report to Colson in San Francisco but with considerable autonomy since their earlier acrimonious encounter. He appreciated the autonomy, but anticipated Colson's knife in his back the first time anything went wrong.

One of Dennis's first tasks in Ireland was to hire a secretary and administrative assistant. He placed an ad in the *Dublin Post* requesting applicants to submit resumes and references.

Fionnoula O'Casey sent a letter seeking an interview. She listed her work experience: currently executive secretary for the managing director of Horst Fenstermaker Transport AG in Dublin and previously customer services officer for First National Farmers Bank in Columbus, Indiana. Curran invited her for an interview.

An auburn-haired woman with green eyes and milky white skin punctuated with a sprinkle of freckles appeared at his door for the interview. She wore a white sweater highlighted by a Celtic cross on a gold chain, a green plaid skirt, and a camel hair jacket. "Now, would ye be Mr. Dennis Curran? My name is Fionnoula O'Casey," she said in a lilting voice. She firmly shook Dennis's offered hand and glided to the chair across from his desk.

Fionnoula's smile radiated enough energy to melt a glacier. She acted as though with an iota of encouragement, she would break into a dance, sing a song, or recite a poem.

Fionnoula had attended Trinity College, but left a year short of graduation and her goal of a degree in Irish music and literature to help care for her sick father. When he died, she moved to America because of the scarcity of jobs in Ireland. After working in the U.S. for several years, she returned to Ireland for a holiday and landed a job with a German transportation firm. She sought a new job because she found her boss too rigid.

Fionnoula listened while Dennis explained the position he needed to fill. "Mr. Curran," she said, "I understand business on both sides of the Atlantic. I can do the work you described—and more."

She then questioned Dennis on all aspects of the job. It seemed to Dennis that Fionnoula was the person conducting the interview.

Dennis was impressed with Fionnoula's experience, confidence, and spirited personality. He knew what an asset a lively assistant could be in giving balance to the deadly seriousness and intensity of an office full of engineers.

Dennis said, "Fionnoula, you're a good fit with our needs. When I've checked out your references you'll hear from me."

The AMSCO Irish fab project was immensely important to the local community and the country. It was the costliest single undertaking in the history of Ireland. Three thousand new jobs were anticipated with several times more for related support activities.

AMSCO issued an information bulletin on the new fab in response to the insatiable public demand for information:

AMERICAN SEMICONDUCTOR CORPORATION (AMSCO) NEW SILICON CHIP FAB

The new AMSCO fab about to be built in the Republic of Ireland will require a 50-hectare site (125 acres) and employ more than 3,000 people.

The fab will manufacture 200-millimeter diameter wafers that resemble medium-sized breakfast waffles. Each wafer will contain hundreds of chips and millions of transistors.

Chip manufacturing equipment will perform complex processes such as chemical vapor deposition, plasma etching, ion implantation, and electro-chemical plating.

Shop floor fab employees will wear white space-age suits resembling Easter Bunny outfits, caps, and masks to control microscopic contaminants.

AMSCO will sell most of its chips to computer manufacturers for microprocessors, the brains inside computers.

The Irish people were proud they had the talent to attract the new high-technology fab, but some were skeptical about it ever really materializing. The spectacular 1982 failure in Dunmurry—near Belfast—of the DeLoreon Motor Company and the loss of twenty-five hundred jobs was still on their minds. The public believed the flamboyant American president of DeLoreon Motors, John Zachary DeLoreon, duped the government of Northern Ireland when their money paid the capital cost of the failed factory. Many believed their money also bankrolled DeLoreon's lavish lifestyle. The Irish rejoiced that the DeLoreon debacle happened in Northern Ireland—a part of the United Kingdom—but on the other hand they redoubled their vigilance to ensure all agreements with AMSCO were sound and promises of good jobs would not turn into another enormous Irish fairy tale.

Dennis and his team had a massive amount of work to accomplish in building the new fab. They had to do it on schedule and within the capital budget. Dennis was a hard driver who accepted no excuses from anyone for not fulfilling his responsibilities. His head-on confrontations with the Irish government officials and contractors to force them to perform faster rankled many of them.

When Paul Mason heard stories of the aggressiveness of the fab project staff and the mounting resentment against them, he invited Dennis to a quiet lunch at the Shelbourne Hotel and tutored him on the realities of the less intense Irish culture. Dennis respectfully listened to Mason, but he still had to build the fab on time. He did not know what to do with Mason's well-intentioned advice.

Dennis brooded most of the night. Business practices in Ireland were, in theory, not unlike those in many other places in the world. Dictionaries showed the same definitions of words as in all English-speaking countries. Contracts were patterned after well-established American and British legal precedents. But in Ireland interpretations had the flexibility of rubber bands. Almost any imaginable event was a valid and acceptable excuse for increasing the time to perform a task. To make a fuss over such things showed insensitivity. Involved parties endorsed schedules, but then nothing much happened. The project schedule couldn't slip any more. Dennis had to find a better way to pick up the pace. But what was it?

Fionnoula sensed Dennis's frustration at his inability to persuade contractors to respond to the urgency of the fab schedule. She understood the difference between the U.S. and Irish way of obtaining action and resolving issues. Late in the afternoon, she prepared a pot of tea and brought it to Dennis's office.

She sat down and said, "Would Himself be agreeable to listen to my observations on some of the issues causing ye and your staff frustration and conflict?" Without waiting for a reply she pushed on. "For eight hundred years, our Irish speaking people—or Gaelic speaking as Americans say—have endured written British laws, decrees, and rules administered in the English language. The British laws were in sharp contrast to our ancient Irish legal system called Brehan Law, and English was a foreign tongue. We felt like insects in a court of birds. The Irish laws, culture, and language were verbally transferred from generation to generation for millennia. We still lean in the direction of distrusting the written word. The spoken word best suits our temperament. Our suspicion of written documents is because they've been used against us for so long."

Fionnoula stopped to sip her tea and continued, "Foreigners sometimes deride us for being inconsistent and purposeless, but in our own way we're firm and tenacious. We're an iron fist in a velvet glove. If we're told the destination for a trip, we're more likely to reach it when we work out our own travel plan.

"The Irish people who work with your staff wonder why they put everything on paper rather than meet for civilized face-to-face discussions and clarifications in a pub while enjoying a tipple. They think drinking a few jars in a nonadversarial forum is a fine way to understand and resolve problems and issues. Maybe if ye have some meetings in pubs or restaurants with no papers present—only words—it'll improve things, or like my Granfar used to say, 'Try digging for a while with the other foot.'"

Fionnoula reached for a package she had brought in with the tea tray and changed her tone. "Now surely ye've heard enough from Myself. Here's a loaf of soda bread and a wee jar of currant jam for ye to take home to Mary Catherine and your dear children for supper tonight. My mum was up at the chirping of the sparrows this morning baking the bread."

Dennis decided to try out Fionnoula's suggestions. He asked her to help coach his team on Irish ways. She said in a staff meeting, "Have ye heard that in Mexico the word *mañana* conveys more urgency than any comparable word known in Ireland? Well, this is a lovely little quip that makes us all chuckle, but it's not the way it really is with modern Irish professionals. We know how to achieve results, but ye must tone down the American in-your-face intensity a wee bit. An American relishes a completed task in terms of the plan, the budget, and the results. To an Irishman these terms are secondary to the friendships developed and the opportunity for *craic*—a combination of talk, drink, and music. Try having some of your meetings in a pub or restaurant and allow time for a little *craic*. The first round is best devoted to football, horse racing, and loathing for the stupidity of the latest British policies in Northern Ireland—no matter what the policies are."

Fionnoula shifted in her chair, glanced at her papers, and continued. "Before the last *Sláinte*—that would be 'Cheers' in England—would be a good time to air problems and issues, but ye should clarify the reasons for required urgent action. The Irish have a history of make-work projects for building roads to nowhere while they were under British domination. They're skeptical of appeals for urgent action until they understand the reasons. And show a little compassion for the explanations of their problems. They live and think in the lumpy world of politics. And don't sound like ye are a priest in the pulpit preaching to them, or they'll become obstinate. Give the lads a chance to do it their own way. To again quote my Granfar, *'Ding de féin a scoilteas an leamhé*: A wedge of its own timber splits the elm.' After they understand your reasons, they will try their best to deliver—sometimes with surprising speed and ingenuity." By this time Fionnoula had won the respect of Dennis's staff so several of them agreed to try out her advice.

They scheduled the next round of meetings with officials and contractors in pubs and restaurants. Even though they chafed to talk business before the waitress took their orders, they followed Fionnoula's advice to hold off. After the pub and restaurant meetings and a reduction of the "in your face" pushiness, somehow, adherence to the work schedules improved.

Each day Dennis's office lobby was mobbed with suppliers and contractors waiting for a chance to talk to him and his engineers to ensure their firms were on the bidder's lists. The amounts of many of the contracts were enormous. The contracts included precision manufacturing equipment capable of controlling chemicals, light, and gasses down to the molecular level.

Representatives of von Kleinschmidt AG were among the frequent visitors. They never tired of saying, "Herr von Kleinschmidt and Herr Doktor Drood are personal friends. They and their wives spend weekends together in Herr von Kleinschmidt's Rhine River castle." This blatant political pressure alienated the engineers. They were trained to objectively evaluate bids and select contractors based solely on merit.

Although Dennis came to Ireland as the project manager for building the new fab, he was spending a growing percentage of his time on government and community liaison and communicating with hordes of job applicants and future fab suppliers. His responsibility was clear-cut on the technical side, but it was vague for everything else. The prevailing attitude at AMSCO headquarters in San Francisco was: "We'll work all of that out later when the fab is closer to completion, and we have established an operating staff in Ireland. In the meantime, let Curran handle it."

A year after Robert Drood took over as the CEO of AMSCO, the board evaluated his performance. They gave him gold stars for dismissing underperforming executives and shifting the company to a more disciplined culture. However, AMSCO's growth rate slowed because of a temporary industry-wide sales slump. The steep upward stock price curve flattened. The compensation committee raised Robert's salary and issued an additional block of stock options, but the options would be of no value until the stock price picked up again. The committee did not declare an executive performance bonus because objectives were not met. Robert was disappointed he would not have immediate access to cash that he urgently needed.

He knew he had to control his rampant personal spending, but no amount of intellectualizing could moderate his Imelda Marcos shoe complex. He invested in speculative high-tech stocks hoping to fix his money problems with quick-hit profits. When the price of the stocks in his portfolio fell, he had to cover the margin calls. His increased salary and loans would carry him for a while, but if his mad spending behavior did not moderate, and the stock market stayed in the doldrums, he was headed for an acute financial crisis.

CHAPTER TWENTY-THREE

Robert dug into the financial reports of some of the large corporations reporting dubious earnings and revenues while paying enormous compensation to their top officers. He became acquainted with their CEOs and learned how they manipulated their financial documents into a Byzantine maze that could be a new chapter for *Alice in Wonderland*.

They reported vaguely anticipated sales as if they were already booked, capitalized expenses to inflate profits, and shifted unsatisfactory businesses to off-the-books never-never-lands.

Their auditing firms were paid high-margin consulting fees for frivolous assignments with the implied threat that if their auditors challenged their spurious financial practices, the consulting contracts would dry up. Greedy senior executives spent corporate money solely for their personal benefit. Their appetites for sumptuous living were as insatiable as an addict craving ever-larger drug doses.

An arrogant CEO, who gulled himself into believing his financial shenanigans were brilliant business innovations, told Robert, "Most of the financial analysts who follow our stock don't have enough intelligence to understand our value-enhancing financial models. Someday they'll wise up and give me credit for pioneering innovative accounting standards. Our financial models will become the industry norms."

Pulling off their financial machinations usually required the chief executive officer and the chief financial officer to work in concert and the lax audit and compensation committees to ignore their oversight responsibilities.

Robert started to initiate financial shenanigans at AMSCO by directing Nate Norton to install several minor bend-the-rules changes. His objective was to hike revenues and profits so the stock price would rise and his options would become valuable. Norton agreed to the changes ordered by Robert recognizing that rising tides lift all ships; his stock options would also become more valuable. The uptick in profits caused by the accounting manipulations was a shot in the arm to the stock price. The shares caught the breeze and rose several points giving Robert momentary financial relief when he exercised some of his options.

He ordered Norton to instigate far more aggressive financial manipulations. Norton leaned back in his chair and took a deep breath while he thought through the changes ordered by Robert. He said, "I agreed to the bend-the-rules changes you ordered, but if I do what you're ordering now, we would be entering a minefield. I can't agree to these fraudulent changes, Robert. When they are revealed—as they eventually will be—we could end up in a barbed wire hotel. I've heard rumors about forthcoming legal action against some of the glamour companies and darlings of Wall Street that follow the miracle business practices you're asking me to introduce; a more realistic term would be actionable practices."

Robert was annoyed, but he remained silent and let Norton continue. "The revenues and earnings these companies are reporting are cotton candy. They pulled off their financial monkeyshines with the collusion of their outside auditors and derelict board oversight committees. Their glitzy reported performances are blinding the common sense of stock analysts and investors. When the glitz fades, there will be a day of reckoning. The companies may fail; their executives and auditors will be discredited; and some will likely do hard time. With the gimlet eyes of Justin Cairncross focused on AMSCO, our chance for pulling off your proposed actions is no better than that of an angleworm crossing a California freeway at rush hour."

Robert steepled his fingers and pursed his lips while he glared at Norton. He said, "Nate, the officers of other companies have foreseen ways to imaginatively enhance their company's value and convince investors they should pay a higher price for their stock. I don't think you know anything those guys don't also know. We're sitting on a company with figures no longer inspiring to Wall Street. If we can't put some fire into our performance soon, we'll be thrown into the same bag with laggards like the U.S. automotive companies. Either make the damn changes, or I'll find a new CFO who isn't a timid rabbit."

Norton's adrenaline surged at the threat of his dismissal. His children attended expensive private schools, and his high-maintenance wife tested the limits of credit card spending. The prospect of being unemployed was unappealing, but the thought of serving jail time was even worse. He braced himself and said, "Robert, I'll bend the rules for you, as I've already done, but if you insist on the fraudulent actions you just told me to take, I won't do it. You have just threatened me, and I have a reciprocal warning for you. If you do professional harm to me, I'll report the reason to Justin Cairncross and the members of the audit committee."

Robert flared, "This meeting is over, Nate. Come back to see me in the morning to sign your termination papers."

After Norton departed, Robert stared out his office windows and regretted he had allowed his dire financial difficulties to get the best of him. It was not wise to have blown up with Norton. Apparently Norton was not the wimp he always appeared to be. If he delivered on his threat to talk to Cairncross, AMSCO would have a new CEO before sundown. The best thing was to immediately make peace with him. But the ruckus with Norton did confirm that he was amenable to continued rule bending. If more substantial benefits were diverted to him, maybe he'd become more pliable. His vain, birdbrain wife would eat it up. Before she married Norton the only job she could hold was at Gump's Department Store spraying perfume samples on shoppers' wrists. Norton was first besotted by her ample display of femininity when he shopped for a bottle of perfume for his sister's birthday present. But Robert's need for money was still urgent. He would have to devise another way to increase his income independent of Norton.

Robert returned to Norton's cubicle and said, "Nate, let's forget our discussion ever happened, okay? I shouldn't have allowed my frustration at our business problems to get the best of me."

"I don't know what discussion you mean, Robert."

Yee was the executive responsible for directing the new Irish fab. While his staff was doing the operational planning in California, many local issues were being deferred until the new fab manager was selected. Yee was in a quandary about whom to pick as the manager. He needed someone who had experience operating a large fab and broad diplomatic skills and sensitivities for dealing with the Irish government and media.

Dennis Curran had the required diplomatic skills but no experience in starting up and running a large fab. Carly Jackson would be a good candidate for the fab manager job. She had successfully started and run a couple of AMSCO's largest fabs, but she recently had taken early retirement to pursue golf and public service.

Since retiring, Carly regretted she could not recapture the satisfaction and thrill she had as an AMSCO executive. After a weekend of boredom, she visited Yee, her old boss. "Ken, when I retired at fifty-one, it was too soon. I'm not cut out for serious golf, and I'm like a football tackle at a tea party when I attend volunteer meetings. I'm going to go nuts if I don't find something better to occupy my time. Do you have anything for me to do? I'm willing to work for room and board."

Yee thought about his need for a manager for the new fab in Ireland and Carly's superb qualifications. He was developing several people, but they were not ready yet for such a key position. With Carly's proven playbook, she would be a godsend. "Yes, Carly, I may have a position for you, but I need some time to work it out. I'll be back to you in a month."

Carly knew Yee had something concrete in mind, but no amount of prodding would force him to reveal it until he was ready.

Carly's rangy, attractive appearance did not hint of her rougher-than-a-corncob childhood in the Oklahoma oil patch where her father worked as a pipeline welder. However, during times of severe work intensity, the rough edges of the oil fields sometimes surfaced. After acrimonious meetings, her detractors occasionally called her "Oklahoma Crude," but they all agreed she knew more about organizing and managing complex fab operations than anyone in the industry. Few people knew her baptismal name was Carrie Lou. She was universally called Carly.

Robert called Bill Beck, the AMSCO security director and said, "Bill, give me the name of the best private investigator in Ireland."

"We once did some work with Seamus Kiely Associates in Dublin. We were quite satisfied with the results. I suggest you try them."

Robert called Kiely for a preliminary interview. He liked his matter-of-fact manner and said, "I'll be in Ireland soon, Seamus. I want to meet you to discuss an investigation for me. I'll give you the details when we meet." If he decided to hire Kiely, he would instruct him to find out if Brian McClellan, the snake who defiled his sister and mother, and George Drood, his father, were still alive and where they lived. Robert did not know what he would do with the information, but it would be a place to start. He felt a small surge of relief for finally doing something that might exert some control over his tormenting demon the next time it pushed him toward the precipice.

Robert called Yee and said, "Inscrutable One, we should go to Ireland soon to have an on-site review of the fab project, settle the outstanding personnel problems, and meet with government officials to smooth out any open issues. Let's go over together on the Gulfstream. And when we finish with our work, we'll need to part ways so I can pursue some personal business while I'm in Ireland."

"Inscrutable One ready to ride on moment's notice when Maximum Bossman say saddle up," replied Yee in mock deference.

Robert always laughed at Yee's whimsical response. "Call Dennis Curran to tell him we're coming and to set up a meeting with top government officials. I think they are still goosey about the DeLoreon car factory fiasco in Belfast even though it happened twenty-five years ago. We can assure them of our intent to stay the course and size them up on their large commitments for supporting our fab." Robert was disingenuous with his explanation for the trip to Ireland. His primary purpose was to revisit the country of his childhood and start the search for his family's malefactors.

Dennis Curran called the office of Patrick O'Kane, Minister of Enterprise, on Kildare Street in Dublin to request that he attend a meeting with Drood and Yee. O'Kane's supercilious administrative assistant said, "I'll speak to the minister, but it isn't likely he'll have time on his schedule for a meeting with AMSCO officials. He's a very busy man."

To Dennis's surprise, Minister O'Kane personally called him back to discuss the purpose of the meeting. Dennis explained, "It is Dr. Drood's habit, when important undertakings are occurring, to meet face-to-face with the key involved parties to ensure there are no open issues."

"Of course, we would be honored to meet with Dr. Drood," the minister replied.

To Curran's even greater astonishment, O'Kane called again and said, "We would like to add Kevin Crossgrove, the Taoiseach, to the meeting agenda. He wants to hear a few words directly from Dr. Drood about your fab project, and, he will likely have his photographer on hand." Curran gulped and acknowledged the agenda change. He knew English had superseded Irish as the everyday language in most of Ireland, but some of the Irish titles for government officials, such as Taoiseach for prime minister, were still universally used. He could not remember how to spell Taoiseach so he phonetically wrote "T-shock" on his note pad. He'd look up the proper spelling later.

Curran suspected O'Kane and Crossgrove were apprehensive about the significant infrastructure investments the Irish government had promised to support the new fab. Political realities in Ireland were as ferocious as in the jungle. If the fab project and its promised jobs should fail to materialize, the press and the opposition party would go into a frenzy of denunciation and censure that would probably cause the government to fall.

Dennis wrote a memorandum with a copy to Drood and Yee noting who the meeting participants from the government would be, the kind of reassurances the Minister of Enterprise and the Taoiseach would likely want, and a list of the possible questions they could ask.

When Robert read Dennis's memorandum, he called Yee. "Dennis Curran doesn't let much grass grow under his feet, does he? Talk to legal, human resources, and financial to see what other issues we should prepare for. Also buy a couple of gifts to take along for the minister and the Taoiseach. People on that side of the Atlantic go nuts over anything related to our Wild West and the Mississippi River."

Robert then changed the subject. "Ken, when are you going to name the Irish fab manager?"

"We should announce the new fab manager right after our Irish trip. I'm not in a good spot with my current availability of managers. They need a couple more years of development before they're strong enough to run a major fab. I've had bad luck last year. One of our fab managers died in a car accident and one resigned. But I also had some good luck. Carly Jackson, a recent retiree and our best large fab manager, wants to come back to work for a few more years. I plan to rehire her to be the Irish fab manager until we're through the start-up period. By then Dennis Curran or several other good, younger people should be ready to succeed her."

Robert nodded while Yee continued, "And we must also improve the current reporting structure. I want Curran and Jackson to both report to me. Diplomacy is not Jackson's strong suit. But Curran has a million-dollar personality, so we should expand his duties to officially cover Irish government liaison and media communications. He would continue to depend on Colson for technology, but I want Dennis to report to me to better handle public relations matters. These changes will overload Curran so I'll ask Colson to send him more help."

Robert asked, "Jackson and Curran will need to work together hand-in-glove. How well do they know each other?"

"We all know each other well. Jackson and Curran worked in close nexus with me on a Singapore project a few years ago. We're symbiotic so there should be no impediments."

"Okay. Let's make the announcements when we return home from Ireland."

When Yee left, Robert chuckled and said to his assistant, "Ken Yee is one of the brainiest people I've ever known. He's read and memorized most of *Webster's Unabridged Dictionary*. Consequently his English vocabulary is enormous, but he occasionally slips in words only a few other people understand or ever use."

CHAPTER TWENTY-FOUR

The AMSCO plane waited on the ramp ready for the flight to Dublin. Six people were scheduled for the trip: two pilots, a flight attendant, a company mechanic, Drood, and Yee. The mechanic was along to monitor an avionics device that had recently been replaced due to an erratic reading. Yee walked the few steps from the waiting room in the AMSCO hanger to the plane when he saw Robert's Bentley stop near the upturned wingtip. An attendant stood by to drive the car into the hanger, wash it, and pamper its pristine finish with a dust-cover. A hangar employee placed Robert's luggage, laptop computer, and briefcase in the plane. The pilots had already filed the flight plan and gone through the pre-takeoff procedures. The plane's auxiliary power unit was running and the cabin temperature was adjusted low to satisfy Robert's preference. Drood and Yee clicked on their seat belts, as the plane taxied to the runway.

The flight attendant set up Robert's computer on the desk at his seat and placed his briefcase within reach. Robert said, "Thanks. I like the orchid you selected, Molly. Is that a Waterford vase that it is in?"

"Yes it is, Dr. Drood. I'm glad you like the orchid, and the vase seemed appropriate for our trip to Ireland. I'll bring you a drink and prepare your dinner when you call me." The galley was stocked with the food and beverage choices suggested by Drood's assistant.

The flight attendant had tucked cloth slippers under Drood's and Yee's seats and stocked the TV cabinet with the kind of historical documentaries she knew Drood liked. Drood and Yee were dressed in Docker slacks and Nike golf shirts. If they became cool during the flight, the attendant would bring them navy blue silk jackets with AMSCO logos.

Robert called up his itinerary on his computer screen. After he read it, he made a copy on the on-board printer and tucked it into his briefcase.

As the plane climbed to its flying altitude of fifty thousand feet, Drood and Yee briefly discussed company issues. Robert glanced at the flight path display monitor to note their position as they crossed the Montana-North Dakota border and were about to enter Canada. After he scanned *The Wall Street Journal, Financial Times, The Economist,* and his e-mail messages, he ordered a Compari and soda in preparation for dinner. During and after dinner they watched a documentary film about Marco Polo's travels. They then slept on the berths made up by the flight attendant until they reached Irish airspace near the River Shannon. The attendant woke them in time to shave and change into business suits while they crossed Ireland to Dublin.

As the plane approached Dublin, it descended through the gray, tattered clouds revealing surrealistic mosaics of sheep-filled fields framed with dark stone fences. Robert was gripped with a feeling of anxiety and vague foreboding when he recalled the misery of his childhood. He broke into a sweat, and his vision blurred. After the plane landed and taxied to the private-aircraft tarmac, he regained his equanimity.

Dennis had arranged for customs and immigration formalities at the plane. He then escorted Drood and Yee a few steps to a waiting white Daimler sedan; his assistant had warned Dennis that Robert did not like dark car colors. Dennis introduced Drood and Yee to Joe Quinlan, the driver, who handed them a card with his mobile telephone number so they could reach him at any time during their visit. Quinn could drive in silence or provide endless historical and cultural information depending on the interests of his passengers.

"We reserved suites for you at the Shelbourne Hotel on St. Stephens Green," Dennis said. "Do you want to check in and freshen up before we go to our office?"

"No, we took care of that on the plane. Let's go to your office right away and get started."

"Good. While we're meeting, Joe will take your luggage to the hotel, check you in, and have the staff unpack for you." Until Dennis set up the hotel arrangements for Drood's visit, he did not know such pampering was available for well-heeled patrons.

When Drood, Yee, and Curran met in Curran's office, Dennis was well prepared, but he waited to see what his visitor's interests were before he launched into his prepared commentary. Drood began, "Dennis, I talked to Jerry Colson before we left home. He brought me up to speed on the technical aspects of the project so unless you have any open issues in that area, we don't need to discuss them again. I suggest you tell us how the project schedule and budget are going, what else you need from us, and what you know about the minister of enterprise and the Taoiseach." Dennis wondered how Drood knew how to correctly pronounce Taoiseach with the accent of a native.

"My staff and I reviewed the entire project a few days ago," Dennis said. "It's on schedule and within budget. Needless to say, we have certain outstanding problems, but we think they are all manageable.

"The appetite of the press and government officials for information about the project is insatiable. If they hear a hint of a quality job, they jump on it as if they discovered a gold nugget. Job applicants and materials and services suppliers are constantly at our door to get in on the ground floor. I've been interviewed so often on TV even my wife is bored.

"Now, on another subject: Ken, your staff is doing a fine job of operational planning in California, but in the absence of any of them in residence here, I must devote half of my time to dealing with their affairs. Frankly it makes me uneasy to be making so many decisions about operating matters that the fab manager and his or her staff will need to live with. The fab will operate with a direct link to our customer's requirements, just-in-time delivery of materials to the fab, and six-sigma quality processes. This necessitates close coordination with the information technology people and others in San Francisco. And we have only a small window of common work hours for communicating between Ireland and California. The sooner we get the new fab manager and his or her staff on board here the better off we'll be."

"Ken and I have some ideas of how to help you in those areas, Dennis," Robert cut in. "We'll share them with you before we leave."

Curran continued, "None of us has ever met the minister of enterprise or the Taoiseach, but I'll tell you what I've learned about them. They worry that our new fab, and the high-quality jobs it will bring, may be too good to be true. They're still getting over centuries of living in an inefficient agrarian economy and on checks mailed home from those who emigrated 'over the waters' to provide a pool of menial laborers for the British Empire and others. Industrial development is still strange to them.

"I'd guess it has even entered their minds you called for a meeting with them to bring bad news about reducing or delaying the fab project—or even canceling it. I think if we could reassure them of our continuing commitment, it would relieve them. Now if you'd like, I'll give you a brief personal profile on Minister O'Kane and the Taoiseach."

Robert nodded his assent. Dennis continued, "Patrick O'Kane, the minister of enterprise, trade, and employment, is a respected businessman who is on temporary leave from Ireland's largest crystal company where he was the vice president of export marketing and sales. His knowledge of international business practices is extensive. He knows Irish history down to the last footnote and has a passionate desire for Ireland to become a partner and eventually a leader in the international information technology industry.

"On the surface, Minister O'Kane appears to be a modern day *seanachie* (pronounced "shawn-a-key) as the ancient storytellers and communicators of Irish history are called; some older people think the *seanachies* are also gifted with the ability to foresee the future. I'd guess tonight when we're at my home for dinner, he will show his *seanachie* side, and tomorrow when we meet in his office he'll be all business. I believe he's determined to carry through on the government's obligations to AMSCO and see that nothing occurs on his side that would impede the completion of the fab project and the creation of the anticipated jobs.

"Incidentally, his wife, Dr. Kathleen O'Kane, is the principal of a secondary school and a language teacher.

"Excuse my lack of brevity on Minister O'Kane, but I want you to be prepared for him. I think he's AMSCO's most important ally in the Irish government."

Yee cut in with a question, "Minister O'Kane's department gave us many promises on roads, water, telephone, and electrical services; legal help for land acquisition; zoning commission approvals; tax concessions; and modification of building codes for our unique fab requirements. Is he delivering on these promises?"

"We're getting things on track now. At first we came on pretty strong to his people when they didn't meet their promised commitments and delivery dates. Since we switched to more oral communications and shared more information, they're coming around.

"Now, in regard to the Taoiseach: his hero is Eamon de Valera, the first prime minister of modern, independent Ireland—of course I mean independent from occupation and rule by Great Britain. Some say they're surprised he doesn't mimic de Valera by dressing in a black cloak and broad brimmed hat while speaking beside an open peat-fueled fire. His other hero is Edmund Burke, the great eighteenth-century Irish parliamentarian. He likes to quote both of them at every opportunity—even if the quotations are not always apropos to the occasion. The Taoiseach gives lip service to the modernization of Ireland, but his heart is stuck in the church-centered traditions of the past. I'd guess he'll use his meeting with us primarily for a photo-op. The Taoiseach never accepts private invitations so he'll not dine with us tonight."

"Dennis, in your short time here you picked up a lot on Irish history and politics," Drood interjected,

"I must credit my remarkable assistant, Fionnoula O'Casey, whom you'll meet this afternoon. When I asked her to give me newspaper clippings on the minister and the Taoiseach, she added a history lesson—but not without inserting her personal insights and colorful comments. Fionnoula is a cross between a muse and an aide-de-camp."

After lunch, Drood and Yee met Curran's staff. When Dennis introduced Fionnoula, Robert said, "I heard the research you did for us on the minister of enterprise and the Taoiseach. It sounds like you believe the minister is quite an able person."

"Ah, indeed I do, Dr. Drood. AMSCO is lucky to have a fine official like Minister O'Kane supporting its interests. He's a clean spot on Ireland's stained political carpet. But unfortunately with that reactionary relic, Mr. Kevin Crossgrove, we have a pig in the parlor of the Taoiseach's offices. If he were ever hung for his intelligence, he'd die innocent."

After the meetings, Joe Quinlan drove Drood and Yee to the Shelbourne Hotel. The elegant Shelbourne was the chosen town residence of patricians and well-heeled visitors for more than a century. Its nineteenth-century facade, glass-roofed entry, and coal-fired lobby fireplaces recalled to its guests the elegance of another time.

Mary Catherine Curran hired extra kitchen and serving help and bought several dinner pieces to fill in the blanks in her own collection. She set a table and selected a menu fit for a sovereign.

When the dinner guests arrived, Mary Catherine's spirited presence catalyzed them to act as if they were lifetime friends gathering for a comfortable evening and dinner party.

Minister O'Kane confirmed his reputation for being a modern day *seanachie*. When he interrupted his storytelling to accept a serving of lox, Mary Catherine and Mrs. O'Kane changed the subject to their passion: teaching.

Mrs. O'Kane noticed Drood paled and fell silent when she boasted of the high quality of teachers in Irish schools. She had been listening to him all evening with her acute ear for languages and detected the faint shadow of a Cork brogue. She guessed her comments on Irish education recalled some kind of a bitter memory for him.

Mrs. O'Kane and Yee discussed the type of education required for modern industry. She could not resist giving him an Irish history lesson: "We Irish were the sole source of intellectualism in Europe during the Dark Ages. However, later, while under the brutal heel of Oliver Cromwell, the devil's earthly envoy from England, we were denied the right to speak our ancient Irish language and to receive an education. To this day, our greatest oath is, 'The curse of Cromwell upon you.' When we finally had our uprising and regained our independence, we had to lash the horses to regain our former high standards for learning."

"We too had our Cromwell in China," Yee responded. "For us it was Mao Tse-Tung and his loony programs to banish intellectualism. China is still recouping the lost ground and catching up with other first-class nations."

When the guests finished their after-dinner coffee and liqueur, O'Kane and Drood called for their drivers and departed. Mason stayed long enough to coordinate his calendar with Dennis for the next day.

As Dennis and Mary Catherine prepared for bed, Dennis said, "Mary Catherine, you did a marvelous job of entertaining our guests and setting a good climate for our meeting tomorrow with Minister O'Kane. I also noticed you set all of the male guests' juices flowing while they took every opportunity for furtive stares at you in your gorgeous new dress. I think you even challenged Ken Yee's inscrutability and clattered his chopsticks."

"I'm glad you noticed all of that, Dennis. And I noticed the red spot on your forehead every time Dr. Drood talked to you. I always know you're anxious when I see that little spot appear. Keep in mind the red spot will shine like Rudolph's red nose on Christmas Eve if you ever cheat on me. Now come over here, Boyo, for a proper good night."

When Robert returned to his hotel, he ordered a cognac and sipped it while staring out his window across the dark, shadowy treetops of St. Stephens Green. He mused: What a contrast between Kathleen O'Kane's description of today's competent Irish teachers and my uncaring schoolmaster who treated students he did not care for—especially me—like pieces of social litter polluting his classroom. Maybe Seamus Kiely can find out if the runty screwworm is still alive. And maybe he can check out Rinty Donlan, the fink who poked fun at classmates like me who were so poor we had to wear his hand-me-down clothes. My satisfaction will be enormous if I can confront my schoolmaster and classmates and show them I didn't grow up to be the worthless nobody they expected.

Although it was only a two-minute walk from the Shelbourne Hotel around the corner to Minister O'Kane's office on Kildare Street, Curran, Drood, and Yee drove in the Daimler. O'Kane's pompous assistant in his cheap blue suit and worn white shirt collar watched for their arrival and escorted them to O'Kane's sumptuous office. The office remained unchanged since the British ran the Irish government and provided their officials with facilities that flaunted the grandeur of the British Empire.

O'Kane and two assistants were seated at a conference table in his large office. The ubiquitous tea service was at the ready on a side table. O'Kane switched to his ministerial manner. "Gentlemen, we're honored because of your visit with us today. We'll do everything possible to make it successful. According to our information, your new fab project—both from the viewpoint of our responsibilities and yours—is proceeding satisfactorily." He paused, dropped his voice, and took a sip of tea.

Drood picked up the cue. "It is we who are honored for the opportunity to meet you today, Minister O'Kane, and for your consideration in setting up a meeting with the Taoiseach. Our commitment to the new fab project continues to be strong. And our manufacturing presence in Ireland still fits a key part of our company strategy." A whiff of an Irish accent crept into Robert's voice.

O'Kane relaxed his shoulders and sighed with relief upon learning Drood did not bring unwelcome news about the fab. Drood continued, "We concur with your observation on the satisfactory work progress. When our project is further along, we'll initiate a comprehensive hiring process to match our jobs to the best Irish applicants. We plan to depend on your government authorities and their staffs for help in identifying and screening the best job candidates."

Drood gave a signal to Yee to go on. "Mr. Minister, we'll soon bring additional high-level management to Ireland to work on the complex preparation needed for the fab operation. Included in their duties will be hiring personnel. Our preference is to hire Irish people for management positions if they have the required skills or can be readily trained. Of course, virtually all of our fab shop workers will be Irish. We also intend to improve and expand our capabilities for communications with the Irish government and the press. We know how important it is for the government and public to be well-informed."

O'Kane wrapped up the meeting. "Dr. Drood, Dr. Yee, and Mr. Curran, this has been a most satisfactory meeting. Your information and clarifications are reassuring as we move ahead with our considerable commitments to support your fab. This project is the capstone of our efforts in Ireland in recent years to build a technical base allowing us to join the league of world-class industrial nations. Mr. Curran, please call me if you see any problems on our side or if you need assistance that we are capable of providing. Mrs. O'Kane and I again thank you and Mrs. Curran—a most beautiful and gracious lady—for the grand evening at your home last night."

Yee pulled a thin package from his oversized case and handed it to Drood. Drood said, "Minister O'Kane here is a token of our thanks for the reception you have given us. This painting by Michael Blaser of a paddle wheel steamer on the Mississippi River recalls the importance of the river to our country's early development. "

O'Kane studied the picture and said, "Thank you, Dr. Drood; this marvelous picture will provide a lasting reminder of your visit. I will hang it in a prominent place in my office. Now, I think it's time to go to the Taoiseach's office. He has a full schedule, but I think a few words on your continuing commitment to the fab project and some time devoted to photographs will be in order."

They drove several blocks and turned through elegant black wrought iron gates and past a pair of guards into a short circular drive to the domed entrance of a magnificent classical building. It housed the offices of Kevin Crossgrove, the Taoiseach of the Republic of Ireland. Lord Lieutenant Fitz Alan, the last Viceroy representing the British Empire in Ireland during the early part of the twentieth century, used the offices on various ceremonial occasions.

After the Taoiseach gave his visitors a pompous greeting, he said, "Although the opposition party tries to make the voters think otherwise, I work tirelessly without fanfare on many fronts to leapfrog Ireland into the twenty-first century." O'Kane winced when Crossgrove launched into one of his trademark quotations:

> *Because a half dozen grasshoppers under a fern make the field ring with their importunate chink, whilst thousands of great cattle, reposed beneath the shadow of the British oak, chew the cud and are silent, pray do not imagine that those who make the noise are the only inhabitants of the field.*

He did not give Edmund Burke attribution for his quotation that he foolishly thought credited him for being the discreet force behind Ireland's technical and economic development.

The Taoiseach impatiently tapped the fingertips of his left hand on his desk while Robert made a brief statement about AMSCO's commitment in Ireland. He then told his assistant to send in his photographer.

At the end of the meeting Drood presented a painting to the Taoiseach of a western cowboy scene by Charles M. Russell. The Taoiseach indifferently glanced at it and handed it off to his assistant.

When the visitors left, the Taoiseach dictated a caption for a photo for the evening newspapers: "The Taoiseach Works Tirelessly to Attract Industry to Ireland."

At Drood's wrap-up lunch with Dennis, he said, "I'm satisfied with the project and can see no hitches with the government. It seems obvious we've a good advocate in court with Minister O'Kane. As for the Taoiseach, in his cloud of pomposity, I think he's clueless about modern business, but I don't think he'll cause us any harm."

Drood looked to Dennis and said, "Now, on another subject; we're going to give you additional work responsibilities. You'll be the official communication link with the Irish government and the press. I'm going to tell Jerry Colson to send you more assistance to take over some of your technical workload. We'll also change your reporting line from Jerry to Ken, but I still want you to continue to depend on Jerry for technical direction and assistance. Ken, will you go on from here?"

Yee went straight to the point. "You've ably handled all aspects of our visit as well as other communications preceding our visit, so the additional public relations duties should not be a challenge for you. Meet with our public relations people in San Francisco the next time you are in town to ensure you keep in step with their policies.

"Now I'm going to jump the gun and tell who I'm going to appoint for the fab manager, but hold it in confidence until I officially announce it in a few days. We're going to rehire Carly Jackson for the position." Dennis raised his eyebrows in surprise and grinned with satisfaction.

Drood concluded, "Okay, Dennis, I think that ends our visit. Please thank Mary Catherine again for her skillful hosting of the dinner last evening. Ken will be leaving right away on a commercial flight home. I'll tend to some personal matters and leave on Sunday. Keep up the good work, Dennis."

On the way back to his office Dennis sighed with relief. Meetings with senior executives often end with mushier conclusions, and it was rare for Dr. Drood to depart without leaving ruffled feathers because of his dissatisfaction with something he observed or heard during his visit. Dennis wondered why the change of character. And why did he seem so remote at times; something other than the fab project preoccupied him. Ken Yee would be a demanding new boss, but there would be no need for politics; everything would be based on unemotional logic.

Robert directed Joe Quinlan to drive to Seamus Kiely's address. His modest office, with a reception area and small conference room, was located in a modern building overlooking the River Liffey. Kiely sat behind his desk looking like James Cagney when he was at the peak of his acting career.

He handed Robert a simple folder containing a brochure outlining his services, a copy of his confidentiality policy, fee scale, and bio. Robert glanced at the bio: seven years of London and Belfast experience with Scotland Yard; three years with the Fraud Division of Paxton Insurance Limited; and nine years operating Kiely Investigators. Kiely asked, "How may I be of service to you, Dr. Drood?"

Robert liked Kiely's efficiency. "I have three areas I want you to investigate. I'll list them in order of priority." Kiely flipped open a well-used leather notebook and uncapped his old-fashioned fountain pen. "First, I want you to locate a man named Brian McClellan. He used to live in Ballincollig or maybe Cork. He should be between sixty-five and seventy now. He raped my sister and sexually abused my mother, but the police were never involved. My mother's maiden name was Mary Garrity; her married name was Mrs. George Drood. She was born in Farranree—in Cork City—in 1942. My sister now lives in Chicago; she is still unable to cope with McClellan's violation of her. My mother died there." Kiely wrote it all down in a stately old-fashioned script.

Robert's voice faltered and his eyes dampened. Kiely stood and looked out the window feigning interest in a pair of swans sailing by on the Liffey. He had seen every sordid sexual crime imaginable and knew how utterly destructive they were to people's lives, especially when children were involved. While he waited for Robert to regain control of his emotions, he observed his impeccably fitted Savile Row suit.

Robert pulled himself together. "Second, I want you to locate my father, George Drood. He may live in Northern Ireland—or he may be dead. He abandoned our family thirty years ago.

Third, I want you to locate Rinty Donlan, a childhood classmate. He probably lives in Cork. I don't know his real first name. He could be a little older than I. At school he was a bully. Also, see if you can find what became of our schoolmaster; he was a twisted little screw-worm of a man named Tweedy."

"Shall I gather information suitable for criminal prosecution?"

"No, I only want it for my information. Please give me regular reports on your findings. I'm coming back to Ireland soon and can visit you again if required. Here's a list of my private and confidential phone numbers and my e-mail address."

"I'll have my first report to you in one month."

While becoming a competent investigator, Kiely had studied psychology. It was obvious to him Drood was still suffering thirty years later from the sexual crimes against his sister and mother. He guessed he was more personally involved than he admitted.

CHAPTER TWENTY-FIVE

When Drood mentioned his Irish trip to Justin Cairncross, he informed his friend, Sir Roderick Kirwan-Swift, CEO and owner of Imperial Textile Limited, the largest textile company in Great Britain. Several days later Kirwan-Swift's secretary called Robert's office and said, "Mr. Cairncross informed us of your trip to Ireland. Sir Roderick will be at his Irish estate the weekend of Dr. Drood's visit to Dublin. He invites Dr. Drood to Rathton Hall to attend a dinner party he's hosting on Saturday evening. If Dr. Drood can attend, I will send detailed information." Robert instructed his assistant to accept the invitation.

She reviewed newspaper clippings on Kirwan-Swift and wrote a note for Robert: married but seldom seen with wife; educated in England and the U.S.; lives on inherited wealth; invites guests who are thinkers and achievers.

Drood arrived at Kirwan-Swift's estate in late afternoon. As he rode down the long gravel drive flanked by ancient, storm-scarred oak trees and looked toward the façade of the stark three-story Palladian mansion, he thought of the light years separating this architectural masterpiece from his childhood hovel—a derelict barn. The injustice of a society that allowed such disparity disgusted him, but at the same time it fascinated him.

As Drood's Daimler crunched to a stop on the raked gravel courtyard in front of Rathton Hall, a servant opened the door and inquired, "Dr. Drood?" When Robert nodded, he announced, "The guests are gathered in the garden; I'll escort you there." He flicked a thumb at Joe Quinlan directing him to park the Daimler behind a hedge. It would not do to have the distraction of parked motorcars in front of the haughty mansion no matter how distinguished their marks. Quinlan could now vacuum the small oriental rugs he always placed on the floor of the back seat of his limo to pamper the feet of his clients and dust off the car with a feather duster.

Drood and the servant entered the house and walked down the seventy-five-foot-long center hall to the rear garden. They passed heedless gazes from portraits of Kirwan-Swift's lordly ancestors who once occupied Rathton Hall and glassy stares from antlered stag heads that once chomped on the lush estate turf.

When Robert stepped into the garden lit by slanting rays of late afternoon sun, Sir Roderick left a cluster of guests to greet him. He wore the standard British gentleman's weekend dress: double-vented plaid jacket, checked shirt, and fashionably clashing socks. After they chatted a few minutes, Sir Roderick introduced Robert to some of his guests: a member of Parliament and his wife; the Lord Mayor of Dublin and a lady who was not his wife; a famous Italian clothing designer and his prissy partner; the president of the Georgian Preservation Society; and Desmond Guinness, whose last name was spoken through parched lips thousands of times each day in the pubs of the world. Thirty guests were invited, as determined by the seating capacity of the dining room. A waiter took Robert's order for Compari and soda.

The gardens were designed by Lancelot "Capability" Brown, the landscaper of dozens of estates throughout Great Britain and Ireland in the eighteenth century. Beyond the gardens were terraces with trees and bushes positioned to focus the view on the distant faux Greek architectural ruins. Capability Brown believed every estate had the "capability" for improvement if the owner would put the landscaping into his talented hands.

Thousands of acres of rich farmland surrounded Rathton Hall. With the aid of an imaginative accounting system and a talented farm manager, Sir Roderick boasted the estate was financially viable in spite of the cost of maintaining the showplace house and gardens. Because of the land's abundant fertility, it was one of the first areas from which the indigenous Irish were evicted by the British when they invaded the country centuries earlier. Kirwan-Swift's guests had an inkling they were on a functioning farm when they arrived and saw Hereford cattle and Suffolk sheep grazing in the fenced meadows beside the driveway.

A few minutes before the guests were summoned to the dining room, Robert met Lady Bennett-Jenkins, a blond, early thirtyish woman and her escort. The inattentiveness of her escort became clear when he was introduced as her brother. Her English sounded as if she had developed it with one foot in Great Britain and the other in New England. She looked like a model for the pricey silk scarves and jewelry advertised in *Vogue* magazines.

As the guests moved toward the house, Robert held back to speak to an irreverent bank director he knew. Robert asked, "Jeffrey, can you give me a thumbnail rundown on Lady Bennett-Jenkins—that blond over there?"

"Lives in Belfast; educated at Oxford and Brown; reeks of old money from textile machinery manufacturing; divorced after a brief and disastrous marriage to a French playboy-industrialist; likes men but is gun-shy about permanent relationships; and likes horse racing. Go slowly Robert old boy, her class lives in another universe; it traces its lineage to Adam and Eve, and it only allows outsiders into its sheep paddocks to shear them of their fleeces."

When they entered the hall to go to dinner and walked past the wall of ancestors and antlers, Jeffrey chuckled and said, "Robert, why do you suppose Roderick's forefathers decided to paint their ancestors' portraits and stuff the stags' heads instead of vice versa on the walls of this snob alley?"

The dinner service was fit for serving royalty as it indeed once had in the late nineteenth century when the Prince of Wales rendezvoused at Rathton Hall with an Irish actress. The blue walls with white bas-relief made the diners feel like they were in an enormous Wedgewood bowl. The elaborate plasterwork appeared delicate even though it weighed tons. An immense Bessarabian carpet softened the formality of the room.

Sir Roderick's sister presided as hostess. The seating place cards showed the escort of the Lord Mayor of Dublin on Robert's left and Lady Pamela Bennett-Jenkins on his right.

Sir Roderick was known for his commanding opinions on a broad spectrum of subjects, and yet at his dinner parties he remained silent except to direct conversations to subjects that interested him. This was his method for developing and refining his opinions.

After a toast to his guests, Sir Roderick boasted, "All of the food you will be served this evening was grown here at Rathton Hall."

Lady Pamela said to Robert, "Please dispense with formality and call me Pamela." They had no trouble finding subjects for conversation; both had read extensively and traveled widely.

After dinner, the party moved to the formal parlor for coffee and liqueur. A plasterwork collection of wild game, watched over by Diana with her bow and arrow, was arranged over the mantle. A fox stared up at the game as if it hoped a partridge would drop. The ceiling displayed classical female figures with ripe swaying bosoms. Paintings by Gainsborough, Van Dyck, and Canaletto boasted of Sir Roderick's excellent taste and abundant financial resources.

Robert and Pamela selected chairs separate from the rest of the guests. From the glances and arched eyebrows of Sir Roderick and his sister, it was evident they anticipated a liaison between them. Robert turned the conversation with Pamela to a more personal note when the evening neared its end. "Pamela, I don't know when I've enjoyed an evening as much as this. I'm in town until Sunday afternoon. May I see you again tomorrow?"

Pamela, not accustomed to being coy, replied, "I hoped you'd ask. Sir Roderick's entertainment for his weekend houseguests will be too tame for my taste: chess, bridge, and garden strolls are not my strong suits. What shall we do with our day together?"

"My hotel brochure notes the horse races are on tomorrow at Leopardstown. My driver can pick you up for lunch, and then we can go to the races. We can work out an evening plan later. I'll check what's playing at the Abbey and Olympic."

"That sounds brilliant. I expect it will be as much fun as this evening has been."

When Robert returned to his hotel, he reflected on his afternoon and evening. Thinking about the meeting with Seamus Kiely brought back the usual depressing memories of his wretched childhood, but this time he had some control of his feelings because he was finally initiating action. He went to sleep with Pamela on his mind.

The next day at the Leopardstown racetrack, Robert and Pamela bet heavily but ended the day near the breakeven point. At the last race they were breathless from the exertion of laughing all afternoon like a pair of exuberant adolescents.

Because of heavy traffic, they were late returning to the Shelbourne. They stepped into the old-fashioned, high-ceilinged bar to the left of the hotel entrance and ordered drinks. When they finished, Robert said, "It's too late for the theater tonight; besides, the offerings looked poor. Will you join me for supper? I can order it served in my parlor."

Pamela agreed. Robert placed his hand on her back while he escorted her through the crowd near the lift door. In the confined space of the lift he observed her perfume.

When Pamela returned from freshening up, Robert handed her a menu to make her selection. "My taste for food is patterned after a buzzard," she said. "Everything tastes good to me; please order me whatever you order for yourself, but in small portions."

Robert and Pamela exchanged their life's history. Pamela spoke of her brief tumultuous marriage to a wealthy Frenchman, his womanizing, and his physical abuse of her when he drank. Robert told his story, but omitted mentioning his early life in Ireland and elementary school days in South Chicago. Pamela sensed there must be a reason for the gap in his chronology.

They agreed to meet the next morning for a walk on the elegant streets lined with multistory Georgian houses surrounding St. Stephens Green. When Pamela said she planned to return to her home via train, Robert said he would tell his pilots to reschedule his San Francisco flight so they could drop her off in Belfast.

Pamela had flown before on private planes and was accustomed to the luxuries of the wealthy, but the size and lavishness of the Gulfstream surprised her. The old British concept that inherited money and family relationships justified hereditary corporate positions seemed less sensible to her now—although that was how she had acquired her board position in her family-owned company.

When they landed in Belfast, the pilots told Robert it would take fifteen minutes to top out the fuel tanks. He walked with Pamela to the unoccupied lounge of the aviation service building. They were both melancholy at seeing their pleasant weekend come to a close. Robert said, "Pamela, it was a marvelous weekend with you. I have another meeting in Europe soon. I'll call you before my next trip."

"I'll anxiously await your call, Robert." They hugged and exchanged an investigative kiss.

CHAPTER TWENTY-SIX

After Ken Yee rehired Carly Jackson to be the new Irish fab manager, she worked a month in San Francisco with the fab operations planning staff to identify key people to move to Ireland with her. She held off as long as possible on permanent staffing appointments until she learned the skills and availability of Irish candidates.

Carly called Dennis. After reminiscences about their previous work together on an earlier project in Singapore, she said, "There's something you can do for me, Dennis. I'm going to give you my office needs. I want you to either pull ahead on completing the fab office construction or rent space for me and my staff."

"We'll need to rent temporary office space for your immediate needs, Carly. We can't complete the new office before you arrive. Shall I also rent a house or flat for you?"

"Yes, go ahead and find me a place. I'd guess Ol' Wally will be around for a visit now and then until I piss him off again and he goes home in a snit, so look at a flat for one person and an occasional visitor. You know I live a minimalist existence; a teepee with a cot and hot plate will cover my needs."

Carly was married for six months after she graduated from the University of Oklahoma with an electrical engineering degree. She was ambitious to develop into a top-notch professional engineer, but her husband wanted a stay-at-home housewife. The marriage soon ended. For many years Carly dated Walter King—she called him "Ol' Wally"—who owned a successful agricultural supply and services business in the Napa Valley. With their strong wills and little inclination for compromise, their time together lasted until a difference of opinion arose. Their separations normally went on until one of them broke the hiatus with a conciliatory phone call and suggestion for a reunion.

When Carly arrived in Ireland with her playbook for running a fab firmly in hand, she marked her territory and became a hub for action. She was a demanding executive and at the same time everyone's mentor and confidant.

Carly and Dennis had a respectful relationship. She recognized Dennis's talent was superior to hers in dealing with the press and the public. Her aggressiveness and flip comments caused public relations gaffes in the past. She preferred to concentrate on planning and organizing for the fab operation.

When Yee told Colson to provide Dennis more technical assistance, he transferred Kim Park Chin to Ireland. Dennis called him and said, "Kim, I'm delighted that you're coming over. With your years of experience in designing, purchasing, and starting up silicon chip manufacturing equipment, I know you'll hit the ground running. Come on over for a few days as soon as you can so we can show you around and rent a flat or house for you and your wife."

Fionnoula O'Casey had a keen sense of when to be serious and when to be the office Puck. She found it unacceptable for people to be down in the dumps unless a serious personal problem existed, a major hangover happened, or a favorite sports team lost a match. She gave each person a nickname. She called Dennis "Himself." Park Chin was "Top Chip." Carly was "Maximum Leader." She also gave several nonstaff people nicknames. Dr. Drood was "His Worship." When Yee first called Dennis's office, Fionnoula answered the phone and said, "Oh, ye are Yee." From then on she referred to him as "Ye Yee." Fionnoula called herself "Myself."

Fionnoula had her own performance rating and reward system. If telling a story, doing her a small favor, or demonstrating knowledge of Irish history or culture pleased her, she brought a small offering from her kitchen. If work-related events went well for an engineer, she gave him a chuck under the chin. If something important happened, such as a promotion, she dispensed two chucks. Her rewards became known as "one-chuckers" and "two-chuckers."

Few were the occasions that did not recall to Fionnoula a song, a poem, or a quotation. When one of the engineers departed on a trip to the U.S., she accompanied him to the door and recalled the departure of so many others during the Irish diaspora by melodramatically singing:

> *Oh, then, fare ye well sweet Donegal, the Rosses and Gweedore,*
> *I'm crossing the main ocean, where the foaming billows roar,*
> *It breaks my heart from ye to part, where I spent many happy days,*
> *Farewell to kind relatives, for I'm bound for "Amerikay."*

Fionnoula's manner of communicating had its basis in the ancient Irish tradition of verbally sharing history, myths, and even laws. Skillful, and especially humorous, oral communication was a valued talent with the Irish and writing was a national passion. In ancient times, travelling storytellers were accepted into homes for long periods of time as honored guests. Writers were honored with more monuments in Dublin than the country's founding fathers. Artistic exaggeration in storytelling was permitted, but the basic facts were preserved inviolate.

At Curran's weekly project meetings, he asked each person to briefly discuss any subject on his or her mind. Because Fionnoula could be counted on as the icebreaker, he always called on her first. She normally spoke on administrative matters, gave advice on Irish business practices, or if she had no pressing company business to report, used her allotted minutes to sing or recite for the staff.

One of Fionnoula's favorite songs, *The Fields of Athenry,* recalled the time of starvation in Ireland during a famine when people were compelled to steal so their families would not starve. When caught, they were hung in the village square or loaded onto squalid prison ships and transported to sparsely inhabited Australia. At a staff meeting, she sang several verses of a sad song about a young man waiting for a prison ship to take him to Botany Bay in far-off Australia:

> *By a lonely prison wall,*
> *I heard a young girl calling, "Michael, they are taking you away."*
> *For you stole Travelyan's corn (grain),*
> *So the young (starving children) might see the morn.*
> *Now a prison ship lies waiting in the bay.*
>
> *Low, lie the fields of Athenry,*
> *Where once we watched the small birds fly free.*
> *Our love was on the wing.*
> *We had dreams and songs to sing.*
> *It's so lonely 'round the Fields of Athenry.*

Singing and reciting poetry was as natural for Fionnoula as was purring for a cat. Dennis did not stifle Fionnoula's puckishness. She brought a tone of humor and calm to balance the intensity that normally prevailed during staff meetings. Dennis's staff learned Fionnoula's observations and judgments could be counted upon. They often ran people-related matters by her before taking action.

AMSCO stock price growth continued but slower than in the past and slower than Wall Street expected. European sales were below projections. The board asked Robert to review and consider delaying the

Irish fab project in the face of lethargic European sales. He scheduled a few days each month in Europe to determine if the slow sales were the result of the poor economy or inadequate performance by AMSCO sales personnel. During each European visit, he met with key clients and attended meetings with AMSCO sales managers.

A visit by Robert was not a pleasant experience for the AMSCO managers. He relentlessly flailed them to improve sales and profitability. They felt they were in a no-win situation when he pressured them to make unrealistically optimistic sales forecasts and in the next meeting excoriated them if the forecasts did not materialize. Managers complained they were spending too much of their time licking their wounds after meetings with Robert and preparing for his next onslaught.

Robert could compartmentalize his mind. After grueling meetings, he could turn off all thoughts of business and think only of his personal interests. He never gave a second thought to the distress he caused his managers.

Seamus Kiely submitted a report showing his progress in locating Brian McClellan and George Drood and requesting more time to confirm his findings. Robert approved the additional time. He did not yet know what he'd do if Kiely found them. It was deeply disturbing for him to think about McClellan and his father.

At the conclusion of Robert's next European trip, he again visited Lady Pamela Bennett-Jenkins. She organized a long weekend at the ancient estate of a friend in Northern Ireland, where they swam in the heated indoor pool, hunted, and rode horseback on the paths through the woods and fields of the estate.

Robert said, "Pamela, this wonderful weekend was like a scene from an Agatha Christie mystery story. I'm thinking of buying an Irish estate similar to this one myself and spending more time here. I could use it during European business trips and for vacations and holidays.

"Are you interested in another weekend together with me when I come back again?"

"Of course I am, Robert. Give me a call anytime."

Robert acquired a list of Irish estates that were on the market. During a trip to Sweden, he stopped in Dublin to tour three estates offered for sale. One was too far from an airport and one was in advanced decay. The third was sixty minutes driving time from Dublin.

The Irish property section of *The Sunday Times* described the third estate:

HOLLYCOURT: An historic country estate—one of the finest in Ireland—is offered for sale. The Georgian house, with one hectare (2.5 acres) of gardens, is set on 30.6 hectares of land—20 hectares are tillable. Built in the early nineteenth century by Sir Thomas Pearce, the 800 square meters (8000 square feet) of living space is in good condition although the new owner may desire to modernize. The house features a flagstone entrance hall, vaulted ceiling drawing room and dining room, study, snooker room, sun room, kitchen, and six bedrooms—two with ensuite facilities (baths.) Included on the estate is a stable converted to a five-car garage with servants' quarters above and an independent caretaker's cottage. The house has oil-fired central heating. The stonewalled garden contains a pond and croquet lawn. A flowing brook borders the estate. Furnishings are available at a price to be determined by negotiations. Riley Auctioneers is seeking offers in the region of 4.6 million euros (4.2 million U.S. dollars.) Phone 01 5550431 for an appointment to view the estate.

The property agent drove Robert to Hollycourt in her Vauxhall sedan. His heart raced when they drove down the tree-lined drive toward the house. The elegance from a by-gone era—classical portico, ram's head friezes, corners sharply defined by granite quoins, Palladian windows, and stylish gardens—struck him like a punch in the solar plexus. When they entered the house and Robert saw the Adams fireplaces, plaster ceiling decorations, and gracefully curving staircase, it looked to him like the work of master builders of old. He was never more taken with the idea of a new possession than he was with Hollycourt.

The agent and Robert spent hours touring the house and walking the land. He imagined the property like it was when it was new and staffed by a platoon of servants. In his euphoria, he filtered out observations on its decrepit condition and the high cost of restoration.

The agent said, "Dr. Drood, if you have a little time for an entertaining diversion, let's meet Paddy and Bridget Lehan. They and their dog Guinness occupy the caretaker's cottage. When Paddy visited the Blarney stone, he was abundantly blessed with its legendary powers for bestowing colorful eloquence to the kissers of the stone."

When the visit was over and they returned to the car, Robert's face ached from laughing at Paddy's stories. He especially enjoyed his rambling tale of a recent incident on his way home from his nightly pub visit when he rammed the side of a parked lorry with his motorcycle. He suffered a twisted wrist and Guinness cut his paw when he flew from his customary sidecar seat against the rear lorry wheel. The police blotter noted, "Drink had been taken by both injured parties in the unfortunate accident." The passive explanation clearly described the circumstances of the accident while showing a hint of compassion for the afflicted cyclists.

As they departed the estate, Robert could only think of his satisfaction if he owned Hollycourt. He felt as good as he did when he first came to Chicago from Ireland and his mother bought him and his sister Bridget complete new outfits of school clothes at Sears and Roebuck. His earlier decision to throttle his spending abandoned him faster than a New Year's resolution.

"Hollycourt is a fine estate and I have some interest in buying it, but not at the asking price," Robert said to the agent when they drove away.

"If you make a reasonable offer, I'll present it to the solicitors who represent the owner."

Robert was so preoccupied with visions of owning Hollycourt, he did not think of what he was willing to offer or what it would cost for rehabilitation. He blurted out, "I'm willing to offer two million U.S. dollars, if the owner includes the household furnishings." Based on his negotiating experience, he thought his offer of less than fifty percent of the asking price was too low for serious consideration and the likelihood of acceptance was almost nil.

"I'll forward your bid to the solicitors, although I don't think they will accept such a discounted offer," the agent responded.

On the flight home Robert shut his eyes and thought about his developing relationship with Pamela. She was attractive and gave him entrée into the exciting world of British and Irish sophistication. He wanted to continue to see her. He was not sure why she was interested in him. It could be affection, money, or just the novelty and adventure of an affair with a presentable person from outside her class and social sphere. He decided to invite her to San Francisco to see how their relationship developed on his turf.

Robert then thought about Hollycourt. He wanted to own Hollycourt more than a fairy-tale frog wanted to be kissed by a beautiful princess. It would be the first house he ever owned. But he must figure out how to obtain the required money. His savings were nonexistent, and he recently took an enormous bath on stock margin calls. If AMSCO sales and profits improved, he expected to receive a large bonus at year's end. If his offer for Hollycourt was accepted, he'd call Hans Bartoluzzi or Karl von Kleinschmidt and ask for a bridge loan to carry him until he received his anticipated year-end bonus. His bank already told him it would not grant him another loan. Bartoluzzi and von Kleinschmidt were major AMSCO suppliers and were accustomed to doing business in cultures where the lines between company and personal interests were blurred.

For the first time in his business life, Robert would be clearly stepping onto the thin ice of financial impropriety. This would be more than bending the rules; it would be a clear conflict of interest. He would be obligated to declare the loan on his AMSCO conflict of interest statement at the end of the year. But before that time his bonus should be paid and final settlement made on the loan so he would overlook declaring it.

Before Robert ordered his dinner from the flight attendant, he read the book on grand Irish houses the property agent had given him because it included several pages on Hollycourt. The book introduction read:

> The grand, Irish country houses and estates are a legacy of the enormous wealth, fine taste, and cultured presence of the Anglo-Irish aristocracy during the Georgian period. The houses were built after the Battle of Boyne when peace and prosperity were restored for a time in Ireland. Hollycourt is a prime example of these estates.

The book further whetted Robert's appetite for acquiring Hollycourt.

CHAPTER TWENTY-SEVEN

A week after Robert returned to San Francisco, the Irish property agent called. "Dr. Drood, the solicitors will sell Hollycourt to you if you raise your offer to two and a half million U.S. dollars." Robert pretended he did not understand. He wanted her to continue talking so he could listen to her voice tone for conviction. Although he was willing to raise his offer, her voice sounded uncertain; he stood pat. He guessed the solicitors had told her to accept his offer and conditions if she could not squeeze him for a better price.

"My offer is firm," Robert bluffed. "The property is run down and will need major additional investment to make it useable. If my offer is not acceptable, I'll remove it from the table."

The property agent half-heartedly attempted to convince Robert to up his offer. She was reluctant, however, to push too hard because the solicitors had told her to keep his bid in play at all cost. She had no other prospective buyers. Robert would not budge, so she accepted his offer.

Robert was euphoric. But he must now find the money for the initial house payment.

He placed a call to Hans Bartoluzzi in Zurich. When Bartoluzzi returned the call, Robert said, "Hello, Hans. We haven't talked since I visited you in San Moritz last winter and enjoyed your fine hospitality. Is everything going well with you?"

"Indeed it is, Robert. I spent last weekend in my house in St. Moritz. My old skiing injury is much improved now. The skiing was outstanding.

"I recently reviewed orders from AMSCO to the Asian factories where we maintain certain interests. I was informed our quality and deliveries have improved, and we'll be rewarded with increased orders from AMSCO next year. I was going to call you in the next few days to tell you how much we appreciate the trust of your company."

Before Bartoluzzi returned Drood's call, he had talked to his sales director for a summary update of the volume and profit from their

AMSCO account. His company's growing business with AMSCO was becoming significant to his income statement. Bartoluzzi went on, "Now Robert, how can I be of service to you?"

Robert cleared his throat and shuffled his feet. "I've just bought an estate in Ireland and I need to borrow a million dollars to temporarily finance it. Due to stringent American laws, I can't borrow it from AMSCO. I read an item in the *Financial Times* about your bank having reserve investment funds. I thought we might work out something to our mutual advantage."

Bartoluzzi and his executives were well informed. Clerks searched the international newspapers and financial information services daily for information related to the people and companies that were their clients and competitors. They recorded intelligence information whenever they read or heard it. They already knew Drood could not obtain normal bank credit because of his compulsive spending.

"It is my good fortune to receive your call, Robert. Several days ago our chief financial officer and I discussed our difficulties in finding sound uses for our funds as you just proposed. When we conclude this conversation, I'll tell him to call you. I'm confident he will share my opinion on your loan request, and you can work out the details to your satisfaction. And of course we'll handle the transaction through our special financial group designed to prevent unnecessary public disclosures. I wish you happiness with your new estate. Please honor me soon with another call."

Bartoluzzi talked to his CFO. "Call Dr. Drood at AMSCO. Give him a million-dollar loan at an interest rate one percent below the market rate, and don't ask for collateral. If for any reason we don't collect on the loan, we're still okay due to the profitability of AMSCO orders to our Asian factories. And call our AMSCO account manager. Tell him to be more aggressive on pricing for the next round of AMSCO contract negotiations. If he meets resistance, tell him to notify me so I can support him with a call to Dr. Drood."

After Robert concluded the documentation for purchasing Hollycourt, he called Desmond Bowen, a Dublin restoration architect, and requested an analysis and cost estimate for refurbishing the house and garden and replacing the run-down household furnishings.

On his next trip to Europe he met Bowen at Hollycourt. Bowen handed Robert an envelope. "Here's a preliminary cost estimate for the restoration. The cost will add forty percent to your purchase price. The electrical service, plumbing, structure, and heating are in appalling condition. The actual cost may vary due to conditions that won't be evident until the restoration work is under way. The work should take about a year to complete. But I must warn you; this is Ireland; cost and time estimates are less definite than you're used to in America."

Robert regretted he had been blinded with his enthusiasm to purchase Hollycourt before he knew the restoration costs. Nevertheless, he was still excited about owning the estate. He scanned the cost estimates and decided, although it would be tight, he could swing it. The initial payments could be paid with the money from the Bartoluzzi loan. By the time the later payments were due, he expected to have his AMSCO bonus and could profitably cash in some of his stock options.

Robert said, "Desmond, go ahead and draw up the specifications and solicit bids for the restoration and modernization."

Robert met with Paddy Lehan and arranged for him to continue managing the farm and controlling contractor access to the estate. Paddy assured Robert the farm income would be enough to pay his and Bridget's wages and the property taxes. Paddy offered Robert a glass of Bushmills Irish whiskey to celebrate their employment agreement. Guinness shared in the gravity of the occasion by lapping from a saucer of water laced with several spoonfuls of Bushmills.

Paddy told Robert a story about how the previous estate owner's aspiring actress wife cuckolded him when he was abroad on business. He unexpectedly returned home and found her *flagrante delicto* with her movie producer lover on the sofa cushions in front of the drawing room fireplace. He lunged for a poker to attack the lover and fell across the edge of the heavy fireplace fender breaking his neck.

She knew the insurance payment to her for her husband's death would be more advantageous if he died of natural causes. When the medical examiner concluded investigating the death, she let her shawl—her only clothing—slip aside, arched her eyebrow, and said, "If you'll write in your official report that my husband died of a heart attack, I'll let you play in my pleasure garden." Before Paddy could expand his story or start another, Robert took his leave.

He spent a few days with Pamela before he returned home. "Pamela, I'd like to invite you to San Francisco to a party I'm giving," he said. "I hope you can attend and stay with me for several weeks. I can schedule a hiatus in my travel schedule while you're there."

"Yes, Robert, I'd love to accept your invitation. It'll be my first trip to San Francisco."

Before Robert departed from Ireland, he flew to Cork for another meeting with Seamus Kiely who had earlier sent a report that he had located

Rinty Donlan, Brian McClellan, and his old schoolmaster. He said he was still searching for George Drood. His report noted that Donlan was a drunk; McClellan lived in a home for advanced Alzheimer's patients; and Tweedy, his old schoolmaster had long ago retired and was in rapidly failing health. Robert was overcome with his dreaded dark feelings when he read the report. He had lived more than thirty years of his life thinking of how these people had abused him and his family and caused such humiliation and how he wanted to confront them.

Kiely and Drood met at the Cork airport and walked to the rented Daimler. Kiely said, "Dr. Drood, are you sure you want to meet these people? Donlan's mind is half mush from the drink and McClellan's brain never emerges from the grip of his Alzheimer's affliction. Their ability to understand what they did more than thirty years ago is doubtful and the Irish statute of limitation is long past for McClellan's crimes. And I'm sorry to report your old schoolmaster has been in the company of his departed ancestors and the holy saints in heaven since a week ago. If I may ask, what purpose will meeting Donlan and McClellan serve?"

Robert stood for a long time with damp eyes and in a soft voice answered, "I've tried with every fiber of my intellect to rid myself of the haunting memories of the bestial behavior of McClellan. I've railed against God for allowing such egregious evil to go unpunished. Meeting McClellan again may or may not mitigate the memories, but I must do it. As for Donlan, I just want to meet him to remind him of his childhood nastiness and the grief he caused me." Robert had never before revealed these feelings to anyone. He was like a traveler telling his most intimate thoughts to a stranger.

They drove to Donlan's sleazy pub. Kiely pointed out Donlan, a dissipated figure slouched alone at a small table staring into his empty glass. Kiely withdrew. Robert sat down across from Donlan and said, "Hello, Rinty; I'm Robert Drood." Donlan gave him an uncomprehending stare but said nothing. "We went to school together when we were seven or eight years old. Do you remember?"

Donlan squinted at Robert in his fine suit, the likes of which had never before passed through the doors of any pubs in this area of town. He hesitated and said in a slurred voice, "I can't recall right off. I'd have to think on it for a time. Maybe a fresh jar would clarify my mind. Maybe it would be even better if the jar was fortified with a wee bit of Bushmills." Robert ordered the drink for Donlan. Although his mind was scrambled, he was cunning as a rat for recognizing a drink-cadging opportunity. He did not have a clue who Robert was, but guessed if he faked remembering him and prolonged the discussion, he could nick him for a few more drinks.

Robert tried to refresh Donlan's memory. "I'm the grubby kid who showed up at our school Christmas party empty-handed in your hand-me-down shirt. I provided laughs and entertainment for you and those nasty little sods in our class after you told them it was your castoff shirt that your mother had donated to the St. Vincent de Paul charity store. You all thought I was a worthless little bugger who would never amount to anything. I was so embarrassed and humiliated, I ran home and did not come back to school for days."

"Oh, yes, now it's coming back to me. How've ye been all of these years? You're looking grand. Some of the old schoolmates are still around—most of them without employment. The smart ones went across the water long ago to find work. The next time ye come by, I'll round up those who are still here for a few jars and some *craic*. Now, what was your name again?"

The pub keeper winked at Robert and shook his head. Further discussion was futile. Robert left two twenties to keep Donlan fueled until closing time while he tried to recall who Robert was and the names of some of his classmates he had not thought of for twenty-five years. Donlan's mind was an alcohol-ruined wasteland.

The pub occupants crowded to the door and windows to watch and wonder who in the world Rinty's grand visitor could be. They asked Rinty who he was as they shared in the bounty of the twenties left by Robert, but he had already forgotten his name.

Kiely and Robert returned to the Daimler parked at the curb for the drive to the home for Alzheimer's patients to visit McClellan.

They rode down a long park-like drive to a grand Georgian building and entered the broad, well-lit reception hall. Kiely explained, "If a man has Alzheimer's disease in Ireland and he's rich, as McClellan obviously is, he can live in splendor. If he's poor, the social system has no more to offer than a dingy cot in a cold, damp, dilapidated barracks."

Kiely had set up an appointment for Robert to meet the head sister. With a thick voice, he said, "Sister, I knew Mr. McClellan in my childhood here in Cork. I want to see him again."

"Dr. Drood, I can allow you to see him if you insist, but it will do you no good. He hasn't had a rational thought for a year. Even his wife and daughters no longer visit him."

They went to his private room. McClellan's cadaverous body was belted into a wheelchair. A thin tube ran from under his bathrobe to a plastic bag. His once hooded eyes were now sunken into their sockets with the unseeing look of a fish market salmon. His toothless mouth gaped and drooled. The jagged scar on his exposed, skinny leg was a reminder of the time Robert slashed him with a pitchfork after he raped Bridget. Like a record with a stuck needle, he said, "Property prices are going up." The sister said he would repeat these words every waking hour. It was hard for Robert to accept that this sorry carcass was once the satyr who ruined his sister, abused his mother, and caused him a life of reliving hellish memories of his crimes.

He stared at McClellan, the target of his hate for more than thirty years, and slowly shook his head. Even though he knew it was useless, he bent over and whispered in McClellan's ear, "When you die, if God is just, he will design a place for you where the fiends of Hell, for all eternity, will use you for their laboratory rat for testing new tortures and agonies." He nodded to Kiely to make the proper exit remarks to the head sister and left the building. When Kiely returned to the car, Robert stood beside it pale and stone-faced while he stared down at the cobblestone pavement.

By the time Kiely and Robert parted at the airport, Robert had recovered control of his emotions. "I could have just as well talked to a pair of cretins. I see no purpose in you investigating Donlan and McClellan any further, but keep on with your efforts to locate my father."

When Robert boarded his plane for the trip back to California, he sat with his eyes closed and his fingers laced behind his head while he thought: What a bitter disappointment it is to be deprived of the satisfaction I dreamed of for so many years when I would finally encounter McClellan and Donlan again. And to make it even worse, I find that my schoolmaster is dead. Now only their victims remember their sins; it all seems so futile. If I could just remove that terrible chapter of my life. A line I once read by Oliver Goldsmith runs through my mind, "Every man has a thousand thoughts that arise without his power to suppress."

Robert unlaced his numb fingers and slipped into a troubled sleep. The flight attendant spread a light blanket over him, and wondered why he tossed and groaned like he was carrying an unbearable load.

The falloff of silicon chip sales that started in Europe now spread around the world. The historical AMSCO two-digit growth rate dropped to a single-digit figure and the stock price tanked. Robert questioned Nathan Norton about the stock price fall. Norton said, "Wall Street investors are ruthless to companies that do not deliver on their expectations; they take them out behind the barn and shoot them if they miss their anticipated numbers—even though the numbers were likely generated by Wall Street hotshots in the first place."

Robert tried to force sales back on track with relentless pressure on his executives to sell harder, develop new products faster, and cut costs. He was merciless with anyone he did not believe was aggressive enough in maintaining AMSCO's historical growth curve.

Robert's motivation for strenuous action was urgent because of his need to receive a large year-end bonus to cover the mounting bills for his Irish estate and losses on his poorly performing and highly margined stock investments.

Robert's party, with Pamela as his guest of honor, was one of the most lavish given in San Francisco for years. AMSCO planes fanned out over the country to ferry out-of-town guests to the party.

Robert received his guests in his enormous condominium. By now he had expanded it to include the entire floor of the building—all at AMSCO expense. Pamela stood at his side in her stunning Dior gown and elegant jewelry. She captivated the guests with her understated elegance and mellifluous voice.

The view across the city to Alcatraz and the Golden Gate Bridge through the windows of the condominium living room and from the expansive balconies was awesome. Champagne flowed from a fountain capped by a trio of mermaids sculpted in ice. In each room there appeared to be life-size human statues. The statues were not what they seemed; they were recent mime graduates from *Ecole Internationale de Mimodrame de Paris Marcel Marceau*. Robert flew them over from France for the party. One "statue" winked at an astonished observer; another flicked a lewd finger at a guest who patted its rump.

Next, the party moved to the top floor banquet hall where the catering staff, borrowed from the Fairmont Hotel, served one of the most elaborate dinners they had ever prepared. Each guest received a gift that would please a Saudi prince; Robert's assistant and the corporate gift advisor at the posh Gump's store selected the gifts.

Pamela and Robert drank nightcaps together after the party. Pamela glowed from the excitement of the evening. They both agreed they were excited about being together and wanted to continue their relationship. Neither, however, could yet say they were in love. Pamela still suffered from the abusive treatment by her ex-husband and was leery about entering a new commitment that might lead to the same end. Robert could not say he loved Pamela with the omnipresent issues of his childhood still gnawing at him. They concluded their nightcaps and agreed to continue seeing each other as often as possible. Pamela planned to return home to Northern Ireland the next day.

Robert received regular calls from Desmond Bowen on Hollycourt's restoration progress. He usually explained new problems requiring additional work and money. Some of the work could have been deferred, but the restoration had become an obsession for Robert; he always authorized the requests. Bowen hired an interior designer experienced with historical decorating. She acquired furnishings and placed them in temporary storage. The costs for restoration, interior decorating, furnishings, and landscaping escalated.

Robert studied historic restorations and period furnishings. During his frequent trips to Ireland, he toured many of the great Irish houses and castles as a guest of the owners who were always helpful to anyone who was preserving another decaying Irish Georgian estate.

After an evening of thinking through every possible way to extricate himself from his dire financial predicament, Robert concocted a convoluted plan to enrich himself at the expense of the AMSCO treasury—a plan that was unequivocally fraudulent.

Seymour Weis, Robert's acerbic personal accountant, called for yet another review of his perilous financial situation. Weis aimed his horsy face at Robert and rasped, "I called for this meeting to again discuss your deteriorating financial condition. You're like a man in a canoe who won't even help himself by paddling backwards when his boat nears a waterfall. You spend money like a forty-niner who discovered the mother lode. How you can piss your bloated salary down a rat hole is beyond me. You don't pay your bills. You pour money into that place in Ireland that you need like a woman needs a fly in her pants, and you blow money on all of those women you squire around like you discovered a secret tunnel into Ft. Knox. And you buy tons of artsy stuff you seldom look at after you take it home.

"Preparations are under way to bring legal action against you for overdue bills, and when it starts it will be an avalanche. The tabloids already are sniffing around for an angle to feature you in one of their lurid articles. I can see the headlines now: Million Dollar Salary Not Enough to Feed CEO's Greed. Your compulsion to spend is like an out-of-control oil well fire. Your only solution is to practice frugality. I've used up my last smoke-and-mirror trick for you. There's nothing more I can do." Weis thumbed his flapping shirttail into his expansive trouser waistband and concluded his scolding. "Now tell me what the hell you plan to do about your foolish financial mess?"

Robert anticipated Weis would flay him. He was prepared for the onslaught. He had tried so many times before to stop his drunken sailor spending without success; he did not consider frugality a viable answer now. He was well down the road executing his imaginative plan to end his financial plight, but he was not going to share it with Weis. "Seymour, you have explained my financial status with singular clarity. I have a plan for solving the problem. Can you buy me four more months of time?"

"I didn't hear the words spending curtailment, shut down the Irish house restoration project, or balance the checkbook. Without these elements, your plan is as suspect as the pleas of innocence by the sauced-up navy officers after the infamous tail-hook incident where they all swore they did not assault the women guests during their drunken binge. I can't wait to hear you explain your intellectually stimulating scheme for turning base metal into gold. I know you can out-think and out-talk any auditor in the country, but eventually you must pay the piper. I hope your plan—or is it a connivance—considers the consequences if it includes graft or corruption."

Weis put on an exasperated look and snapped his briefcase shut. "I don't know why every meeting with you turns out like the biblical scene in *The Parable of the Prodigal Son* where the boy foolishly squanders his inheritance on wild living. Yes, I can buy you four more months, but that's the limit."

When Robert did not receive his anticipated year-end bonus, he thought of how the AMSCO compensation committee had unfairly compensated him: Why don't they pay a bonus during down business cycles? It's harder to manage in a down market than when business is good. It was a difficult year at AMSCO. The results would have been a lot worse if the company did not receive my imaginative management. Other companies allow their CEOs to write their own executive pay plans that their compensation committees automatically endorse. Something needs to be done soon to provide the infusions of cash required for Hollycourt and to pay off my stock margin calls. It is getting more difficult—and even scarier—by the day.

Robert again reviewed every detail of the fraudulent plan for acquiring money that he had been developing in his mind for several months and assessed the risks. The plan was as crooked as a dog's hind leg, but it seemed to be foolproof with almost no chance of detection.

CHAPTER TWENTY-EIGHT

Robert initiated his scheme for acquiring four to five million dollars. He would skim money from the enormous Irish fab appropriation. The amount would be less than a quarter of one percent of the project cost; it should be nearly undetectable.

He put the first step in place by calling for a meeting of the executive committee of the Georgian Preservation Society. He presented them with a proposition: "I will donate Hollycourt and the funds for completing its restoration to our society with the condition that I may reside in the house until my death. Another condition is that the donation must not be revealed to the public. If this is agreeable, I will draw up documents for the transfer of ownership."

The board was stunned; it had never before been offered such a valuable donation. Although it did not like the idea of Robert using the estate for such a long time, it would not look a gift horse in the mouth. It accepted the donation along with its conditions.

Robert proceeded to the second step of his plan by calling Colson. Colson went to Robert's office with outward calm, but those who knew him could tell he was nervous when he hoisted up his trousers, tightly tucked in his shirttail, and ran his fingertips over his close-cropped hair.

Colson was relieved when Robert offered him a chocolate mint from the dish on his credenza. "Jerry, I want you to brief me on the major manufacturing equipment orders you're ready to issue for the Irish fab. We can only expect several years of advantage over our competitors when we place the new state-of-the-art fab in operation. If equipment problems cause start-up delays, our advantage is shaved away. We can minimize delays by purchasing the equipment only from companies with superior performance records. Which suppliers are you planning to use for the major equipment?"

"Applied Materials in Santa Clara is the recognized supplier for sophisticated high-end equipment. They are obsessive about selling only proven products. We plan to negotiate solely with them for the most critical equipment.

"We plan to request competitive bids for the less critical equipment. Companies such as von Kleinschmidt AG in Germany will be on the bidder's list for a great deal of this category of equipment. Von Kleinschmidt is better than its competitors by a narrow margin, but we don't think their advantage is sufficient to justify working solely with them."

"If we do purchase from von Kleinschmidt, what would be the value of the orders?"

When Colson mentioned a figure, Robert calculated how much it would be possible to skim from a contract of that magnitude. "Jerry, considering von Kleinschmidt has an edge on equipment reliability over its competition, even though it's narrow, I want you to order from them. We must minimize all risks every way we can."

"Okay, Robert, I think that's a good decision. I'll get right on it."

"Incidentally tell Dennis Curran that Jan Van Hook from our European finance group will occasionally visit him to review the status of the fab contracts. Van Hook is doing some special work for me, and I want him to gain exposure to this side of our business. Tell Curran to show Van Hook the books on anything he requests."

As Colson left, Robert thought of how Nikita Khrushchev once described his obedient aide. He said, "If I tell him to drop his pants and sit on a block of ice, he squats and sits on it until I tell him to stand." Robert smiled and thought this was how he would picture Colson in the future.

Colson often discussed his work with his wife, who was also an engineer, over their evening cocktails. "I wonder what was in Dr. Drood's bonnet today when I met with him. He wants me to place a large equipment order with von Kleinschmidt AG, a German equipment firm, without subjecting it to competitive bidding. He seems to have something up his sleeve, but I can't figure out what it is. It was a relief though when he didn't take a bite out of my butt as he usually does."

"Well, I only met him once; he made me very uneasy. I don't think I'd ever allow a fox like him to have access to my hen house."

Robert called Karl von Kleinschmidt. His call was put through as fast as if the chancellor of Germany was on the line. Von Kleinschmidt hoped to land large orders for the Irish fab, but he anticipated a bruising bidding contest against his competitors.

"Hello Karl, how are you," Robert said. "I was just thinking about our last visit when you asked if AMSCO could offer a person to serve on the Save the World Rainforests board. If the need is still open, we're now at a point where we can offer an AMSCO person for the position."

"Yes, Herr Dr. Drood, we still have an opening. We'd be honored to have an AMSCO individual on our board." Although there was no opening at the moment, von Kleinschmidt would expand the board to accommodate another person—anything to please Drood and to increase the likelihood for large orders.

"Good, we'll provide Jan Van Hook, one of our bright financial managers from AMSCO's European operations. We assume you'll use his expertise for financial committee work.

"Now, on a different subject; I know you're working through Mr. Curran in our Irish fab office in Dublin on equipment proposals. Of course, it is appropriate for you to continue working through his office. But, while the project proceeds there could be sensitive and confidential information or instructions I'd like to communicate to you. I may sometimes contact you through Mr. Van Hook."

"That sounds fine to me, Dr. Drood. Please have Mr. Van Hook call me, and I'll make the necessary arrangements for him to serve on the Save the World Rainforests board. Of course, we'll take full advantage of his financial expertise. And thank you for your call. I'm always available to talk to you and your staff in Ireland."

When von Kleinschmidt finished the call from Robert, he asked his sales vice president to come to his office. "I just had a call from Dr. Drood at AMSCO to offer a person for the Save the World Rainforests board. I wish the call had been to inform me of positive news about our pending equipment order for their Irish fab. However, it's never a bad sign when the CEO of such an important company calls during the middle of a bidding and negotiating process."

"What do you think he really wants?" his vice president skeptically asked.

"My sixth sense tells me there is more than meets the eye in regard to his call and offer of a new member for the Save the World Rainforests board.

"I'd guess a matter will arise that will fall outside the lily-white business practices espoused in the AMSCO ethics manuals. Oh, well, I'm accustomed to special arrangements with Eastern European, Chinese, and Latin American customers. The special arrangements always seem to end up with a request for us to transfer money to a private bank account in a dubious country. We'll wait to see what happens next."

Robert thought about Van Hook: I plan to use him to handle part of the scam I'm setting up with von Kleinschmidt AG. With his jellyfish spine, he is ideal for the task. But putting up with his repulsive toadying is the high price I must pay to pull off the scam.

Robert asked his assistant to schedule a meeting with Van Hook in his Berlin Hotel suite when he visited Europe a few days later. He told her to tell Van Hook not to speak to anyone, including his boss, about the meeting.

Before leaving on his trip, Robert read Van Hook's personnel file. It noted his high intelligence and unusual loyalty, but it also commented on his low self-confidence and constant sucking up to his superiors.

Van Hook could not sleep because of excitement and anxiety after he received the call to meet Dr. Drood. When they met, Robert calmed him down with small talk and then went on to the purpose of the meeting. "Jan, von Kleinschmidt AG, a German chip equipment company, has a high interest in supporting a nonprofit natural resources conservation group. Karl von Kleinschmidt is the owner of von Kleinschmidt AG and the chairman of a non-profit group called Save the World Rainforests. He contributes a small percentage of his company's revenue to this organization. I'm interested in this group and also in an organization in Ireland called the Georgian Preservation Society where I'm a board member. I want AMSCO to support both of these organizations through orders we are about to place for von Kleinschmidt equipment for our new Irish fab.

"I've arranged for you to serve on the Save the World Rainforests board. I hope this is agreeable to you." Van Hook vigorously shook his head in assent. "I told Mr. von Kleinschmidt you should play an active role in the financial affairs of the group. And Jan, I do not want my interests revealed to anyone within our company or to the public. It is absolutely essential that keep this information to yourself.

"Jerry Colson will direct Dennis Curran, the Irish fab project manager, to order a large volume of equipment from von Kleinschmidt AG. I want you to meet with Curran and get in the loop in regard to the von Kleinschmidt orders. Curran will be informed of your visit to his office and asked to show you all information on equipment orders status."

"Does Mr. Curran know the purpose of my visit?" Van Hook asked.

"Absolutely not and don't reveal it to him. Just say you need fab equipment cost information for a confidential project you are working on for me.

"Then meet with Karl von Kleinschmidt. Tell him we expect him to include in his bid for the Irish fab equipment his normal donation for the Save the World Rainforests, but he should also add a five million dollar contribution to the Georgian Preservation Society. The contribution to the Georgian Preservation Society should be passed through you to me. I again stress you are not to tell anyone about this. And don't mention it to your boss. I've already told him of your new position on the Save the World Rainforests board, and that is all he needs to know.

"If there is an information leak, your career will be in peril. You're a smart accountant, so I expect you'll do all of this without a paper trail; do not put anything in writing. When the final check to the Georgian Preservation Society is written, your salary will increase by fifteen percent and you'll be promoted one level."

"Dr. Drood, am I free to call you if anything arises requiring your attention?"

"Of course, Jan. I may also want to meet with you now and then for briefings."

After the meeting with Van Hook, Robert once again reviewed his scam plan: Only von Kleinschmidt and Van Hook know what is happening, and they have compelling incentives to remain silent. Colson and Bartoluzzi know a few pieces of the plan, but not enough for them to piece it all together. The risk of the scam backfiring is close to nil. Actually, due to my dire need for money, there is no choice but to go ahead with the scam. The only viable alternative is personal bankruptcy, and that is untenable.

Robert recalled a history lesson from his school days at St. Ignatius in Chicago: When Julius Caesar anxiously prepared to cross the river Rubicon and lead his armies from Gaul into the forbidden territories of Italy, he shuddered, prayed to the Gods, and said, "*Alea iacta est* (The die is cast)." Robert thought: And the die is now also cast for me.

The Irish fab building construction was under way and the major chip manufacturing equipment orders were rapidly being issued. The schedule and cost estimates were in good shape. Curran's engineers planned to solicit competitive bids for the manufacturing equipment except for the sophisticated items from Applied Materials, Inc. Von Kleinschmidt AG was on the bidder's list for a major portion of the other equipment. Curran and his engineers were depending on aggressive competitive bidding and negotiating to keep the project within the estimated costs.

Curran was surprised when Colson called and directed him to buy von Kleinschmidt equipment without competitive bidding. When he asked for clarification, Colson gave a vague explanation. His directive did not cause Curran much concern because his engineers were skilled negotiators, and he thought they would bargain the price of the von Kleinschmidt equipment down to their budget estimates even without competitive bidding.

As the AMSCO engineers negotiated with von Kleinschmidt, they ran into difficulties. Based on their intimate knowledge of industry costs, they knew the price from von Kleinschmidt was several million dollars too high. Time was running out. Orders had to be placed soon to meet the project schedule.

Curran received a call from Van Hook requesting a visit to review the financial status of the Irish fab project. This seemed like an unusual request, but in a large company, it is not always possible to know the responsibilities and interests of everyone. Curran had his project cost accountant review the details of the cost control records with Van Hook. He seemed interested only in the items related to the stalled negotiations with von Kleinschmidt. He did not explain why he focused only on von Kleinschmidt.

Dennis and Carly periodically met for lunch. They liked to share their problems and business concerns. When Dennis brought up Van Hook's visit, some of Carly's Oklahoma oil-field lingo from her youth came through. "When I seen that conceited rooster prancin' down the hall yesterday in his hoisted-up pinstripe pants, I remembered him from the Polish project we worked on together a few years back. Every time Van Hook met anyone he thought might have a little horsepower, his knees went wobbly. If he had to explain unfavorable financial figures to management, he slumped around for days looking like a wildcatter on his way to tell his banker he just drilled another dry hole. What do you think the pesky little weasel really wanted?"

"I can't figure it out, Carly. For some reason he seemed to be only interested in von Kleinschmidt AG, the firm that won't quote us reasonable equipment prices. Colson said we must negotiate exclusively with them. Their reputation is good but not that much better than the competitors. "

"Well, Dennis, I'd watch Van Hook like a hawk. I wouldn't trust the pompous peacock any farther than I could throw a bull by the tail.

"And to completely change the subject before we go back to work, I'm pleased you're doing all the communicating with the government bureaucrats. I never learned to speak 'governmentese.'"

"That's okay, I learned 'political speak' in the Air Force. With practice you can say all of that stuff you have to say with a straight face. And, Carly, I appreciate you inviting me to your staff meetings and all of the time you take to mentor me on fab operations management. I feel like I'm being tutored by a master."

As they concluded lunch, Dennis said, "Carly, if you and Wally haven't had your next final squabble before Friday, come over to my house to see Mary Catherine and me after work for a drink, and then we can go out to supper. Mary Catherine has heard of a new restaurant that serves great roast lamb. She says that there is a remarkable lyric Irish tenor named Paddy Homan performing this weekend."

"It usually takes at least three weeks for me to piss Ol' Wally off bad enough for him to hightail it back to California, and he has only been here for ten days. We'll take you up on the invitation. And I promise there will be no shop talk."

Dennis's daughters were delighted to hear of Carly's Friday evening visit. She always brought them extravagant gifts.

Even though Carly was wealthy from her AMSCO stock options and high salary, she lived as if she had the income of a beginning engineer. She covertly gave away her money by the tons. Every needy church, family with a sick child, and orphanage in her small hometown in Oklahoma received anonymous checks from an obscure California bank. It did not take much of a detective to guess the source of the gifts, but the recipients respected her wish for anonymity. Knowing Carly was a subscriber to the local newspaper, they often expressed their gratitude for their "unknown benefactor" by writing an appreciation letter to the editor. One of the letter writers with good sense of humor noted at the bottom of her letters, "Carbon copy: God."

Van Hook met Karl von Kleinschmidt at a Save the World Rainforests board meeting. Afterward they had a drink in Van Hook's hotel. "Mr. Van Hook, we're in negotiations on equipment for the AMSCO Irish fab project," von Kleinschmidt said. "The pressure on us to reduce our prices is intense. Your Mr. Kim Park Chin knows what competitive equipment prices should be, and he's quite unhappy with us because our quoted prices are high. I know the project is not in your province, but perhaps you could advise me on AMSCO's business culture so I'll know how to proceed. We could lower our price four to five million dollars and conclude the negotiations, but we can't do it if we must stick to your direction to make a five million dollar donation to the Georgian Preservation Society. My people want to lower the price. Naturally they don't know about the need for the five million dollar donation."

If there was one thing Van Hook did well, it was take orders from his CEO as if he were a Nazi *Wehrmacht* officer receiving directions from the General Staff and High Command. "Mr. von Kleinschmidt, you must hold the line in regard to reserving moneys in your proposal for the donation to the Georgian Preservation Society. You may alienate Mr. Park Chin, but I think you can count on receiving orders soon. I again remind you, this must be handled in strict confidence, and I must be the conduit for the transfer of funds to the Georgian Preservation Society."

A few weeks later, Curran's engineers were still at loggerheads because of the bloated von Kleinschmidt equipment prices. He said, "I called Colson again to see if he would relent on issuing equipment orders to von Kleinschmidt AG. He stuck to his guns. We'll have our knuckles wrapped for overrunning our cost estimates on this equipment, but if we miss the project completion schedule, Carly and Ken Yee will boil us in oil. Let's release the orders to von Kleinschmidt even though we know the prices are too high."

Kim said, "I know when Colson gives his imperious orders, we must follow them, but I'm going to write a confidential memorandum with copies only for you and me. If we're ever called on the carpet because of von Kleinschmidt's overpriced equipment, this memo will record why it happened. We're getting the shaft. Yesterday in our umpteenth negotiating meeting with von Kleinschmidt, I tried to break the logjam by requesting a look at their cost estimates. Their response was an unqualified *Nein*."

"The memo is a good idea, Kim. Let me also initial it."

Fionnoula took a call for Dennis from California. He was urgently occupied and told her he'd return the call later. Fionnoula would not be put off. "I know Himself is working on urgent matters, but His Worship is on the line and you should take the call." By now Dennis knew Fionnoula's nicknames for people and the caller was Dr. Drood.

Dennis stepped into his office and said, "Hello, Dr. Drood."

"Hello, Dennis. We're having a board meeting soon, and I want to make some comments on the fab project. I'd like you and Carly to give Ken Yee and me an on-site review of the project before the meeting. We'll be in your office next week."

"We're pleased to hear of your visit, Dr. Drood. We'll be prepared to give you a project status report. By the way, the Irish have an insatiable appetite for information about the project. Would you be willing to participate in a meeting with the media while you're here?"

"Of course, Dennis, if you think it will be of value."

Dennis and Carly met to arrange Drood's visit. They decided to invite several members of their staffs including Fionnoula to the meeting with Drood and Yee. Dennis was now loaning her half time to Carly to work in her human resources group. She was proving to be a whiz at interviewing and evaluating people for jobs. Carly planned to promote her to Human Resources Manager of the new fab in the near future.

Carly coached Fionnoula on executive meeting protocol. She said, "I can suppress my Oklahoma oil field personality when I meet with the company suits. Do you think if we invite you to the meeting with Dr. Drood and Dr. Yee, you can put a lid on your free-spirited behavior?"

"When I worked in the U.S. in a bank, I once had to meet with the bank president. My boss told me to 'cool my jets' before the meeting. After I learned what that expression meant, I took a tranquilizer and pretended my dog had just died. I was able to pull it off so I'm confident I can do it again with His Worship and Ye Yee."

After Dennis set up the press conference to be held during Drood's visit, he received a call from Minister O'Kane's officious administrative assistant, who had sniffed out information on the AMSCO media meeting. He demanded, "Minister O'Kane will attend your press conference and the photographing session after the conference. He will stand beside Dr. Drood—in fact slightly ahead of him—when the photos are taken." Dennis reluctantly agreed, but he was concerned because he did not know O'Kane's purpose.

Dennis and Carly co-chaired the project review meeting and site tour for Drood and Yee. When Dennis reported on the project cost he said, "The costs for each portion of the projects are within the budget estimates, except we'll be four to five million high on equipment from von Kleinschmidt AG. We don't have much leverage with their price because they are the sole source supplier for their equipment."

Drood was undisturbed when he cut in, "I know von Kleinschmidt equipment from my days when I was a fab manager in Poughkeepsie. Their equipment is reliable, and I think Jerry Colson called the right shot when he decided to order from them. The overrun is a small percentage of the overall project cost and is not enough to necessitate resubmitting a revised appropriation request to the board for approval."

Dennis was startled at Drood's response. It was contrary to AMSCO culture to be complacent with cost overruns no matter how small. And he wondered how Drood already knew Colson had directed him to buy equipment from von Kleinschmidt.

When Carly reported on the status of staffing for the new fab, Yee asked, "What percentage of our professional workforce do you expect will be Irish, and how many will be repatriates from abroad?"

Carly nodded to Fionnoula to answer Yee's question. "I'll answer your question, Dr. Yee, but I must first give you a word of historical perspective on why so many gifted people left Ireland. The tradition for massive emigration started two hundred years ago with 'The Flight of the Wild Geese' as the exodus of the cream of Irish youth was called. After a valiant fight and defeat by a merciless British army, the Irish survivors were forced into exile. The closing lines of an old verse about a boatload of exiles discovered at sea tell of their dreams for returning to Ireland:

Jesus save you gentry! Why are ye so white?
Sitting so strange and still in the misty light?
Nothing ails us brother, joyous souls are we,
Sailing home together on the morning sea.

"Many emigrants still have a visceral desire to sail home to Ireland. Some are returning now that worthwhile jobs are becoming available.

"Now to directly answer your question, Dr. Yee: From the job applications coming to us, I believe initially seventy percent of our professionals will be Irish with half of them being citizens returning home—and it looks like a goodly number will be women. In three years, about ninety-five percent of our professionals should be Irish."

Yee normally would not have tolerated such a circuitous answer, but he let it stand because of his similar feelings about his Chinese countrymen.

Robert asked an intricate technical question about future chip designs and the flexibility of the Irish fab to manufacture them. Dennis knew of Robert's deep technical knowledge and interest so he signaled Kim to answer.

Kim kept in close touch with his friend Nathan Veldthoff, the company research and development wizard, so he could launch into an answer brimming with esoteric technical facts. Kim looked like Oddjob, the hulking Korean chauffeur in the James Bond movie *Goldfinger* who could cut off his adversary's head with his razor-edged derby hat brim when he tossed it frisbee-fashion. Kim was one of the few engineers who could design methods for manufacturing the devices conceived by Veldthoff. When Kim completed his complex answer, Fionnoula whispered out of the corner of her mouth to Carly, "And that's why we call him 'Our Top Chip.'"

When the press conference convened and the photographers were about to take pictures, Minister O'Kane stepped to the microphone. "We're not only fortunate to have AMSCO as one of Ireland's principal industrial citizens, we're honored Dr. Robert Drood is its chairman.

He's a modern day 'Wild Goose' who returned to Ireland since his childhood emigration from Cork. We're also honored he has become an active member of the Georgian Preservation Society board and is doing such a marvelous job of restoring Hollycourt, one of our national treasures."

Robert reddened and jabbed his fingertips to his forehead. Now that O'Kane had revealed his birthplace and his ownership of Hollycourt, his detractors could say the new fab was located in Ireland to make him look like a returning Yankee hotshot. A senior officer of Titan Motors suffered the same charge when he was ridiculed for building an automobile factory in his native Spain. And the risk just increased that someone might figure out his fraudulent arrangement for financing Hollycourt. Robert whispered to Dennis, "Shut this goddamn press conference down—now!"

After the meeting, he motioned with a thumb jab for Dennis, Carly, and Yee to return to the conference room. He slammed the door and while standing fumed, "Never again do I want to be involved with a conference that goes out of control like this one just did. My private life is not for public display." He glared at Carly and Dennis and demanded, "Who told O'Kane of my birthplace and my involvement with Hollycourt?"

Carly said, "I don't know who did it. I was unaware you were born in Ireland or owned a place here until O'Kane spoke."

Dennis said, "Minister O'Kane has a lickspittle administrative assistant with political aspirations. My guess is he dug up the information somehow and told O'Kane. Like with Carly, the information was news to me."

To Robert's surprise and relief, there was no public or stockholder reaction to O'Kane's remarks. He decided it was safe to let the fraudulent financing for Hollycourt proceed according to his plan.

Drood met with Van Hook to review the status of the fraudulent scheme for ripping off the fab project. "I've set up a money transfer system that leaves no audit trail," Van Hook explained. "Money from von Kleinschmidt AG will go to Save the World Rainforests according to the normal von Kleinschmidt practice. Money for the Georgian Preservation Society will be laundered through an Istanbul bank. The bank can send checks to the Georgian Preservation Society or to any other designated place. The balance in the Istanbul bank account now stands at well over one million dollars." Van Hook looked like a puppy expecting a pat on the head for performing a trick.

Robert could not stand being around Van Hook, but he forced himself to pretend satisfaction, "Well done, Jan. Now draw two checks on the Istanbul bank: one to Hans Bartoluzzi in Zurich for one million dollars—it will pay off a private loan that he has made to me; and one with the rest of the account balance—through me—to the Georgian Preservation Society. Later when von Kleinschmidt makes his full payment to the Istanbul account, close it out with a final check to the Georgian Preservation Society. And, Jan, I again remind you not to discuss this with anyone and leave no paper trail. By the way, take ten thousand dollars from the Istanbul bank for yourself. You have earned a consulting fee." Robert thought: This dip into the till for Van Hook's personal benefit helps reduce the risk that the little creep will leak information about the scam of the fab project.

Robert reflected on the status of his fraudulent manipulation of AMSCO funds: The scam is now fully in action and my money worries will soon be over. Van Hook's the only other person with knowledge of all of the pieces. All he needs to keep him from singing is regular strokes of his ridiculous ego. The plan still should be detection-proof.

CHAPTER TWENTY-NINE

On his next trip to Europe, Robert visited Hollycourt. Now that adequate money was available from his scam, work was progressing rapidly. The house restoration was nearly complete, and the garden rebuilding was under way.

Pamela accompanied Robert. Ever-vigilant Guinness greeted them with a welcoming bark and a canine jig. He remembered Robert's earlier visit and hoped he would call on Paddy to celebrate with another round or two of Bushmills. His bark aroused Paddy who rocked to greet them with his peculiar side-to-side gait.

When the house and garden tour was completed, Paddy insisted on taking Robert and Pamela to the meadow to see the latest crop of calves. This reminded him of a story about an aging bull that was a laggard in performing his duties until the farmer had his veterinarian threaten him by revealing artificial insemination apparatus. It dawned on the bull that he could be declared redundant and hauled away to slaughter. He briskly pawed the ground and mounted the first heifer he saw with the hope that his spirited demonstration of youthful vigor would prolong his residency in his owner's meadow.

After the story, Paddy escorted them to his house to examine the farm records and honor their visit with a tot of Bushmills. Guinness was grateful for Paddy's customary thoughtfulness of rewarding him with a dollop. To Robert's surprise, the farm financial books were meticulous and showed a modest profit. It took an hour and a half for Robert and Pamela to depart from Paddy's captivating hospitality.

Robert and Pamela felt a warm glow after their day of visiting Hollycourt and hiking down quiet country roads. While they sat before an open fire in Robert's hotel suite, they sipped their evening drinks. It seemed like it was the right time to discuss their relationship. Although they had previously discussed marriage, they had not reached a definitive agreement. Pamela took on a serious look and said, "Robert, I love you more than I've ever loved anyone before. I can't imagine ever being happier than when I'm with you, and I can't stop thinking of how welcome you made me feel when I visited San Francisco. I know if we were together permanently, we would have to live in San

Francisco. I'm not sure I'm ready for that, especially with you away so much of the time. I need more time to think about it. But I can't bear the thought of another marriage going on the rocks."

Robert took a sip of his drink and said, "Pamela, I also have never cared for anyone this much. When we're apart, I constantly think of our next time together. And yet my record for personal bonding and commitment is poor. Maybe with more time, I can improve upon it. Let's go on like this for a while longer."

"Oh, Robert, I hoped you would feel that way."

When the restoration, furnishing, and landscaping of Hollycourt were complete, Robert occupied the house at every opportunity. He used it for parties and to entertain visitors, but he found he could also enjoy it when only he and Pamela shared it—and when she was unavailable he was quite satisfied to be alone basking in the pleasure of proprietorship.

During a weekend at Hollycourt, Robert's euphoria ended and his mood shifted to the downside. As often happened when he had a surge of good feelings, it was countered with memories of the torments of his childhood and the strangling fear that his good fortune could end. He lamented that he couldn't bond with Pamela—or anyone else. He wished his relationship with her could be like the one between Dennis and Mary Catherine Curran. When they were together it was like watching a soap opera love scene. Life seemed so unjust. He followed the American dream and succeeded beyond imagination, and yet it did not lead to a feeling of personal fulfillment. The dark and depressing memories clung to him all weekend like a damp spider web, and he didn't have the power to dispel them.

Kiely sent Robert a report on his father:

SEARCH FOR GEORGE DROOD

> George Drood is a motorcar salesman in Belfast. His health is good, but he shows the physical limitations that go with being more than sixty years old. He remains unmarried. His comfortable flat at 45 North Mill Road, where he lives alone, does not have a telephone. He meets his friends several times a week at their pub although he drinks sparingly. His life is confined to the few blocks between his flat and the automobile agency where he works. When the weather is fine on weekends and holidays, he usually sits on a park bench and reads or talks with friends.

Robert thought about a meeting with his father. But would it turn out to be futile as it was with Rinty Donlan and Brian McClellan? For more than thirty years he imagined a confrontation with them might dispel some of the resentment that haunted his mind and controlled his emotions. Because Donlan's mind was ruined with drink and McClellan's was eaten away with Alzheimer's disease, his confrontations with them had no more meaning than threats to a dog for yesterday's misconduct. He decided to sit on the information about his father for the present time. If he delayed the meeting, he could go on resenting him and savoring the satisfaction of a confrontation. He'd tell Kiely to bill him for his services and end his investigations.

The Irish fab went into production with minimum fanfare. Carly continued to manage it through the hectic start-up period. Dennis and part of his staff stayed on in Ireland to resolve remaining equipment problems while he waited for his next work assignment. Sales in Europe were recovering and it was now obvious building the new fab in Ireland had been a wise business decision.

Problems were still occurring with some of the von Kleinschmidt equipment. Several machines were so balky they had to be taken out of service. The von Kleinschmidt engineers claimed the problem was faulty operation by AMSCO personnel, and they declined to make restitution for the nonperforming machines. Dennis talked to the AMSCO lawyers who concurred that legal action could be taken to recover the cost of the machines.

Karl von Kleinschmidt called Drood. "Dr. Drood, I received your note some time ago thanking me for sending you several cases of wine from my vineyard. I hope you enjoyed it. And I trust our donations to the Georgian Preservation Society were all satisfactorily handled through the hands of Mr. Van Hook.

"Now I must bring up an unfortunate problem and ask your assistance in solving it. Your Irish fab people have taken legal action to resolve a dispute about the functioning of several of our machines. We respectfully disagree with them. We have ample evidence the fault is not with our machines. Perhaps you'd be so kind as to look into this matter yourself even though I know you have many other pressing matters on your agenda."

Robert winced knowing this was the price he must pay for von Kleinschmidt's cooperation in funneling money to the Georgian Preservation Society. "Karl, I'll look into this matter," he said. "And I'll direct our people to suspend legal action and to negotiate a resolution."

When Robert hung up, he called Colson and said, "I received a call from Karl von Kleinschmidt complaining that our people in Ireland are taking legal action over a dispute about the functioning of their equipment. Discontinue legal action, Jerry; settle the dispute by negotiation."

"Okay, Robert, that sounds like the best way to handle it."

Colson's direction to stop the legal action against von Kleinschmidt did not make sense to Dennis: Colson insisted on buying von Kleinschmidt equipment at a high price without competitive bidding because of its superiority. Some of it turned out to be junk, and now we must not take legal action to settle the matter. The whole business with von Kleinschmidt has stunk to high heaven from the beginning.

Dennis came home and mixed evening drinks. Mary Catherine knew he had something on his mind when she saw the small red spot on his forehead. She dreaded he was going to tell her of his next work assignment in a location away from her paradise in Ireland. He handed her a sheet of paper and said, "Read this. If I agree to it, it will be posted Monday."

The paper was a bulletin appointing him assistant manager of the Irish fab.

Mary Catherine let out a war hoop loud enough to be heard in the next county. "Tell me this is real and not a dream," she exclaimed. "Can you call Carly right now, and tell her you'll take the job before she changes her mind? My life since we moved to Ireland is like a trip to fairyland. I'm so happy it won't end yet. Congratulations, Dennis my lad. If you continue to treat me this way, I'll reward you by giving up my other lovers."

"I'm not worried about the other lovers. Where would you find a better one than the one you already have? And Mary Catherine, this is the first step to a bigger deal. Carly will likely leave when the fab is fully operational, and I'm in a strong position to be her successor."

Since Robert completed rehabilitating Hollycourt, his compulsion for material acquisitions did not wane. When he learned more about how other unprincipled CEOs lived at the expense of their companies, it whetted his appetite for more homes, lavish parties, rented yachts, and prestigious golf club memberships. He learned how they lived like billionaires even though their companies did not excessively compensate them. Robert sought out these CEOs.

After he gained their confidence, they explained how they manipulated their companies to buy whatever they wanted and used the acquisitions for their personal purposes. One CEO who managed a large conglomerate of industrial companies was especially interesting to

Robert. His company owned fancy condominiums in big cities around the world, sprawling estates in glamorous locations, a yacht, a private golf course, and a wide-bodied jet. His parties, held in exotic locations, would be the envy of Roman emperors. Almost all of the acquisitions were bought without board approvals. Robert decided acquiring new possessions this way was simpler and less risky than the dangerous manipulations he had used to pay for Hollycourt.

He used his newly acquired information to go on a rampage of senseless acquisitions: condominiums in New York, London, and Paris; a mansion in Palm Beach; and a Boeing Business Jet. Norton set aside his qualms about Robert's foolish acquisition spree after Robert told him to buy an estate with AMSCO funds in the Bahamas for his personal use. Robert and Norton reasoned they were not really stealing because the new acquisitions were secretly held on AMSCO books.

Even though the rampant acquisitions were carried out without board approval, some of the board members knew about them and accepted Robert's invitation to enjoy them for their own purposes.

Soon after Robert became the AMSCO chairman and the terms of the existing board members expired, he replaced them with new members who would be loyal to him and give him carte blanche authority for managing AMSCO. He did not, however, try to squeeze Justin Cairncross off the board because he was too powerful to alienate. Cairncross would normally have learned of Robert's acquisition binges and squelched them, but he was spending almost all of his time fending off mounting competitive threats to Titan Motors from offshore auto companies.

Van Hook called Dennis to request another visit to the Irish fab. He again said he wanted to look over the cost control records. Dennis asked the fab financial controller to learn more about Van Hook. "Van Hook's responsibilities don't in any way include the fab capital costs." But he added, "He hints of his special relationship with Dr. Drood any time anyone will listen to him. This may be true. They have been seen together several times."

When Van Hook arrived at the fab office, Dennis pulled out the project cost control records. Again, Van Hook only showed interest in the amount of the von Kleinschmidt equipment purchases. He jotted down the contract and final invoice payment amounts.

Dennis asked, "Jan, can you tell me more about von Kleinschmidt A.G.? They have caused us more grief than any other contractor on the fab project. We paid too much for their equipment, and some of it functioned so badly we had to remove it from operation. We're trying to negotiate a settlement with them, but we're not making any headway."

Van Hook said, "They are a reputable company; I don't know more than that."

He did not want to talk about von Kleinschmidt; he jumped to his feet and pranced out of the office.

Dennis had asked Fionnoula to sit with him in the meeting with Van Hook. Her ability to see what was on people's minds was extraordinary. After the meeting she said, "Dennis, Van Hook is as neurotic as a hen the first day she takes her chicks from the nest into the barnyard. Something is bothering him."

"What do you think he really wants?"

"I don't know. I can't speak of his purpose, but I'm of the mind he'll eventually let something slip out of his mouth and cut his throat with his own tongue."

Dennis borrowed unused equipment from other AMSCO fabs to temporarily replace the unsatisfactory von Kleinschmidt machinery after receiving Colson's authorization. The older technology replacement equipment caused a reduction of chip quality and efficiency and prevented the fab from reaching some of its objectives.

Carly called Dennis to her office and with a grim look shut the door. "Ken Yee called me last evening. He said the board is dissatisfied with our tardiness in coming up to the fab's projected profitability. They say the fab is overdue on delivering the promised quality and profitability—as if we didn't already know it. They've hired Harlan, Bonesteel, and Hawkins, a consulting firm, to come here to assess our problems. We're to cooperate with them. Their team will be here Monday."

The small patch on Dennis's forehead flashed fiery red. "Why in the world would they do that? Didn't Colson explain what we have so often reported to him? The problem is the von Kleinschmidt equipment, and that's because Colson shoved them up our nose and made us order from them without competitive bidding."

"I brought that up to Ken. He said Colson claims it was your decision, and you should be able to explain why you bought the von Kleinschmidt equipment."

"That lying bastard! He's the one who told me to do it. I even called back several times to ask him if we could consider another supplier. And don't you remember when Dr. Drood was here, he said, 'Colson made a good decision to contract with von Kleinschmidt.' Apparently we're faced with memories of convenience from both Colson and Drood."

"Do you have anything from Colson in writing?"

"No, we only have Kim's internal memorandum on what happened. All of Colson's directions were verbal."

"Dennis, for some reason someone is trying to set you up as a scapegoat. I suggest you cooperate with the consultants. Don't appear defensive, and wait to see what their report says before you go ballistic. It could be a tempest in a teapot. I know the consulting firm. They'll be thorough and honest with their findings. Meanwhile let's continue to give high priority to fixing our remaining fab start-up problems."

Drood had unsuccessfully tried to dissuade the board from hiring Harlan, Bonesteel, and Hawkins. He did not want the spotlight to shine on the fab and possibly illuminate his scam of the von Kleinschmidt equipment orders. He spoke with Colson, von Kleinschmidt, and Van Hook requesting them to seal their lips on providing meaningful information to the consultants related to the decision to award equipment orders to von Kleinschmidt.

CHAPTER THIRTY

After weeks of interrogation and review of thousands of documents, the consulting firm submitted its report to the board on the reasons for the Irish fab not achieving its production and quality objectives. The report was supported with substantiating evidence for its findings.

Carly received a numbered and registered copy of the consultant's confidential report. She called Dennis to her office and said, "Read this."

HARLAN, BONESTEEL, & HAWKINS
Industrial Consultants
5000 Eight Mile Road
Detroit, MI, U.S.A.

November 3, 2004

Copy 6 of 15
Registered with
C. L. Jackson

CONFIDENTIAL

EXECUTIVE SUMMARY

1.0 OBJECTIVES
    A Determine why the AMSCO Irish fab is not meeting its quality and cost objectives.
    B Determine if the fab is capable of operating at its specified capacity.

2.0 FINDINGS
    A The major outstanding problems with the fab lie with manufacturing equipment supplied by von Kleinschmidt AG.
    B When work that is under way to replace the von Kleinschmidt equipment is completed, the fab should reach its objectives.

3.0 RECOMMENDATIONS
- A Negotiate financial resolution with von Kleinschmidt AG. (It is unclear why a decision was made to order equipment from von Kleinschmidt AG without competitive bidding.)
- B Allow the competent current Irish fab management team to continue working to achieve the fab objectives.

When Dennis finished reading, Carly said, "Dennis, if you do nothing, this whole thing will die when we get our productivity and profitability up, but your career may have a shadow over it. Only you can remove it. I think Colson is the snake in the grass on this problem, but my opinion will carry little weight in the AMSCO power corridors. I don't know who else may be involved with Colson. The senior level of the company runs with a different playbook that I never could understand. If you decide to fight this, I'm willing to take on some of your work to give you time to find out who's behind it all. If you decide to run down the rat that caused this mess, it may turn nastier than a mad rattlesnake."

"Carly, when I was at the Air Force Academy, we were indoctrinated with the words 'Honor and Duty.' I believed those words then, and I'm old-fashioned enough to still believe them. I'm going to the mat on this—and I'm grateful to have a boss like you to support me."

That evening, Dennis explained his predicament to Mary Catherine and asked her to help prop him up during the difficult months ahead. "I'll keep the oil boiling for you to dump from the castle turrets onto the heads of those slimy snakes," she said. "We won't let the slithery bastards get the best of our Dennis."

Dennis had a few sleepless nights before he made his first move. He called Bill Beck, the AMSCO security director.

After Dennis explained his situation, Beck said, "You can't get your hands on enough investigators and lawyers to dig up all of the required facts and evidence on all related subjects; I suggest you list everything that has happened since you moved to Ireland that seems odd or unusual. This may narrow down the number of mouse holes we need to watch. We often use this procedure, and it sometimes leads us to the guilty mouse. I'll be in Paris in ten days to meet with the French authorities on computer-related crimes of mutual interest. Can you come over from Ireland and meet me there to review your list and work out the next step?"

"Yes, Bill, I'll sure be there."

Dennis developed his list of unusual events and sent it to Beck in preparation for their Paris meeting:

November 2004
D. Curran

CONFIDENTIAL

LIST OF UNUSUAL EVENTS RELATED TO SELECTION OF VON KLEINSCHMIDT AG EQUIPMENT FOR IRISH FAB

1.0 Something is fishy about Jan Van Hook's repeated visits to the Irish fab and his singular focus on von Kleinschmidt AG contract payments.

2.0 Why does Van Hook hint of his personal relationship with Dr. Drood? Dr. Drood has a reputation for being a lady's man whereas Van Hook is thought to be gay.

3.0 Why did Jerry Colson give direction to order equipment from von Kleinschmidt and then lie about it when something went wrong? And why did Dr. Drood not jump in to clarify matters? He knows Colson directed us to buy the von Kleinschmidt equipment without competitive bidding.

4.0 Why was Dr. Drood so accepting of von Kleinschmidt equipment problems and cost overruns?

5.0 Fionnoula O'Casey (a superb judge of human nature) observed during the last project review meeting that Dr. Drood was nervous and edgy when von Kleinschmidt and the project cost overrun were mentioned.

6.0 Why did Dr. Drood have a conniption when Minister O'Kane mentioned his birth in Ireland and his ownership of Hollycourt?

7.0 How can Dr. Drood live like a billionaire when he is not from a wealthy family?

cc: William Beck

Curran and Beck met in Paris. "Dennis, I've kept my ear to the rail since we last talked. I did some checking on the character of the people you mentioned in our preliminary discussions. Colson is noted for micromanaging his employees' work, and if senior people disagree with the results, he pretends it is all new to him. Dr. Drood intimidates him. He will claim black is white and up is down if he thinks that is what Dr. Drood wants to hear. He lives a modest personal life. Both Colson and his wife have good incomes. We'd have to take a look at his financial records to find out if he's on the take, but we've not yet found any evidence that he is.

"Van Hook's a wizard with figures, but he's not capable of managing or strategic thinking so his corporate growth potential is limited. Nevertheless, his drive to reach executive status is relentless. He circulates in the tawdry homosexual community of Berlin where he lives, but at work he remains in the closet. For important company social affairs, he hires unemployed actresses for his dates so he will appear to be straight. A gay man under these conditions is susceptible to blackmail. He recently received a promotion, and no one can figure out why. He seems to have impressed Dr. Drood for some reason."

Dennis said, "That partly explains why he acts like such a creep."

Beck went on. "Dr. Drood provides grist for the gossip mill with his womanizing, rampant spending, and lavish living. The source of his wealth is a mystery. Although some call him a discerning art collector, most say he's only a haphazard accumulator of stuff. Drood is an intellectual elitist. He puts anyone down who can't keep up with his enviable thinking speed unless he thinks they can do something for him.

"Firing employees whom Dr. Drood does not respect is as easy for him as sacrificing pawns in a chess game. Most people are on their guard in his presence. Yee is the only AMSCO executive he respects. The only time he is civil to other employees, for some inexplicable reason, is when he teaches company management courses. Teaching seems to trigger his good side."

Dennis said, "He's never treated me badly on any of his visits to the Irish fab. Maybe he thinks I can do something for him."

"Maybe that's a clue," Beck said. "Let's add that as a point on your list of unusual things."

"Karl von Kleinschmidt is from a wealthy, ancient German family. He prides himself on his moralistic Catholicism. Nevertheless, he deals all over the world and has a different viewpoint from Americans on what moral business behavior is. He loves to focus his attention on sales and is relentless in doing whatever it takes to land orders for his company. Von Kleinschmidt and Drood have socialized together on at least one occasion."

"I just can't figure out what von Kleinschmidt's hold is on Colson and Drood," Dennis mused.

"None of my information, however, solves our problem," Beck said. "Although the crux of the difficulty may not be with any of the people on your list, I have a hunch some of them are involved. I always keep an open mind, but I've learned to follow up on hunches. This suggests a couple of actions. I can obtain records of Colson's phone calls and find out if he talks to von Kleinschmidt. This may not prove anything, but it could lead us in the right direction."

Beck yawned and stood up to stretch. "I can handle jet lag pretty well, but lately my travel has been nonstop. I'm bushed.

"The next action is a little riskier. Van Hook may be a player in whatever is going on. All CPAs I know keep meticulous records of financial transactions. I think it's in their genes. I'll bet you a buck if Van Hook is doing anything shady, he can't resist recording it. I have a long shot in mind. I sometimes use a talented Berlin computer crime investigator. If you want me to, I'll turn him loose to see if Van Hook has financial records that might help us understand what's going on."

"I want you to go ahead, Bill."

"Okay. It'll take a couple of weeks for results. I suggest you go back to work. I'll call you if anything interesting turns up."

Beck called Dennis ten days later and said, "I've found no record of calls between Colson and von Kleinschmidt so I see no reason to pursue that angle any further. As for the Berlin investigator, he could not hack into Van Hook's computer, so he hired a gay man to approach him in his favorite bar. They hit it off well and spent a long weekend together in Copenhagen."

"Well, that confirms he's gay," said Dennis.

"It sure did," said Beck. "While they were in Copenhagen, the investigator picked the lock on Van Hook's flat and searched his computer. It did not contain information related to von Kleinschmidt. He then searched the flat and found a fireproof safe in the back of a wardrobe. He picked the lock, opened the safe, and found a CD labeled, "Dr. Drood Agreement and Financial Disbursements." After viewing the CD, he guessed it was what we wanted, so he burned a copy. Of course all of this wouldn't look good if it ever came to light in the newspapers or a court of law, but without taking some risks in my game, there's often no gain."

"Yes, I know, Bill, but the CD could be a gold nugget."

"It sure could be. He also copied several cryptically labeled voice recorder tapes he found in the safe, but he did not audit them. You'll understand better than I what is on the CD and the tapes. I instructed the Berlin investigator to fly to Dublin and personally hand them over to you. Can you meet him at the airport?"

"You bet, Bill."

Dennis met the investigator at the Dublin airport and took the CD and tapes from him. He drove home and impatiently ate his dinner with Mary Catherine and their daughters before loading the CD into his computer. After reading it twice with mounting excitement, he knew he had found a corporate version of the deep-throat information that destroyed President Nixon's administration. He roused Mary Catherine from her doze in front of the tellie.

Dennis showed her some of the files and said, "This is the mother lode of incriminating information. It contains detailed records on Van Hook's meetings with Dr. Drood to commit big-time fraud. It includes complete financial records—check numbers, names, and dates—for passing millions of dollars through an Istanbul bank to the Georgian Preservation Society in Ireland. It shows a number of references to a Swiss man named Bartoluzzi, von Kleinschmidt, Van Hook, and Dr. Drood. It includes commentary about Dr. Drood asking Van Hook to become a board member of the Save the World Rainforests organization and how he should instruct von Kleinschmidt on the illegal money flow. It seems quite clear money was transferred from the Istanbul bank to the Georgian Preservation Society and earmarked for Hollycourt for the sole benefit of Dr. Drood. Mary Catherine, do you remember me telling you of the hissy fit Dr. Drood threw at the press conference when Minister O'Kane mentioned his position on the board of the Georgian Preservation Society, his ownership of Hollycourt, and his Irish origin?"

"Yes, I do, Dennis. You thought Dr. Drood grossly overreacted."

"Now I think I know why we had all of that grief with von Kleinschmidt AG. It was part of a scheme to scam the contract for millions of dollars. My God, Mary Catherine, I don't know what to do with this information. If it becomes public, Dr. Drood will be ruined and I'd guess if the information goes public, investor confidence in AMSCO will plunge, sending the stock price into a dive. Billions of dollars are at stake. I need to sleep on this and get some advice. I feel like I'm a mouse dancing with an elephant. If this information is publicly revealed, it'll be in the headlines of every business newspaper in the world."

Dennis mulled over the CD information for a few minutes and went on, "This started out being an issue of why the fab wasn't producing according to plans and whether Colson or I lied. Now it's an issue of massive corruption at the highest level. How I handle this will affect the fate of Dr. Drood and others, and it could crush me like a bug on a bumper. It's a situation beyond anything I've ever faced before. If I were a politician, I'd be thinking of manipulative courses of action, but I'm not, so I must work it through on the basis of what is the right thing to do—old-fashioned as that seems. Mary Catherine, if I'm squashed before this is over, are you still going to remain in my camp?"

"Dennis, if you don't carry it through, I'll abandon your camp and tent and ride into the desert with the next caravan to leave the oasis. Go for it. I'm with you to the end."

The next day he called Bill Beck. "Bill, I need to see you right away."

"What's up?"

"I think I now know which mouse hole we need to watch more closely."

Beck said, "OK. I'll be in Boston in two days—it's more or less a midpoint between San Francisco and Dublin. Can you meet me at the Marriott-Boston Hotel?"

"I'll be there. Please keep several hours open for me on your schedule. There's a lot of very smelly stuff to look at and to discuss."

"Will do, Dennis."

When Dennis and Beck met, Dennis loaded the CD into his laptop computer, and they watched it while Dennis interjected comments based on his familiarity with the information.

"This is a bombshell," Beck exclaimed. "We now know how the von Kleinschmidt equipment deal financed Hollycourt. This also tells us if Drood didn't have enough money to buy and restore Hollycourt, he must have also committed some kind of skullduggery to buy all of those other fancy homes in New York, London, and Palm Beach, and to support his high-living habits. He could not have done this alone. He has to be in cahoots with Nate Norton or some other high level financial officer in the company. I'll speculate the fancy homes are on the company books, and they were bought without board approval."

"Boy, this is getting scarier by the minute, Bill."

"It sure is, Dennis. I can have my staff accountant check the company books to look for the homes, but we need to get more corroboration of the CD information. A smart lawyer could prove to a jury the information on Van Hook's CD is a setup.

"Dennis, I'll help you any way I can, but you need to understand this may turn into a head-on challenge of the AMSCO alpha lion. It may make *Gunfight at the OK Corral* look like a boy's playground game. Do you want to go on?"

"I'm in clear over my head, Bill, but I've decided to bring this out in the open to clear my name even if I don't survive with my job.

"I'll put all of this in a report when I return to Ireland tomorrow ready to present to someone who has the power to act. Of course it must be someone outside the company. Dr. Stepanek comes to mind, but he's too far removed from the company and has resigned from the board so I don't think he's a good choice. From what I've read and heard, Cairncross is the strongest board member and is a straight arrow. I'd like to take this to him, but I suppose it'll be as hard to get to him as it would be to make an appointment in the White House. And of course I understand we must also first find independent corroboration of the information on Van Hook's CD."

"I can get you to Cairncross. The Titan Motors security director is a friend from our time training together at the FBI Academy. Considering the gravity of this matter, I'm sure he can set up a meeting, but let's slow down until we have more of our ducks in a row. I'll check out the company books on the ownership of Drood's fancy houses and try to look at the Georgian Preservation Society records. This will all help, but I wish we could clinch the CD information with more evidence. And Dennis, continue to play all of your cards close to your chest. I don't think you should even mention anything to Carly. We can't afford a leak."

"Bill, I can't thank you enough for your assistance and advice. I know the stakes are high, and you may be putting your thumb into the same vise with mine."

"I've never shied away from tough political investigations before. I'm used to having my job and sometimes my life on the line. That's why I always sit in a room with my back to the wall. We'll fly through some heavy flack, but I think we'll soon have enough solid evidence to prevail. I agree with you that we're now watching the right mouse hole."

"I'll go to work on my report right away and have it done in a few days," Dennis said. "I'll also try to find a way to make our case foolproof."

Dennis did not entirely follow Beck's advice about talking to Carly. He believed it would be a betrayal of her trust if he did not tell her something was up. The next day he told her his investigation was going to be a bombshell, but gave her no details. She said, "Okay, but if you can tell me anything, even at the last minute, I should warn Yee before the stuff hits the fan."

The next night Dennis considered Beck's concern that a smart lawyer could discredit Van Hook's journal. He slapped the side of his head with his hand when he remembered the voice recordings the Berlin investigator had given him at the Dublin airport. When he played them in his study and heard Drood's voice giving Van Hook directions, he tipped over his cup of coffee and hollered, "Mary Catherine, I just hit the jackpot!"

She worked most of the night helping him transcribe the recordings. The next morning, he sent a copy to Beck via courier.

Beck called Dennis the next afternoon and said, "Dennis, after I read your transcripts, I reviewed them with my staff lawyer with strict direction on confidentiality. Now, if we can confirm Drood's fancy houses and other playthings are on the company books, we think your case will be solid as a granite tombstone."

A week later Beck called Dennis again and said, "We've checked the ownership of the New York, London, Paris and Palm Beach properties, and some of the paintings and antique furnishings. They are all hidden deep in the crevasses and folds of the AMSCO accounting books—and the board did not approve them. We also discovered Norton has the exclusive use of a company-owned estate in the Bahamas. It's probably his payoff for helping with the unauthorized property acquisitions. My lawyer advised me some of the transactions are legally actionable, and others were within the law but in violation of company policies and rules."

Beck set up a meeting for Dennis with Cairncross. Cairncross requested a copy of Dennis's report and substantiating information before the meeting. Dennis included in his report appendix a copy of the memorandum he and Kim Park Chin signed at the time Colson ordered them to buy the von Kleinschmidt equipment. With Cairncross's compulsion for knowing the character of the people he dealt with, he also requested a copy of Dennis's personnel file.

CHAPTER THIRTY-ONE

Cairncross met with Curran in the Titan Motors building in New York. Cairncross immediately cut to the chase, "Mr. Curran, the information in your report is so stunning I sent it and your substantiating information to our chief legal counsel for review. She had our Middle East counsel check out and confirm the Istanbul bank records. He was once an employee of the bank and knew how to grease the palms of susceptible employees who gave him access to the bank's murky record-keeping books. I also talked to my friend Sir Roderick Kirwin-Swift who looked at the records of the Georgian Preservation Society relative to Hollycourt. Their findings confirm many of the accusations you made in your report against Robert Drood." Cairncross's assistant interrupted with an urgent call.

After the call, Cairncross resumed exactly where he left off. "If I decide to act on this information, it will destroy a brilliant man's career. If there are any flaws in your report, it may also destroy yours. The stakes are high. I'm inclined to convene an emergency AMSCO board meeting to dismiss Dr. Drood and appoint a new CEO and Chairman. Do you think the information in your report is strong enough to support such drastic and harsh actions?"

Dennis gulped and said, "Yes, sir, it is. I've crosschecked my information with the help and guidance of our chief of security, and I know it's valid."

Cairncross abruptly changed pace. "How do you and your family like living in Ireland?" he asked.

"I enjoy it, and my wife thinks she lives in paradise."

"I know how she must feel to find such a place. My wife and I have our paradise at our Wyoming ranch."

Cairncross sat with his eyes half-closed for thirty seconds while he rubbed his arthritic hands. Then he said, "Okay, Mr. Curran, I'm going to move on this matter. If I don't, there may be a leak, and serious harm may be done to AMSCO. My experience is timidity or delay in making hard decisions always ends up being regrettable."

Cairncross told his assistant, "Set up an AMSCO special teleconference board meeting as soon as possible—no make that an emergency meeting; it should take less than fifteen minutes. Do not notify Dr. Drood. Tell the board members the agenda for the meeting will consist of three points: (1) To hear incriminating evidence of massive fraud and corruption by Dr. Robert Drood and to request a board vote to dismiss him from his CEO, Chairman, and board positions; (2) To elect Dr. Ken Yee the new CEO; and (3) To elect a new Chairman. Before the board meeting I want to make a courtesy call to John Stepanek to inform him of the agenda."

He turned to Dennis and said, "Be here for the teleconference board meeting and stand by for the next several days. At the board meeting, I'll introduce you and ask you to present a summary of the information contained in your report. When you're through, stay for possible questions. Hold your presentation to less than four minutes. Let me review it right after lunch. Write the presentation so you can give the corporate secretary a copy to include in the meeting minutes. When you are through, I'll call for a vote on Dr. Drood's dismissal followed by a vote on electing Dr. Yee the new CEO and selection of a new Chairman—I assume the chairmanship will be hung on me as my 'reward' for acting on your information even though I'd rather be enjoying my retirement cattle ranching in Wyoming."

Dennis spent the rest of the morning writing his board presentation. When Cairncross reviewed it, he changed only a few words.

The teleconference board meeting convened the next day. After a brief, calm discussion, it voted to accept all of the actions on the Cairncross agenda and to elect Cairncross Chairman. The meeting was over in fifteen minutes. Dennis later told Carly the board meeting, in spite of the gravity of the agenda, had about as much visible excitement as a village traffic committee deciding on the installation of a new stop sign.

After the board meeting, Cairncross gave his assistant detailed instructions for having Drood and Yee come to his office in New York.

Cairncross met with Yee at 8:30 a.m. "Dr. Yee, thank you for coming on such short notice. I'm going to speak to you as the representative of the American Semiconductor Corporation Board of Directors. Your Dennis Curran was accused of making a poor buying decision related to a major purchase of von Kleinschmidt equipment for your Irish fab. While investigating the charges to clear his name, he came upon a far more serious matter. He has courageously presented credible evidence of massive fraud and unauthorized use of company assets by Robert Drood. Several other people including Nate Norton aided Drood with his reprehensible activities."

"That is quite unbelievable!" exclaimed Yee.

"Yes, it's hard to believe, but the evidence is unequivocal. The board has decided to accept Drood's resignation. It will be up to AMSCO's new management to sort out what action to take with Norton and possibly other involved employees. I'll tell Drood of his dismissal when we are through with this conversation. He's waiting to see me in another office. The Titan chief legal counsel will be my witness. Our security officer is standing by in my assistant's office."

As Yee sat wide-eyed, Cairncross continued, "Dr. Yee, the Board of Directors of American Semiconductor Corporation has unanimously elected you to succeed Dr. Drood. You're ready for the job. You will be the new Chief Executive Officer and a member of the board. We're all impressed with your rapid executive growth the last year, and already had you on top of our succession list for the CEO position. We saw no reason to again search outside the company for Drood's successor. Congratulations."

Cairncross waited a moment for Yee to absorb his statements and then he went on. "The board has elected me as Chairman. I've already publicly announced I'm retiring next month from Titan Motors and will have more time for AMSCO. The company needs an independent chairman for a while to steady the market while you plant your feet on the ground and the investment community gets to know you."

The normally unflappable Yee was speechless. Cairncross said, "Mr. Curran is in the next room waiting for you to review his presentation to the board that precipitated these actions. Here is a copy of the resignation documents I intend to show Drood. Right after I finish with Drood, I'll participate, along with you, in a teleconference with AMSCO management. My assistant has already set up the meeting. I'll announce Drood's resignation, your election as CEO, and my election as Chairman. You can then lead the rest of the meeting. I'll have another word with you when I'm through dismissing Drood. I know I'm taking summary action, but I've learned in my years in management when someone commits deliberate crimes, it demands immediate redress."

Yee said, "When I regain my composure, I'll express my gratitude to you for your inestimable trust in me."

Yee was devastated to learn Robert, whom he regarded as his mentor and friend, had committed criminal acts. He went into the men's room to clear his head and say a prayer for the wisdom needed for his new job. When he came out, he knew what he would say in the teleconference and the actions he would take in the next few days.

When Drood entered the room for his 9:00 a.m. meeting with Cairncross, the assistant shut the whispery-silent door. Cairncross stood behind the conference table. The Titan Motors chief legal counsel sat at his right in the only chair in the room with her laptop computer open. Her job was to witness and record the meeting.

Robert wondered why, if Cairncross was going to offer him a career advancement, he looked so grim. Cairncross spoke without a greeting or handshake. "Dr. Drood, we have irrefutable documentation of your fraudulent and unauthorized use of AMSCO money and assets for your personal use. We have read Mr. Van Hook's comprehensive journal entries and financial records and listened to incriminating wire recordings of your instructions to him."

Robert froze in his tracks as he neared the conference table and watched Cairncross glance at his papers. "We know the details of your concealed loan from Hans Bartoluzzi and shameless machinations with Karl von Kleinschmidt to commit grand larceny. We also have comprehensive information on your circumvention of AMSCO procedures to buy properties for your personal use aided by connivance with Mr. Norton."

Drood started to tremble. "I warned you in our last meeting if you tried to manipulate your compensation, I'd deal with you harshly. The board met in an emergency session to discuss your egregious and reprehensible behavior and your betrayal of its trust in you. It elected to accept your immediate resignation. Its decision is irrevocable."

Drood turned pale and opened his mouth to speak, but his vocal cords were paralyzed. He thought: This can't be happening to the CEO of one of the largest corporations in the world. Something important was in the wind for Cairncross to call this meeting in New York, but who would have dreamed it would be for this purpose. The deals with Bartoluzzi and von Kleinschmidt seemed so well concealed. It wasn't likely that Van Hook would sing, but the fruity idiot must have disobeyed his orders to not leave a paper trail. It is unbelievable that this information is now out in the open. It must be a dream that will go away.

A lesson from a nun who taught Robert his boyhood catechism class flashed through his mind. She said if a person prayed hard enough and promised a worthwhile penance to God, he could miraculously forestall impending disaster. He would pledge everything he owned to the Lord if it would stop this terrible thing that was happening. But of course that was all fairy-tale talk.

For the first time since his school days, Robert stammered and his body turned cold and sweaty. His legs weakened. He placed his fingertips on the edge of the conference tabletop to take some of the load off his shaking knees and to help him keep his balance.

Finally Robert could speak as he repeatedly moistened his dry lips with his tongue. He tried to mount a defense. "Justin, I—I t-tried—Umh, if I-I had been c-compensated more fairly—Ah, c-can you wait a few days so we can w-work something out?"

Cairncross shook his head while Drood sputtered. He said, "Please withhold comments until I'm finished. Here are four documents for you to sign: (1) a letter to the board acknowledging you committed these crimes and violated AMSCO policies; (2) a letter of resignation stating you're resigning for personal reasons; (3) a letter stating you accept the offered severance settlement and its conditions; and (4) a document stating you'll keep all matters related to your departure confidential.

"The financial settlement will be generous: (1) payment of your current salary for six months; (2) a severance payment of three million dollars spread out over ten years; and (3) a cash settlement for your outstanding options. If you say anything to any person or to the public beyond what it says in your resignation letter, all payments to you will stop, and we'll initiate harsh legal action. This generous settlement is to avoid public disclosure, which could precipitate an adverse reaction to the AMSCO stock value. Mr. Beck is in the next room to inform you of arrangements for vacating your office and company-owned properties."

Drood searched for a way to mitigate the harshness of the board decision, but he could think of nothing to ease his dire and ignominious situation. For one of the few times in his life, he was indecisive. His professional life just tumbled into an abyss. His throat felt like it was packed with cotton and his heart pounded. The resignation documents on the table undulated before his unfocused eyes. His career was melting away as fast as an ice cube on the pavement on a hot August day.

Cairncross switched to a more conciliatory tone. "Robert, this is no doubt the worst setback of your professional life, but your world will go on. I suggest you talk to someone you can trust, either in your spiritual or personal life or a professional who can help you think through where you have been and what you should do next. You should put this behind you and find a way to use your considerable talents. When you have read and signed the documents, please give them to my assistant before you leave. This meeting is concluded."

Cairncross and the chief legal counsel marched out of the room and clicked the door shut.

Robert stood by the conference table in stunned disbelief. His career, which he spent his entire life creating, was just snatched from him in less than five minutes—and he couldn't think of a single thing to do about it. It was a catastrophe. He was probably in shock. He needed counsel before signing the documents. He would call his personal lawyer, Martin Blanski, in San Francisco. Blanski would likely still be home before going to work at his law office. It would be the worst time of the day for him; he would be feeling cruddy from last night's booze and edgy because his first cigarette of the day had not yet kicked in. Blanski's advice could always be counted on to be explicit and probably irreverent.

Blanski took Robert's call in his bathroom. Robert, having regained enough control to speak, explained his situation. Blanski, who had seen almost every seamy facet of human nature in his long, colorful legal career, listened without interruption and growled a response in his nasal New Jersey accent. "Robbie baby, it looks like you tripped a rat trap on your dangly parts when you raided the till. Seymour Weis and I've been wondering what kind of damn-fool scheme you'd contrive to feed your overstimulated appetite for unaffordable playthings. Lately, you've been like an unrestrained French pig rooting and snuffling for more tasty goodies in a freshly discovered truffle patch. It's too late for us to give you much help now. Hold on a minute; I'll throw a nicotine fit if I don't go to another room for a pack of cigarettes."

When he returned he continued, "As for the settlement offer, you could hold out for more, but if I were you, I'd accept it right now. You're lucky they're not going to throw you in the slammer for a decade of hard time, and it wouldn't be a cushy 'Federal Club.' A pretty boy like you'd be a fresh shipment of choice meat for the established prison denizens. A couple of young 275-pound dudes with the urgency and stamina of a pair of young bulls would be your welcoming committee. Damn, there's a special delivery at the door; I have to sign for it. I'll be right back, old boy—hold on a minute.

"You're also lucky they want to hold this matter in confidence. If it becomes public, you won't be able to get a feather-plucking job in a poultry slaughterhouse. When you sign the papers, I think you should skip town until the media feeding frenzy is over, and you should start thinking about a new career that won't involve working the till. And do sign the severance documents *muy rapido, Roberto*, before Cairncross thinks about applying his Parable of the Coyote to you—you remember the story you once told me about him shooting a stalking coyote in Wyoming. Cairncross is a dangerous man—he's honest."

"Uh, thanks, Martin."

"*De nada* old boy. Call me again in a few days so we can tie up the loose ends."

With a wobbly hand, Drood signed and dated the documents on the yellow-tabbed pages and handed them to Cairncross's assistant. She checked the signatures and handed him an air ticket to San Francisco. It appeared she was showing him a courtesy by escorting him to the elevator reserved for occupants of the executive floors, but she was following the orders of the security officer who had instructed her to stay with him until he left the building.

A beefy man with a bulging inside breast pocket said, "'scuse' me," as he pushed his way to the rear of the elevator. He was planted there to provide muscular intervention if needed. Security officers know fired employees sometimes go on rampages of destruction and violence. The muscle man remained in the lobby to ensure Drood did not re-enter the building. While Cairncross's assistant was returning to her office, she noticed the pungent smell of Robert's panic still permeating the elevator. Late in the afternoon she told the muscle man Drood was at the airport waiting to board his plane to California, and he could leave his post in the lobby. He said, "Jeeze, I thought that guy would never get to the airport. I gotta get home on time tonight for our anniversary, or my wife's going to make me sleep on a pile of rags under the basement stairs."

When Dennis finished explaining his incriminating report to Yee, he assumed the need for his presence at the Titan Motors offices was over. Cairncross's assistant stopped him when he prepared to depart and asked him to wait for Cairncross and Yee.

Cairncross met again with Yee. "Robert Drood has signed his resignation documents and departed," he said. "Now, you can proceed with our teleconference with the AMSCO executives."

Yee opened the teleconference with the staff who had reported to Drood. "Thank you for being available for this urgent conference on such short notice. Mr. Justin Cairncross will start the meeting."

Cairncross cleared his throat and said, "Good morning, ladies and gentlemen. Dr. Drood, for personal reasons, submitted his resignation as chief executive officer, chairman, and a member of the board of directors of American Semiconductor Corporation this morning." He paused for a long moment to let his shocking announcement sink in. "The board of directors has accepted his resignation and unanimously elected Dr. Ken Yee the new AMSCO chief executive officer and a member of the board of directors. Simultaneously they elected me to be the non-executive chairman of the board of directors. The board is confident the superb executive team of AMSCO will continue to excel during the seamless transition to your new CEO. I now turn the meeting back to Dr. Yee."

When the teleconference was over, Cairncross and Yee met with Curran. Cairncross said, "Mr. Curran, I live in a world of people who worry so much about company politics and self-interest, I sometimes despair. It is refreshing to know you, a person who sticks to guiding principles even if it could imperil your career. You have courageously and intelligently handled this difficult matter. I've directed Dr. Yee not to allow any reference of these proceedings to enter your personnel file. I'm aware of the dismal record of many corporations for adversely handling whistle-blower's careers when they report malfeasances."

Yee added, "Dennis, I endorse Mr. Cairncross' statements. You're indeed a *rara avis* (rare bird). I assure you your career at AMSCO will continue on track. However, if you ever run into problems resulting from your actions of the last few weeks, please immediately come to me. Congratulations for your splendid work."

Dennis was sure these two righteous men meant what they were saying, but if word ever got out, he'd be branded the whistleblower who destroyed a CEO. He knew people in the Air Force who tried to right injustices, and they were harassed until they resigned. If there was no leak, he'd be safe—but if there was, he'd not be a *rara avis* but instead he'd be a *mortuus avis* (dead bird)—to continue with Yee's choice of words.

Dennis returned to his hotel to pack and call Carly to give her a summary of the happenings of the last few days. Carly sighed, and with a quiet voice said, "Damn well done, Dennis. Take a couple of days off before you come back to work."

When Dennis returned home and told Mary Catherine about the events in New York, she said, "I'm so proud of how you managed it all, and I'm so happy this nightmare is over. I'd have turned to mush if I had to handle it. I'll bet those evil snakes will think twice before they hiss or strike at our Dennis again."

"I'm not sure I'd have had the guts to go through with this if you hadn't been there for me, Mary Catherine. Right now I'm pretty disgusted with having worked my butt off for the last several years building a successful fab—except for the von Kleinschmidt equipment that was crammed up my nose—and then having to defend myself for lying. I'm also surprised I wasn't pulverized for blowing the whistle."

Yee took over running the company without a ripple. He reprimanded Colson for not having the spine to stick to professional conduct. "Jerry, I too am an engineer and our code of ethics calls for us to stick to principles over politics. I've not heard or seen any evidence of you resisting Dr. Drood's corrupt direction to you about the von Kleinschmidt order. And your habit of shifting blame for everything that goes badly onto your people, even when you're the source of the problem, must stop. A manager who doesn't support his people isn't up to AMSCO standards. If I hear of it happening again, I'll take you out of your job. Stick to your strengths of executing projects on schedule and within budget and you'll have no trouble with me."

As Colson stood to leave, Yee handed him a copy of the memorandum signed by Kim Park Chin and Dennis Curran noting Colson's instructions to hire von Kleinschmidt without competitive bidding. He said, "And I never want to see a document like this again. The English language has many synonyms to describe your repudiation of the direction you gave to Dennis Curran to buy equipment from von Kleinschmidt; 'prevarication' is one of the milder ones."

Yee called Norton to his cubicle. Yee had resumed Stepanek and Budak's custom of working in a standard size cubicle like all other company employees. "Nate, you knew the purchase of most of those fancy properties needed board approval, but you bought them anyhow because you wanted to curry favor from Dr. Drood. You also knew your personal use of the fancy estate in the Bahamas was wrong. I must have a CFO whose integrity is above reproach. You have the integrity of a South China Sea pirate. I give you the choice of demotion or resignation. If you choose resignation, I'll give you a suitable financial settlement. Let me know your decision tomorrow."

Norton returned the next day, read the financial settlement offer, and resigned.

In Yee's first meeting with Norton's successor he said, "Sell all of the trappings of grandeur—the company-owned condominiums and houses, and the Boeing Business Jet; replace it with a less commodious plane—maybe a Cessna Ten. And establish a policy that no executive can use company planes for personal travel without my approval—and my approval will be as rare as a balanced budget in Washington."

One of Cairncross's first tasks as chairman was to purge the board of the "pet rock" members who did not seriously carry out their oversight responsibilities.

Yee and Cairncross hired a vice president of corporate governance who reported to the board. They instructed her to establish procedures for employees to anonymously report ethics violations. They also told her to strengthen the AMSCO Codes of Business Conduct and Ethics and conduct an obligatory ethics-training course for every employee.

As Van Hook read the AMSCO green bulletin on Robert Drood's resignation, he turned white and his knees went weak. His alarm and dismay were compounded because his lover, a low-level employee of the Russian consulate, had abandoned their affair. The day Yee instructed Van Hook's manager to dismiss him, he jumped from the thirtieth floor window of his Berlin office. Bill Beck sent an agent to his flat to comb it for all of the original records related to transactions with Robert Drood.

The business media went into a frenzy trying to discover the reason for Robert Drood's abrupt resignation. In spite of their vigorous efforts, they could not find an informed person who would talk to them. Many of the reporters speculated the board removed him because of his abrasiveness and aggressiveness with his executive team. Cairncross lent credibility to their speculation by making a vague public reference to the wear and tear on the AMSCO executive staff because of Dr. Drood's intimidating management style. None learned the real reason. After several months, the media moved on to fresher quests. AMSCO stock maintained its price.

CHAPTER THIRTY-TWO

After Robert left the Titan Motors building, he grumbled that he hadn't ridden in a taxi or on a commercial airline for years: It was ridiculous to have sent the AMSCO jet deadheading back to San Francisco without me aboard. At least that bastard, Cairncross, ordered me a first-class commercial air ticket for my trip home.

During the three-hour flight delay, Robert sat alone at a small round table in the airport bar and brooded; he drank more than he had since high school days. He thought: A laborer on a construction gang would be dismissed with more respect than I was allowed. And Cairncross's self-righteous attitude was damn hypocritical—he sure as hell didn't get to be CEO of Titan Motors by always taking the high road. Other companies recognize the effort it takes to manage a company in bad times and find a way to reward their CEOs for their efforts. All the compensation committee at AMSCO did was rigidly apply the rules like a clueless government bureaucrat.

He ordered another drink and tried to figure out how his scheme backfired. He wondered: Who all was involved? Colson could probably be ruled out because it was not in his career interest to talk. And it couldn't be Norton, because his dopey wife was too pleased with the Bahamas estate. Bartoluzzi and von Kleinschmidt wouldn't squeal with all of the AMSCO business they enjoy. That sycophant Van Hook wouldn't have talked, but someone must have suspected him and discovered where the damn fairy cached his records even though I absolutely forbade him to put anything in writing. Curran, the Eagle Scout, could have somehow sleuthed out the truth when his feelings were hurt for being accused of making the decision to order the faulty von Kleinschmidt equipment. And our chief centurion, Beck, could have had his oar in the water helping Curran.

Robert ordered another drink and went on with his brooding: The bastards at AMSCO might even fire my assistant. It'll be a cold day in hell before they ever see me in my office or condo again. They can pack my personal stuff and send it to Hollycourt; it is the only available place I have to go. They can sell all of the cars except the Bentley; I'll have it shipped to me. It is best to leave town right away to avoid having a bunch of curiosity seekers digging around in the muck and clucking over my fall. Many will rejoice that I fell. What a hell of a way to end a career. I've been royally screwed. After all of this, I have as much chance of finding a suitable new job as a felon just sprung from prison. What a freaking, god-awful, stinking, bloody mess!

At no time in his brooding did it occur to Robert to personally shoulder any of the blame for his transgressions.

By the time he downed his last drink, he had worked himself into a state of self-pity worthy of a prima donna high school senior without a date on prom night.

When Robert arrived back in San Francisco, he checked into the Fairmont Hotel and immediately fell asleep. The next morning, wakefulness started to slowly seep into him, but then he sat bolt upright with a feeling around his chest like the grip of a constrictor. The full realization hit him that his life had taken its worst turn since the horrible times of his childhood in Ireland. He would leave for Hollycourt immediately. He dreaded the possibility some of his colleagues might call him. He did not know they had already switched their allegiance to Ken Yee and he was yesterday's news.

After Robert called room service for breakfast, he asked the hotel concierge to order him a first-class one-way ticket to Dublin for afternoon departure.

He called Sarah and Pamela to tell them of his resignation and that his new address would be Hollycourt; he did not tell them the reason. Pamela agreed to come to Hollycourt for an extended visit soon after he arrived.

Out of the blue, Robert thought about his sister Bridget. He had hardly thought of her during the last year. Maybe she came to mind because she had once been his childhood confidant long ago in Ireland. He called her group home in Chicago. The administrator said, "Bridget is getting along fine, but our psychologist doesn't think she can go back to work or live alone. She seems to be happy living here except in late afternoons and evenings when she has 'sundowner' depressions. With her positive attitude, she's a good influence on our other residents. Do you want to talk to our psychologist?"

"No. Perhaps at another time. You told me everything I wanted to know. Thanks."

Robert finished eating his breakfast and called his assistant at AMSCO to tell her he would be moving to Hollycourt. He was pleased she had not been fired because of her close association with him. She promised to continue to handle his calls and mail.

Robert was on the boards of seven companies and institutions. Their CEOs were already calling Cairncross to ask him what happened to Robert. Cairncross did not tell them, but he hinted they should quickly remove him from their boards. Robert saved them the trouble. He dictated resignation letters to each company and institution where he was a board member.

His assistant cried when Robert thanked her for her loyal service to him, but she asked no questions. In corporate executive suites bosses only tell assistants and secretaries what they want them to know.

Robert went to the men's shop on the ground floor of his hotel and bought enough to last until his clothing would be shipped to Hollycourt. He did not want to try to go to the company-owned condominium where he lived to pack a bag. The place probably already had a new lock. He checked out of the hotel and took a limo to the airport.

As his fuel-laden plane ponderously gained altitude for the long flight to Dublin, Robert stewed about his dismissal: So long to those narrow-minded sons of bitches on the AMSCO board. I know some things about some of them that I could tell their wives and cause them many nights of sleeping in the spare bedroom. And I know a few who drew a very vague line between their assets and their company's. AMSCO lost the best executive they'll ever have when they canned me. What a miserable fiasco! Sweet Jesus in heaven, I wonder what's going to happen to me now.

CHAPTER THIRTY-THREE

Robert rented a Jaguar at the Dublin airport and drove to Hollycourt. It was the first time in years no one met him when he arrived at his destination.

After he settled in at Hollycourt, he took long, gloomy walks each day around his estate and on country lanes while he brooded and blamed others for his fate. He had a difficult time sleeping.

The thought of his dismissal from AMSCO smothered him with its relentless presence. He felt like he was stumbling into an abyss. There was no one he could turn to for understanding or sympathy. He could not talk to Yee because of the stipulations in his termination agreement. His pride prevented him from turning to Pamela. He could not talk to Bridget as he did in his childhood because their intimate relationship was long dormant. Another call to Sarah was tempting, but he did not want to disturb her new marriage.

At the end of each day of walking, Robert stopped at the caretaker's house. Paddy's endless tales provided a momentary respite from his consuming resentment of the people who he believed tossed his career away as if it were a soiled rag.

Robert took slow, solitary drives around the community. Each evening he drove to an ancient pub in a nearby village for a pint of Guinness and his supper. At first, by his accent, he was taken for an American or a Canadian, but day by day the Cork brogue of his childhood became stronger. He even remembered a little of the Irish language he had learned at his mother's knee and spoke a few words to Irish-speaking patrons of the pub.

On a sunny morning, after his second cup of coffee, Robert noticed the numbing shock of his dismissal from AMSCO had diminished. The strangeness of not going to work each day did not seem so odd, and the pressure on his chest and head was more bearable.

He thought about his future: I could seek the CEO position at another major corporation, but only a few such jobs exist and none is open now. Anyhow, a large company would not hire me until I could explain why I left AMSCO—and that is not possible or else I'd lose the financially advantageous benefits of my dismissal. Small start-up companies might take on a CEO without too much investigation, but why take a step backward? And why re-enter the rat race anyhow? Who needs to enter a tournament that has already been played and won before? And besides the phone is not ringing with offers—in fact it hardly ever rings for any reason. It's hard to get much adrenaline flowing about the prospect of another CEO position. There must be some other worthwhile thing to do. But indefinitely sitting fallow and brooding in Hollycourt is not the answer.

Pamela called and said she would come to Hollycourt for a visit. It was strange for her to have to take the train from her home in Belfast. For the first time in their relationship, Robert could not send a plane for her.

Robert and Pamela spent a few leisurely days together. They talked of the enjoyment of having time together without a schedule hanging over them. Neither brought up Robert's future or the future of their relationship. The third day of Pamela's visit, Robert became morose. She had never before seen him in a gloomy mood. She let it go for a while and then cut her visit short. They parted with feigned cheerfulness and hearty assurances they would soon meet again, but they did not specify a time or place.

Early one morning when Robert could not sleep, he made a cup of coffee and drove to an area of the surrounding community that was new to him. He noticed an obscure marker along a remote road pointing to a Benedictine monastery. To satisfy his curiosity, he drove down the short entrance road and parked his car. The pale moon near the horizon, looking like an oversized communion wafer pinned to a tree branch, lighted the path to the monastery. Robert tiptoed into the lighted chapel intending to stay only long enough to have a look around.

Morning mass was being celebrated with about twenty monks in attendance—the few remaining residents of what had once been a teeming community of priests and brothers. When he turned to leave the chapel, the monks started to sing their praise of God with a timeless Gregorian chant. It evoked memories of his school days in Chicago. He slipped into a back pew to listen, but stayed until the mass ended and a few minutes more for reflection and contemplation. When he rose to depart, a middle-aged monk was also leaving. They nodded to each other and Robert paused to allow the monk to pass. The monk stopped and said, "I'm Father Finbar Finley. I hope you found fulfillment by sharing the mass with us today. I'm on my way to breakfast. Would you care to join me?"

Robert opened his mouth to decline the invitation and then changed his mind. "Why not? My day is free. Thanks."

They ate a simple breakfast and talked for two hours. Robert questioned Father Finbar about his work within the monastery. "I'm a teacher and philosopher. I write books and lecture on ways to look at spirituality and philosophy in a modern world that is abandoning the thinking and practices of the past. My abbot doesn't understand my murky manuscripts and monographs, but he lets me cut my own swath as long as the checks from my literary agent continue to flow into the monastery counting house."

Robert was attracted to Father Finbar because of his ability to scrape away nonessentials from his intellectual deliberations. He was also drawn to him by a compelling need to associate with another intelligent, understanding human being.

Robert asked, "Father Finbar, would you join me for supper some evening soon?"

"I'd be happy to. Brother Kevin's supper recipe book has been stuck too long on the same page."

While Robert was in the port of Cobh to pick up his shipped Bentley, he stayed a few days in nearby Cork. He visited the mound of rubble that had once been his wretched home. He then visited his mother's childhood home in Farrenree. He remembered the address from the flyleaf of her prayer book. He strolled around the neighborhood trying to envision his beautiful young mother in her youth.

When he checked out of the Garnish House Bed and Breakfast to return to Hollycourt, he overheard one of the guests say, "I wonder why a chap who can afford to drive a Bentley wouldn't be staying at a more upmarket hotel like the Hayfield Manor or the Imperial Hotel."

Robert departed from Cork with an odd feeling of calm.

As he drove back to Hollycourt, he reviewed his financial situation: When I pay off my outstanding debts, I'll still have a hefty bank account and substantial income from the AMSCO settlement—and this does not consider the salary I could receive if I ever find a job. I've frequently made financial projections in the past, but they all flew out the window when I went on foolish spending binges. But I don't seem to have a compulsion to acquire stuff any more. Whatever I do with my talents in the future, the decision apparently does not need to be driven by a requirement for additional income.

Robert swerved to avoid a man wobbling on his bicycle and resumed reviewing his finances. He decided he had lost all perspective on the value of money the last few years. It seemed when numbers had a lot of zeros after them, they had no meaning. His Bentley cost more than what ten average American families earn in a year. Replacing it with a less showy and noticeable car made sense. Besides it was awkward to drive on the left side of the road when the steering wheel was on the left. And the community gossip would diminish when they no longer saw the Bentley tooling around the neighborhood. Some people think living in the country is a life of seclusion, but the neighbors have the prying eyes of the jungle and the wagging tongues of a sewing circle.

Robert turned his thoughts to his personal future. His relationship with Pamela seemed to be on the wane. He still wasn't capable of bonding with her—or anyone else—and he guessed that without his previous platform of a high-powered job with its perks and his large income, her interest in him would not last much longer.

As he turned into the driveway to Hollycourt he neared the end of his reflections. His satisfaction with living in Ireland continued to grow and thoughts of returning to the U.S. were less appealing each day. One of these days he'd have to decide what to do with his life. After all, he was only at the midpoint of a normal working life. Maybe the next thing he should do was visit his father now that he knew where he lived although he didn't hold much hope it would be any more productive than his visits had been with Donlan and McClellan.

When Robert dined with Father Finbar, they exchanged information on their lives. After Robert summarized his life, omitting the painful parts, Finbar said, "It sounds like your education was as extensive as mine. After becoming a Benedictine priest, I earned my masters degree in Celtic history at Trinity College and a Ph.D. in philosophy at Oxford. Since then my métier has been writing and teaching about the fast-changing modern world." Finbar did not mention his advanced degree in psychology. When many people learned of it, they became unsettled and suspected he would manipulate their minds like a psycho-geek in a Hollywood film.

Finbar sensed Robert was in turmoil and searching for a purpose for his existence. He guessed if he brought up any of the obvious anchor points of life such as spirituality, family values, or Aristotelian teachings, he would lose him. It was evident to Finbar that Robert was an intelligent man who knew all about the Christian faith and its philosophical teachings from his boyhood school days so he would not sail into those waters. When they finished presenting their biographical sketches, they talked for the rest of the evening about the relationship of Ireland to the European Economic Community.

Each of them was impressed with the acuity of the other's mind. They agreed to meet weekly for supper and to continue their unstructured conversations.

Robert swallowed his apprehension about meeting his father and drove to Belfast to see him. He was too young when his father abandoned his family to remember him. His father's landlady, at the address provided by Kiely, said, "On nice weekend days, Mr. Drood sits on a bench in the park. It's only a stone's throw away. You'll know him by his bare head of gray hair and a blue windbreaker jacket. He will be reading or talking to a friend or a passerby." She wondered about the striking similarity in looks between Mr. Drood and his visitor.

When Robert saw his father sitting on a bench reading a folded newspaper, he was surprised that his excitement and emotions at the prospect of finally meeting and confronting him had subsided. He sat down beside his father and when he looked up after a few moments softly said, "My name is Robert Drood; I'm your son."

George Drood gave a startled and searching look at Robert. After a long pause he laid down his newspaper and said, "I always hoped some day we'd meet again."

They told their life stories. Robert said, "As a young boy, I turned your picture to the wall, figuratively speaking, but it did no good. I continued to think of you; I could not understand why you abandoned us when we were in such dire circumstances and why you did not take the responsibility for your own family. My beautiful mother, Bridget, and I desperately needed you. My resentment of you has burned into my psyche ever since; I obsessively hated you.

"But lately, I have had an epiphany in my own imperfect and often shameful life. My imperfections may have even been worse than yours. I finally realized I was in no position to sit on the sidelines and cast scorn at you. So after much deliberation and with no specific purpose or objective in my mind, I decided to come to see you after a detective that I hired ran you down."

George Drood reflected for a long pause on Robert's listing of his failings and said, "I'd have felt the same way. I shouldn't have walked away from my family and my responsibilities. As time went by and until this day, I bitterly chastise myself for my reprehensible behavior. I'd be lying if I said I loved your mother, but I respected her, and I loved you and Bridget. Maybe your mother and I could have worked out our squabbling if we were left alone. But we were young, and it was a terrible strain on her to raise two children with me on the road working most of the time. I was able to accept your uncles beating me half to death to force me to marry her when she was carrying you, but I wasn't strong enough to endure their constant ridicule and verbal abuse. I just quit coming home. For a while I sent money to the Garritys to give to Mary, but I suspect they filched it. Except for Liam and your mother, the Garritys were a bin of rotten potatoes. After your Uncle Liam took you to Chicago, I lost touch with your mother and you. I know it's futile at this late date to express regret and remorse to you so I won't try; in fact if I did, it would be suspect as well as unbelievable. But let me say with all my heart how grateful I am to have the chance to talk to you today. I never dreamed we'd meet again."

Robert's emotions were so unsettling and overwhelming, he soon ended the discussion and departed. On his drive back to Hollycourt, Robert reflected on the meeting with his father. He was not the ogre he envisioned for the last thirty years. This was the first time he knew he was almost born a bastard. And it was the first time he knew about his rowdy uncles; he always assumed they were gentle fellows like Uncle Liam. On one hand the meeting with his father was a letdown, but on the other hand he was relieved to learn he had a father with more character than he had imagined. He'd write a letter to Bridget tomorrow and tell her of their meeting.

George Drood sat on his bench until long after dark. He reviewed in his mind every word of his extraordinary meeting with Robert. He doubted he would ever see him again and the chances were even slimmer he would ever see Bridget. He walked home light-headed and happy.

CHAPTER THIRTY-FOUR

During one of Finbar and Robert's weekly pub suppers, they did not slip into their normal conversation on a period of history or an issue of the day. Robert was withdrawn and pensive.

As they drank their after-dinner tea, Robert abruptly poured out the story of his personal life from the time of his first childhood memory. He recounted his wretched childhood in Cork; the abuse of his sister and his mother; his humiliation because of his family's poverty; the disrespect from his schoolmaster and classmates; his hatred of his father for abandoning his family; his failed marriage to Sarah; his womanizing; and his foolish aping of high-rolling corporate crooks. He admitted to his ridiculous pride, intellectual snobbery, and gluttony for material goods.

Moving to a more emotional level, he lamented that he could never experience a full measure of satisfaction for his remarkable academic and professional achievements; never bond with anyone; and never accept any kind of meaningful spirituality in spite of his years of exposure to philosophy and theology. He dreaded his conviction that at the time of his death, it would be like a roomful of light vanishing without leaving a residual trace of his life on earth when the last candle was snuffed out. He wondered if the common dung beetle did not leave behind a more meaningful contribution during its tenure on earth.

After a few more sips of tea, Robert twisted his back to the other pub patrons and leaned across the table to Finbar. He erupted with the remainder of his story about the sex abuse of his beloved mother; the rape of his adored sister; his guilt for failing to defend them; his inability to excise the memory from his mind; and his obsessive frustration because McClellan was never brought to justice for his heinous crimes. He told of the haunting specter perched on his shoulder, always ready to recall the dark unspeakable evils committed so long ago and how it could warp and twist his psyche to its will. He likened himself to the tormented man in Edgar Allen Poe's poem, *The Raven*, who could never be free of the tortured memories for his lost Lenore and whose soul must forever live in the shadow of the sinister raven with its haunting, one-word vocabulary: Nevermore!

His story flowed in torrents punctuated with tears, momentary silences, and periodic emotional gasps. For a half-hour Robert poured out his story.

When his outburst neared the end, he said, "The first time I visited St. Peter's Basilica in Rome, I was mesmerized by the Bernini Altar with its four soaring, writhing, helical columns symbolically and mysteriously beckoning the faithful to eternity in the unblemished heavens above. Later in a dark dream I saw the columns again, but this time inverted, leading to Dante's inferno below. They seemed to define the path that I would follow when my life on earth ended. This dark Stygian image still haunts me when I'm visited by the beasties of the night."

Robert sat exhausted but calm. He was astonished he told Finbar more about himself than he had ever told another soul; he was relieved to be unburdened of his crushing load. By telling his story to another human, perhaps he had transferred part of his unbearable load to other shoulders. A feeling of euphoria swept over him.

When Robert mentioned the sex abuse of his childhood, Finbar knew it was probably the crux of his difficulties. Of all the psychological problems he had studied and dealt with in his life, childhood sex abuse caused the most profound and enduring damage.

Finbar was accustomed to the secrets and responsibilities of the confessional. He guessed he had just witnessed the once-in-a-lifetime catharsis of a psychologically crippled and suffering man. Any words of consolation or benediction would be a waste. With Robert's passionate outpouring, the thing of most value had happened; he was finally able to share his story with another receptive and understanding human being. The process of sharing would not solve Robert's problems, but it could help him diminish his torments and accept his condition.

Robert paid the pub bill. Finbar touched him on the shoulder and they parted.

Finbar was a man who knew from study, experience, and his uncanny intuition, a great deal about the psyche of humans. He sensed, from the first time he met Robert, he was carrying a heavy load of psychological agony. He anticipated when their friendship eventually built to the point of trust, he would hear Robert's outpouring of feelings.

The next day it rained as if the sullen sky was a giant vessel of water with a screen for a bottom. While Robert waited for the rains to abate, he reflected on the previous evening with Finbar: What could have triggered my eruption? It was like a water-saturated levee collapsing without warning. And why was Finbar the recipient of my flood of emotions? For the first time since my childhood, I started to personally connect with another person. Maybe Finbar was a psychological catalyst who allowed me to face the events of my life that had been locked away in the hidden chamber of my mind for so many years. It is now a little easier to accept the past, but I still have no idea what to do with the future.

As dusk approached and the rain subsided, Robert pulled on his coat and Wellingtons and went out into the fading light of the dusk for a walk around his estate. When he returned to the welcoming light of his house entrance, he thought more about his dismissal from AMSCO: I am damn lucky not to be waiting for a criminal trial or sitting in prison like several other top officers who gorged themselves at corporate troughs. And I'm also lucky to have received such a generous financial settlement; I should have been forced to repay the AMSCO treasury for all of my costly shenanigans. My earlier rationalization that AMSCO owed me what I took from the company was utter nonsense. I was guilty of civil crimes and a gross violation of AMSCO policies. Why couldn't I see this before? I can't believe I didn't grasp what any person with average wits and common sense would have easily understood was wrong and actionable. Why didn't I, with my celebrated intellect, understand that I was wallowing in a fetid pit of corruption?

Robert sent Finbar a one-word note. It read: "Thanks."

When they met again, they did not speak of Robert's emotional revelations during their previous meeting. These two articulate men, with their towering intellects, sensed the best way to draw the curtain on the incident was in silence. They continued their weekly meetings with their usual informal conversations peppered with good-natured bantering.

At a weekly supper meeting, Finbar brought a guest. "Robert, this is my star student whom I taught at University College Cork—Dr. Michael Hennessey. Michael is now Ireland's minister of education and my prime advisor on thorny education issues." Hennessy effortlessly joined into the flow of free-ranging conversation. He refrained from mentioning he knew all about Robert from his fellow Irish minister, Patrick O'Kane.

Near the conclusion of the evening, Hennessey said, "Robert, we're having serious difficulties in Cork finding qualified mathematics and physics teachers. Many of our best people have left to work for the information technology companies relocating to Ireland or gone off to better jobs in other countries. I have a meeting in Cork next week to discuss its teacher shortage. Would you like to accompany me? It could be an interesting diversion for you."

"Thanks for the invitation, Michael. I'd be happy to come with you. I've done some teaching and always found it appealing."

Drood and Hennessey met for breakfast at the Hayfield Manor in Cork. "Robert, while I'm meeting with the education authorities here, how about you auditing a mathematics class at North Monastery School on the other side of town? Locally they call the school MONS. By the way, here in Ireland the Catholic Church runs ninety-five percent of the schools even though they're funded with government taxes. The remaining five percent are called multi-cultural schools. In America you'd call MONS a high school; here we call it a secondary school."

Robert met Eamon Dugan, a mathematics teacher, and audited several of his classes. In the middle of the morning, one of his bright students asked Dugan how to solve a problem not in the textbook. Dugan said, "Caitlan, the solution to your problem would require the use of mathematics beyond what we're covering in this course. In fact I'd have to review my old university calculus books to answer your question—unless Dr. Drood, who has a mathematics background, would care to give you an answer." Robert walked to the blackboard and explained the elementary calculus needed to solve Caitlan's problem. He was exhilarated to again have the opportunity to teach.

During the lunch break in the teacher's dining room, Hennessey overheard Dugan say to a colleague, "It's too bad we can't get our hands on the likes of Dr. Drood to help us with our shortage of mathematics and science teachers. He's a natural teacher."

Before Hennessey and Drood parted at the end of the day, Hennessy said, "Robert, we're desperate here in Cork for technical teachers, and I have no immediate solution to the problem. I understand for the moment you're not professionally engaged. Would you agree to a trial period of teaching? I have the right to waive the normal teaching certification requirements for capable candidates."

During the week while Robert deliberated on Hennessy's request, he thought about Steven Wozniak, the technical wizard who cofounded Apple Computer Inc. with Steve Jobs. When Wozniak resigned from Apple due to poor health, he taught computer science to children. With mounting enthusiasm, Robert imagined himself also teaching. He called Hennessey and agreed to a three-month trial teaching period at MONS.

Teaching was like a shot of adrenaline into Robert's system. In recollection of his childhood neglect by his schoolmaster, he liked to give extra help to students who were struggling and falling between the cracks.

He slept better and his "downers" diminished. It now seemed like his previous life happened to some other person in some other world.

Robert again reviewed what he should do with his life. His intellect and experience could be best used if he brought his management skills to a large company or taught advanced mathematics and science at a top level university. But others were standing in line to fill those positions and MONS urgently needed mathematics and science teachers. Young people were being frozen out of technical careers due to the dearth of capable teachers. He loved to teach at MONS as much as he did in the past when he tutored students at MIT and taught management development classes at AMSCO. He decided to bite the bullet and tell Hennessey he was available for an indefinitely long teaching position at MONS.

Robert leased a three-bedroom flat overlooking the River Lee in the Sunday's Well area of Cork. The flat was in a restored building with large bow front windows and a classical Palladian entrance behind a green-painted cast iron fence. The rooms, with ten-foot ceilings, plaster cornices, and oak herringbone-pattern floors exuded the elegance of yesterday. Robert hired a decorator and instructed her to furnish and decorate the flat in an appropriate style but with living comfort in mind. He wanted to live modestly to minimize the apparent disparity between his and his school peers' incomes. He found he no longer had any desire to live in a grand style.

During his first year of teaching, Robert enjoyed the companionship of women although it was with the understanding that long-term relationships were not in the cards. He and Pamela had long since ceased seeing each other.

Students from difficult home environments became the target of Robert's attention. He bought a jacket for a boy who had none. "Sean," he said, "I walked in a park last weekend and found an abandoned package on a bench. It contains a jacket that's too small for me. If it fits you, would you be willing to take it? I don't know what else to do with it."

A girl in his class could not do her homework because of a disruptive and abusive home environment. Robert said, "Catherine, the halls and stairs in my flat are always in need of cleaning and waxing. Could I hire you to attend to them?" When Catherine came to work, he assigned her tasks that only occupied a small part of the agreed-upon work time. He invited her to his study to do her homework during the remainder of her time.

Robert had a special talent for devising simple methods for making the students understand that complex subjects were self-evident when looked at from a different perspective. He taught them to fashion simple devices from string, protractors, straws, and candles to perform experiments. Some thought they were modern-day Galileos after they performed assigned nocturnal observations on the moon's orbits and phases with simple homemade instruments. Robert wrote papers on his teaching methods that were widely distributed and eventually became the standards for teaching in schools throughout Ireland.

Dr. Hennessey heard reports of Robert's extraordinary teaching methods and skills. He invited him to join his staff in Dublin to improve teaching courses for the entire country. Robert offered to freely share his innovative teaching programs, but declined to move away from his classroom and students.

On a weekend while alone at Hollycourt, Robert did all of the usual things that he had enjoyed in the past: A visit with Paddy, walks in the fields, and a meal with Finbar. But it did not give him the pleasure it had in the past. He was anxious to leave Hollycourt after an unsatisfying weekend. Hollycourt had become a closed chapter in his life. And it was a reminder of his financial shenanigans that caused his fall from the chairmanship of AMSCO. He would not return.

He wrote a letter to the Georgian Preservation Society:

> Lee Mews Apartment
> 64 North Mall
> Cork City
>
> April 15, 2007

Board of Directors
Georgian Preservation Society
63 Sheridan Street
Dublin

Dear Sirs:

It has been my privilege to serve on the board of directors of the Georgian Preservation Society for the last several years.

For personal reasons, however, I submit my resignation from the board.

I no longer have need for the use of Hollycourt. Therefore, I modify the previous agreement giving me use of the estate until my death. The Georgian Preservation Society may immediately take unrestricted ownership of the estate and its furnishings.

I hope for success to the Georgian Preservation Society while it continues its worthwhile work.

Sincerely,
Robert G. Drood

After Robert visited his father in Belfast, he wrote to Bridget to tell her about their meeting. It opened a flood of letter exchanges.

While reading a long letter from Bridget, an idea jumped into Robert's mind: What if I bring Bridget to Cork to live with me? I wonder if it would work with my lifestyle, but when I think further, I don't really have a lifestyle. I spend most of my time working on student papers and lesson plans.

He set the letter aside and made a cup of tea before resuming his musings: Could I properly care for Bridget? But maybe that was not the right question. I am the one who really needs care. I eat lousy food and my flat looks like it is still moving day. I am turning into an eccentric bachelor. Maybe it would be beneficial to both of us if Bridget and I lived together. And living together might allow us to re-establish the bonds of our childhood days when we were inseparable pals.

Robert called Bridget's group home in Chicago and talked to the administrator. She said, "Bridget spends her days reading, watching television, and assisting the staff. Working in the kitchen and helping prepare meals is one of her favorite tasks. She's a good samaritan who listens to residents who need a sympathetic ear. Something that happened in her childhood depresses her. She keeps a little verse by Louis MacNeice taped on the wall over her desk that reads: 'When I was five the black dreams came; nothing after was quite the same.' She's happy each day until late in the afternoon when she becomes gloomy and depressed."

"I'm going to come to Chicago to visit Bridget," Robert replied. "If it goes well I want to bring her to Cork, here in Ireland, to live with me. Do you think that is feasible?"

"We always try to find a way for our residents to resume normal lives. It is possible for Bridget to come with you if you can shield her from strangers whom she always finds threatening, see that she takes her medication, and provide a domestic routine for her."

During Robert's next school break, he flew to Chicago to visit Bridget.

On a sunny day, at a time of minimum city traffic, he and Bridget visited their mother's grave.

Robert stood for a long time staring at Mary's tombstone. The gravesite also included her husband, Matt, and Uncle Liam Garrity. The tombstones already showed signs of weathering. He was overwhelmed with memories.

He turned his head up to look at a singing robin and then returned to his reveries: Since Bridget's rape, I never allowed myself to form a relationship with my mother, Bridget, or anyone else because I did not want to be hurt if grave harm came to any of them again. Because of this selfish resolution, I never again demonstrated affection for my mother, and I never expressed gratitude to her for her countless efforts on my behalf. It must have caused her unimaginable anguish—and surely Matt also deserved consideration for his endless supportiveness. I thought only of myself. What a self-centered schmuck I have been. Although I have doubts about God, I'll still pray for my mother. If I could only turn back the clock!

That evening Robert said, "Bridget, I'm going to ask you a question. Sleep on it tonight and if you can, give me your answer tomorrow. Would you like to return to Ireland to live with me in Cork?"

Bridget did not wait for morning. Before she went to bed she said, "I don't need to think any longer, Robert. I'd like for us to be together and happy again in Ireland."

Before their trip to O'Hare Airport to start their nonstop flight to Ireland, the nurse sedated Bridget to reduce her anxiety. The trip went without a hitch.

Bridget thought Robert's Cork flat, with its view of the graceful River Lee, was as classy as a building and setting could be. The sentimental anthem of County Cork, *The Banks of My Own Lovely Lee*, became her favorite song when she watched the river each day from their flat window. She loved her new routine of caring for the flat and bringing order to Robert's domestic life. She settled into her new living circumstances as effortlessly as a cat curling up on a pillow.

Maggie Flynn, an older woman who lived upstairs in their building, and Bridget became friends. When Robert stayed late at school or went away for a few days, Maggie watched over her.

Bridget continued to be nervous she might encounter strangers who would harm her, but she was able to start going out for weekend rides with Robert. She entered the car while it was parked in the brick-walled lot behind their flat and felt secure if he locked her in the car while he went about his errands.

CHAPTER THIRTY-FIVE

During one of Finbar's periodic visits to Cork, Robert ordered two glasses of Guinness and said, "Finbar, you crafty old fox clothed in the hooded cloak of a friar, I am, at long last, on to your devious designs. My scientifically educated mind is the tortoise, and your wisdom-stuffed cranium is the hare in races where we compete. I concede fate ordained our first meeting at your monastery, but after that I was a marionette on your string. By some means you induced me to reveal to you the foul demon that had, heretofore, controlled the dark chamber of my mind. You responded with a torrent of silence. You used your diabolical faculties to enter the forbidden chamber in my mind, which always denied me entry, and you curbed the vile forces residing there. Later you gave me a cock and bull story about how I'd enjoy a trip to Cork with Michael Hennessey. And now, due to that trip, I'm a mathematics and physics teacher with the weirdest résumé of any teacher in the Republic of Ireland."

"You better stop to relubricate yourself, Robert; I think you're running a couple quarts low on oil," said Finbar.

After another sip of Guinness, Robert resumed. "Somehow through your Machiavellian methods, I've learned to accept the fact that I can't confront the people who harmed my family and me during my childhood. I regret the years I foolishly wasted raging against them. And I've come to the realization that a suitable penance for my sins against the many unfortunate people who had to contend with me would be to repeatedly recite the ancient prayer of the confessional that goes: 'I have sinned in what I have done and what I have failed to do through my most grievous faults.' I've squelched my compulsion for chasing the holy grail of material possessions and learned how to coexist with my subdued demon even though it is still with me."

Robert took another swig. "On a more serious note, Finbar, maybe I should say you're the best listener I ever met. I bow to you in awe of your wisdom and methods. My gratitude is without bounds. I can add you to my list of most-admired people. The list, until I met you, included only one person—Ken Yee, a respected colleague from my previous life."

"Well, Robert, that was an interesting exposition. Who am I to deny the extraordinary powers you attribute to me even though they are fanciful? And also on a more serious note, I'm delighted to see the tormented, care-ridden person I first met in my monastery chapel is now transformed into one of the most dedicated and capable teachers in the country. Ireland should be grateful to have you for a teacher, and I'm grateful to have you for a friend."

Robert again assumed a somber look. "Finbar, I want to be serious for one moment more. Since my epiphany, I remembered an incident from my days at MIT. When a Jewish classmate celebrated Yom Kippur, I asked him to explain the holiday to me.

"It's the Day of Atonement," he told me. "It's a day of last appeal; a time to repent and amend the judgments written in the book of life for an individual's poor behavior before the book is closed and sealed forever."

"That concept made me think before my book of life is closed and sealed, I have time to amend my relationship with my remaining family and to try to redeem myself for the unconscionable fraud I committed in my business career."

"That's an interesting way to look at it, Robert," Finbar said.

"I've reestablished a close relationship with my sister and I'm trying to reconnect with my father. Unfortunately, all I can do for my mother and her husband, Matt, is to reflect on their goodness and regret my lack of gratitude to them while they were still alive.

"To help compensate for my greed and fraud, I've instructed AMSCO to give most of my remaining termination payments to the AMSCO Charitable Foundation; the company certainly doesn't owe me anything—actually I owe them. And I've relinquished all rights to Hollycourt.

"I just may have finally cut the Gordian knot that bound me for so terribly long to my binful of psychological encumbrances.

"Now, I think that's enough of my *mea culpa* declaration and atonement plan. I promise; you won't hear of it again."

Finbar sat for a long time in silence and finally spoke, "If I may put my response in terms appropriate for the confessional, you've declared a more profound penance than I could ever conceive for you. By the way, why did you not include your decision to teach here as part of your penance?"

"Frankly, because I've found more satisfaction from teaching young people than from managing corporations. It's not a penance; I feel the opportunity to teach is a blessing and it is my destiny. After I die and take my final ride across the River Styx to the underworld of afterlife—or whatever other place fate ordains for me—I want the epitaph on my tomb to only read: Robert Garrity Drood—Teacher.

"And just in case you think the old, sarcastic Robert Drood has shed his fangs and blunted his claws, you should attend one of our school staff meetings where the dim-witted school administrators waste the teachers' time on bureaucratic twaddle. I suggest more productive pursuits for them and hasten the conclusion of the meetings by spearheading a mass teaching staff exit."

CHAPTER THIRTY-SIX

Late on a sunny Friday afternoon, a short time after Drood's departure from AMSCO, Carly called Dennis to her spartan office. She shut the door and poured him a cup of coffee from the pot she always kept on her credenza. She unlocked a drawer and removed an unopened bottle of Bushmills Irish whiskey even though alcohol in the fab was forbidden. She said, "It's past quitting time and the front office staff has gone home except for us so let's improve the octane rating of our coffee. I'm too nervous to go on in a state of complete sobriety." She poured a generous splash of whiskey into each cup and switched to her Oklahoma oil field dialect. "I'm goin' to tell you somethin' that'll, sure as hogs stink, make your spurs spin." After an uneasy pause she went on. "Ol' Wally and me have been together now for three months without pissin' each other off. I set him up a telecommunication system in my flat so he's been remotely runnin' his business in Napa from there. Maybe we just stopped noticin' what we was doin' to each other to cause our flare-ups in the past. I can't believe what I'm about to tell you now." She took a worthwhile sip of coffee and Bushmills and nervously went on. "Next month I'm goin' to put on my cowboy boots and white Stetson hat and go back to the oil patch in Oklahoma where I was raised. Wally's goin' to meet me there; we're a goin' to get married."

"My good God in heaven, Carly, I can't believe it! Congratulations!" Dennis ran around her desk, gave her a bear hug, and planted a kiss on her. "Before you leave for Oklahoma, Mary Catherine and I will put on a celebration for you and Wally to remember for the rest of your days."

"And me and Ol' Wally will be there like a pair of high-schoolers steppin' out on prom night."

As Carly drank the last sip of her coffee, she cut out the Oklahoma dialect and switched back to business. "The fab is now up to speed, our quality problems are behind us, and we're on the road to making our profit objectives. I'm going to retire again like I told Ken I would when this place was up and running. I'm sure you guessed Ken has had me mentor you for some time on how to run a large fab—although you didn't need much mentoring. He has not appointed a successor to his old job, so he's still wearing his old hat as my boss along with being the CEO. I told Ken you're ripe to take over my job. Tomorrow Ken will be here to officially offer you the job face-to-face. According to company procedures, I'm not supposed to tell you this in advance so act surprised when he offers it to you."

"Carly, I can't say the offer is a complete surprise. Before the nightmare surrounding Dr. Drood's departure, I'd have been walking on air with what you just told me, but now I'm not so sure. I'm still in shock such duplicity existed in our company. Just after this mess all happened, I was so disgusted I'd probably have resigned if it weren't for you and Mary Catherine holding my hand. Please give me until tomorrow morning to think about the offer."

Early the next morning Dennis and Carly met again. "Carly, I thought about my situation most of last night. The world's not a perfect place, and if I want to work in the domain of big people I have to live with its imperfections. I'd be nuts not to accept the job offer. And Mary Catherine will be in ecstasy at the opportunity to continue living in her Irish fairyland a few more years."

"I knew you'd come around to accepting the offer, Dennis. You'll make an outstanding fab manager."

When the announcement was made about Carly's retirement and Dennis's promotion, Fionnoula, who was now the human resources manager, came to his office and said, "We're so pleased Himself is our new Maximum Leader. When we first read the bulletin about Carly's retirement, our hearts flinched for fear we would be sent one of those efficient-as-a-robot managers with no more sensitivity than a hedgehog."

Late on a rainy Friday afternoon in early December, while Robert sat in his classroom grading student papers with his door open, Fionnoula O'Casey glided in. "Hello, Dr. Drood. It's grand to see ye again. I hope ye remember me from your visits to the new AMSCO fab here in Ireland."

Robert was startled to see the first AMSCO employee since his dismissal. "Of course I remember you Finnoula. How could I ever forget your colorful and memorable lessons on Irish history and culture?"

"I inquired about ye at Hollycourt, and Paddy gave me your address. I'm here for a weekend visit with my boyfriend who is earning his Ph.D. at University College Cork. By now I'm sure ye have found education of the Irish is a bit peculiar. We're poets; we're often deficient in the hard-nosed logic and discipline that comes from studying mathematics and science. Maybe, through your teaching, ye can help us disprove the sentiments expressed by James Froude who said, 'Order is an exotic in Ireland. It is imported from England, but it will not grow. It suits neither soil nor climate.'"

Robert chuckled and said, "Fionnoula, you know more about Irish history, culture, politics, songs, poetry, and the ways of the people than anyone I know. Now, I want to ask you a question that's been on my mind for many years. "My mother told me when I was born in Cork, a soothsayer foretold my destiny. She said I'd gain wisdom from the 'Salmon of Knowledge'; I'd be the leader of many people in many lands; and someday I'd return, like the salmon, to the place of my birth in Ireland. All of her prophecies turned out to be true. Based on my life of scientific education and experience this is all pure nonsense and falls in league with those who believe in leprechauns. Now, tell me from your viewpoint, do you think the accurate prophecy of the soothsayer was a lucky guess or do you think she really knew my destiny?"

"Oh, surely she knew. There are special people in Ireland who the Lord blessed with the gift to prophesize. Ye must never deny their wisdom.

"Now, I wish ye a Merry and Holy Christmas, Dr. Drood. It's grand to see ye again in health and happiness; may Jesus and the Holy Saints in heaven always bless ye." She hugged him and slipped to the door of his classroom with the grace of a ballet dancer.

Robert said, "Wait a minute, Fionnoula. I have been carrying an envelope for Dennis Curran in my briefcase for a long time. It's high time to deliver it. Will you please hand carry it to him?"

"Of course, Dr. Drood."

The undated confidential note read:

Dennis,

After I departed from AMSCO, I surmised you were the person who discovered and courageously—at substantial risk to yourself—revealed my malfeasances that lead to my downfall. You had every right—and indeed the responsibility—to disclose my despicable deception to clear your good name when you were falsely accused of improper equipment selection for the Irish fab.

Since that difficult time, I have had an epiphany in my life; it has led me to my current fulfilling role as a mathematics and science teacher here in Ireland. I owe inestimable gratitude to you for courageously taking action that eventually removed the scales from my eyes allowing me to clearly see the folly of much of my life. I sincerely apologize to you for the grief I caused you.

I wish you all the best with your career and your personal life.

Most sincerely yours,

Robert Drood

Fionnoula's visit made Robert realize the earlier chapters of his life were now as decisively closed and sealed as the book of life is to the Jewish faithful each year on Yom Kippur (The Day of Atonement).

CHAPTER THIRTY-SEVEN

As they drank their after-dinner cup of tea, Robert said, "Bridget, what do you think of inviting our father to come here from Belfast to spend Christmas with us? He could sleep in my room and I could sleep on the sofa in my study."

Bridget closed her eyes and thought about it for a long time. "I like the idea very much, Robert. Let's do it," she finally said.

They sent an invitation to George Drood inviting him to Cork for a Christmas visit. He accepted by return mail. He had not yet entered into the world of computers and e-mail.

Bridget went on a maniacal flat-cleaning and meal-planning spree and sent an order to Marshall Field in Chicago. She ordered Christmas decorations and presents—books and a mathematics game for Robert, a cashmere scarf and fur-lined gloves for their father, and a box of Field's famous Frango mint chocolates for Finbar. She asked Robert to buy a basket of fruit and marmalade at the English Market for her to take upstairs to Maggie Flynn.

At breakfast on the day of George Drood's scheduled arrival, Bridget gravely said, "Robert, I want to ride with you when you drive to the train depot to pick up Father."

It was a raw, cold-to-the-bone day when they drove the short distance through wintry sleet to the Cork railroad depot to meet the train. The car wipers flapped to clear the slush from the windshield. Bridget folded her gloved hands together and rested them in her lap. She was anxious but calm. While Robert parked the car near the depot, she said, "I'll wait in the car, Robert, while you go to the train to meet Father and help him with his baggage. Please leave the engine running with the heater on so it'll be nice and warm for him when he gets in the car with us."

The Die Is Cast is an examination of the human condition with goodness and evil in competition for the soul. Frank Lyons' portrayal of a high flying corporate executive and his struggles with his past and himself makes for a good read. It is a journey home to place, family, and goodness that fulfills the prophecy of a *seanachie* [soothsayer.] It is an Irish tale told by an Irishman that is a lesson for all who read *The Die Is Cast*.

James T. Barry, Ed.D.,
President, Mount Marty College

ABOUT THE AUTHOR

Frank Lyons understands large multinational corporations from working as an executive of a Fortune 100 corporation and president of an international consulting company. He lives on the Mississippi River in Rock Island, Illinois, where he continues to write.

Books by the same author:

William and Mary—Their Lives and Times

South Dakota Days
(Available for purchase on Amazon.)

Made in the USA
San Bernardino, CA
20 December 2012